Praise for
New York Times and USA Today Bestselling Author

Diane Capri

"Full of thrills and tension, but smart and human, too."
Lee Child, #1 New York Times Bestselling Author of Jack Reacher Thrillers

"[A] welcome surprise….[W]orks from the first page to 'The End'."
Larry King

"Swift pacing and ongoing suspense are always present…[L]ikable protagonist who uses her political connections for a good cause…Readers should eagerly anticipate the next [book]."
Top Pick, Romantic Times

"…offers tense legal drama with courtroom overtones, twisty plot, and loads of Florida atmosphere. Recommended."
Library Journal

"[A] fast-paced legal thriller…energetic prose…an appealing heroine…clever and capable supporting cast…[that will] keep readers waiting for the next [book]."
Publishers Weekly

"Expertise shines on every page."
Margaret Maron, Edgar, Anthony, Agatha and Macavity Award Winning MWA Past President

FATAL GAME

by DIANE CAPRI

Published by: AugustBooks
http://www.AugustBooks.com
ISBN-13: 978-1-940768-76-2
ISBN-10: 1-940768-76-4

Original Cover Design: Cory Clubb
Digital Formatting: Author E.M.S.

Published in the United States of America.

Visit the author website:
http://www.DianeCapri.com

ALSO BY DIANE CAPRI

The Hunt for Jack Reacher Series
(in publication order with Lee Child source books in parentheses)

Don't Know Jack (The Killing Floor)

Jack in a Box (*novella*)

Jack and Kill (*novella*)

Get Back Jack (Bad Luck & Trouble)

Jack in the Green (*novella*)

Jack and Joe (The Enemy)

Deep Cover Jack (Persuader)

Jack the Reaper (The Hard Way)

Black Jack (Running Blind/The Visitor)

Ten Two Jack (The Midnight Line)

The Jess Kimball Thrillers Series

Fatal Enemy (*novella*)

Fatal Distraction

Fatal Demand

Fatal Error

Fatal Fall

Fatal Edge

Fatal Game

Fatal Bond

Fatal Past (*novella*)

Fatal Dawn

The Hunt for Justice Series
Due Justice
Twisted Justice
Secret Justice
Wasted Justice
Raw Justice
Mistaken Justice (*novella*)
Cold Justice (*novella*)
False Justice (*novella*)
Fair Justice (*novella*)
True Justice (*novella*)

The Heir Hunter Series
Blood Trails
Trace Evidence

CAST OF PRIMARY CHARACTERS

Jessica Kimball
Carter Pierce
Mandy Donovan
Thelma Baxter
Henry Morris
Donald Warner
Karen Warner
Roy Mercer
Hades
Cora
Simon Lawson
Melissa Green

FATAL GAME

CHAPTER ONE

Friday, May 12, 9:30 p.m.
Santa Irene, Arizona

CORA FELT HIS EYES on her. She was the first woman who'd ever stood by Hades and he'd always done the same for her. The deep keloid scars on his face made him ugly to most women, but to Cora, they were proof of his fidelity.

Earlier today, at his brother's funeral, she knew he'd felt a sliver of comfort, having her hand in his once again. Maybe his luck and hers were beginning to change.

When this job was over, they'd go away. Somewhere exotic, where neither had been before. Just the two of them. They'd have plenty of money. His brother would have approved, and that was the only motivation Hades craved right now. Cora nodded. Decision made.

Cora had worked hard, and she'd achieved the best physical condition of her life. Even in the moon's cool blue aura, she felt beautiful. The line of her jaw, her neck, bountiful hair brushed back from her face. The curves of her figure, the delicacy of her fingers, the tone of her muscles.

Many men had praised her beauty. But not Hades.

He didn't have the words.

Nor would he have ever uttered them.

For he was no god. Nor she the daughter of Zeus.

She grinned. They weren't even Greek.

They were pure Arizona low-class trailer trash, born and raised. And they were perfectly comfortable standing in this bus shelter, waiting for the right moment. For Benny.

Across the road was a lounge. It's neon sign read *ndy's Bar*, the *A* having long since disappeared.

The parking lot was stuffed with an assortment of old cars and older trucks. So they waited.

Trucks drove in. Cars left. People walked down the street and entered through the front door. Cora ignored them all.

After fifteen minutes, a white panel van pulled into the lot. Hades nodded toward the tired looking vehicle. "There it is."

His voice was low and sexy, and she loved it.

"Yep," Cora replied.

The choice was made. She knew what to do. Hades walked off. He trusted her. They'd rehearsed the plan countless times.

Cora watched as he turned to his right, and disappeared around the corner.

The van's driver was finishing his paperwork before he finally called it a day.

Cora crossed the street and used the front entrance. Andy's was a busy bar on Friday nights. No one paid the least attention to her. She eased around the edges of the room, squeezing between the patrons, to the rear door that led to the parking lot.

The wig curled in waves that spilled down onto her shoulders. She wore a trench coat over a red silk dress that shimmered as it touched every one of her curves. She had donned thick black eyelashes, and her vibrant wet-look red lipstick was pure seduction from a tube.

She stood by a window, a few feet from the rear door, and unbuttoned her coat to show off the dress and the sizzling body it revealed.

The driver stepped out of the van and shrugged into his jacket. He dropped the keys in his pocket as he walked to the door.

She waited until he was three paces away to move.

The driver pulled the heavy steel door open. His head was down. He swung his right foot over the threshold.

Cora kept her pace, reaching the threshold at the same moment, and walked through as if he'd been holding the door open for her. They met in the archway. She put her hands up, pressing them against his chest as she tried to squeeze through. The man jerked his head up while his eyes swept her body from heels to cleavage, where his gaze stopped.

She slid her right hand over his shoulder and giggled. He raised his chin and stared into her eyes. She blinked her thick eyelashes. A long, slow, deliberate movement.

He pushed himself back onto the doorframe. "I—"

She leaned forward. Her gaze locked on his. "Who said chivalry is dead?"

"Er—"

She pulled him to her and kissed his cheek. He didn't back away. She slid her left hand over his thin nylon jacket. Her fingertips felt the flap that covered his pocket.

She kept her face close to his. Two cheeks just touching. She squeezed his shoulder with her right hand and lifted the pocket flap with her left.

He pulled away a fraction, and she pushed closer to him and wiggled her hips.

Her fingers wrapped around the metal key ring in his pocket. She tucked the keys into the palm of her hand, squeezing to quiet the rattle.

She eased her hand out of his pocket and leaned back. His mouth was slack. His hooded eyes were unfocused.

She giggled and blinked her big eyelashes. "Sorry." She dropped her gaze a fraction. "I couldn't resist."

The man licked his lips. "Sorry. I—"

She turned away, and walked out of the bar, keeping her hand and his keys in front of her. She strode purposefully, opening her purse as if to search for her own keys. She heard the door thump shut as he went inside and she glanced back to be sure. She was prepared to deal with him if he followed. But he didn't.

She kept moving, weaving through the vehicles, on her way to the panel van.

To avoid electronic bleeps, she used the mechanical key. She slipped into the driver's seat and twisted the key in the ignition at the same time as she pulled on the seat belt.

She was rolling within seconds.

The rear of the parking lot led to a two-lane road. She feathered the accelerator as she crept out into the traffic, turning right for the freeway a half mile down.

The van was old, but the engine was strong. It was a workhorse, and had power and torque to spare. Perfect for their needs.

She entered the freeway. A line of eighteen-wheelers, doing a steady sixty-five miles an hour, kept her pinned to the inside lane. She slowed to let them pass before moving into the left lane to accelerate.

The freeway speed limit was sixty-five, but she pushed it to seventy-five to clear the trucks. She pulled into the middle lane, in front of the trucks, and slowed to their speed.

She glanced in the rearview mirror. Her heart skipped a beat. A black and white police cruiser was fifty yards behind, passing the convoy of trucks, gaining fast.

The cruiser was probably responding to a call miles away. But she couldn't risk being stopped.

The next exit was half a mile. She eased into the slow lane and used the trucks to shield her from the cruiser's view.

She'd take the next exit, spend a minute waiting at traffic lights, and rejoin the highway. The cruiser would be far gone by then.

She heard the whoop of a siren. "Dammit!"

She moved over to the right-hand exit lane. Behind her, the trucks separated, and the cruiser darted through the gap.

She weaved around a blue Nissan, keeping her speed up as she covered the off-ramp. The road narrowed again before the cruiser could pass.

"Damn driver." He must have reported his van already. Bad luck. Nothing more.

She took the first right. A single lane street. She needed buildings for cover. There was no way she would outrun the pursuit. This one cruiser, perhaps, but he would be calling for assistance already. She had less than a minute to ditch the van and put a good deal of distance between her and the police officers chasing her.

She touched the brakes as she approached a four-way stop. Traffic was sparse. Two cars were stopped, waiting their turn. She took the opposite lane, passed the cars, and swung left at the four way.

The van's wide tires chirped at the strain in the fast corner, but they held the line, catapulting her through the intersection and onto another single lane road.

She floored the accelerator. The engine's rumble became a full-blown roar. The van's rear end squatted down. The distance to the next intersection passed in a flash.

The cruiser was a good hundred yards behind her. Another few blocks and she would have enough distance to dump the van and run.

She weaved around a stationary car at the next four-way stop sign, and raced alongside a car crossing the intersection, pushing ahead. She swerved into the right lane, ahead of the car.

A police siren wailed. Close. She glanced in her mirror. The original cruiser was still behind at the last intersection, but a second cruiser must have been at the stop.

The second cruiser fishtailed a ninety-degree turn, and raced after her.

Her slight advantage was gone. She gripped the wheel harder and cussed every word she'd learned in that broken-down trailer park playground at the age of six. If these worthless donut eaters wanted to play, she would play.

She eased off the gas. The engine groaned as it slowed the van's weight. The second cruiser gained and moved into the opposing lane to pass.

Cora stomped on the gas. The big engine growled as it dumped fuel into its cylinders. The rear wheels broke traction. She flipped the steering wheel right.

Both back tires slid sideways across the pavement. The heavy van smashed hard into the second cruiser's front wheel. The officer braked and turned his steering wheel.

But the van's speed and force pushed the cruiser, and it

whipped around, beyond human control. The cruiser's rear smashed into a line of parked cars, bubbling over the hood of a mid-sized sedan, and smashing through a glass storefront. Pedestrians scattered, covering their heads to protect themselves from flying glass shards.

The second cruiser was permanently out of commission.

Cora eased off the gas. The van slithered back into a straight line as the tires regained their grip. The mayhem behind her slowed but did not stop the first cruiser.

She reached an area where the buildings were bigger and closer together. If she could gain enough distance, she could ditch the vehicle and blend in with the night crowds. She smiled. The odds were swinging in her favor. Her luck had improved.

Traffic lights marked the next intersection. The freeway was to the left, the denser city streets to the right. She gripped the wheel and decided to go right.

The lights were red. A line of traffic waited. The first cruiser was pressing hard behind her. She moved out to overtake the stationary traffic. A police car was blocking the right exit, red and blue lights flashing.

Another cruiser raced to block the road ahead but wasn't yet in place.

A minivan wandered across the intersection. Cora eased left, judging the minivan's progress, and matted the accelerator. She whipped by the waiting cars. The intersection cleared.

And the minivan stopped.

"Damn! Damn! Damn!" She jinked the wheel, but she couldn't deflect the van's mass. She hit the minivan's rear quarter panel at full speed. The minivan spun as if a giant had flicked a toy with his finger.

Cora's airbag exploded. The force shoved her hands from

the wheel. The van pirouetted and hit three cars waiting on the other side of the traffic light. The van scraped along the sides of the vehicles before lurching around the last car and hammering into the front of a flower shop.

Cora shoved the deflated airbag from her face. Steam poured from under the hood. The engine had died. The windshield was a mosaic of cracks.

The front of the van was buried in the storefront. Flowers were scattered everywhere.

She leaned all her weight on the door. It creaked open. Her left hand throbbed. In the dim light, she saw blood dripping onto the airbag and the steering wheel and down to the dirty carpet.

She struggled out of the van and landed on solid ground. Her legs were weak, but she was inside the flower shop. There was no time to torch the van. She had to go. Now.

Behind the counter was a door. She put her weight on the counter, rolled over, and pushed through the rear door.

It led into a stockroom, and another door led outside. She grabbed a handful of paper towels for her bleeding hand.

Outside an alleyway led to another street. More shops and a bus collecting passengers. She hurried to reach the bus a moment before the doors closed. She fished a few coins from her pocket and dropped them into the fare box. She walked down the aisle and slid into a seat near the rear door.

Passengers chattered about the noise and confusion of the big crash. A few pointed back to the intersection. She heard sirens headed toward the carnage. The bus drove in the opposite direction. Gradually the siren song subsided, and the passengers quieted.

Cora folded her arms and gazed out the window. She kept her injured hand covered with the paper towels and waited for her blood to clot. A bored commuter, blending into the fabric of life. The very life she had been so desperate to leave behind was now her means of escape. She smiled at the irony. As her adrenaline levels began to subside, the throbbing in her hand became more intense, but she ignored it. Nothing more she could do about it now.

In a couple of miles, she changed buses. She tossed the wig in a trash can on the street and cleaned off the makeup with a few swipes of the tissues in her pocket.

Two buses later, she made the call.

Hades would rescue her at the next bus stop. She'd get a lecture, and he would worry about the evidence she'd left behind. He worried about everything. Damn cop chasing her in that first cruiser was to blame. People must have died in that crash. What the hell did he think he was doing?

She shrugged. None of that was her problem. She'd calm Hades down. She always did. Their plans would be derailed for a week, but they were safe. And that slime ball Lawson wasn't going anywhere with the money he stole from Benny, anyway. At least, not yet.

She looked at the bloody paper towels, dried now, adhered to her wound. If only she hadn't hurt her hand.

CHAPTER TWO

Sunday, May 21, 8:30 p.m.
Santa Irene, Arizona

HADES RAISED A PAIR of binoculars to his eyes. A half mile away sat Simon Lawson's modern, two-story home on a gentle upslope. The closest neighbors were a hundred feet of lawn away from the house, separated by thick pines.

The property had a commanding view. The lawn swept upward from the street. A waist-high brick wall and a wrought iron gate separated the green manicured perfection from the daily road grime.

The solid front door was set deep into the front porch. The drapes were open, but plantation blinds shielded the interior from view. Light spilled from between the slats.

A three-car garage was nestled behind the house. Only two of the spaces were filled. Lawson had recently sold his Porsche and scoured the Internet for a late model Ferrari California to fill the vacant slot.

Hades grinned. He had different plans for that empty space.

Cora's left hand still bore the wound of her first failed attempt to steal a white panel van. A broad bandage covered the gash. For the first few days, she had winced with the slightest movement. The wound was still fresh, but not as painful.

Last night, from a different bar in another part of town, she'd completed the theft easily. Before this night ended, the stolen van would rest in the spot Lawson had optimistically reserved for the Ferrari.

Hades took a deep breath to quell his nerves. Not because he feared the consequences. Far from it. He relished the stakes. The greatest risk for the greatest reward. Always one step ahead, one second from tragedy, one brush from the razor's edge. Nothing else was worthy. Nothing else stirred his blood. Nothing else fired his imagination.

For the Greek god and his queen, nothing was as important as winning the game. Especially this time. *For Benny.*

A half mile away, the lights behind the plantation blinds in Lawson's house went dark.

Now was the point Hades relished. The game began. He would balance on the razor-thin edge between life and death. The adrenaline almost fizzed in his blood.

He rapped twice on the metal wall behind him, between the van's front seats and the two men waiting in the rear. "We begin," he said.

"Ready." Both men tapped once on the wall. "Ready."

Cora started the van. The engine rattled and knocked before settling out in a rough idle. She pulled out from the roadside spot where they had parked onto the planned route through the streets to the house with the now-darkened windows.

She drove easily. No high revs, no crunching the manual gearbox. The rough engine purred under her right foot. She was as in touch with the mechanics of a vehicle as anyone Hades had ever encountered. She was no trophy, no pampered debutante, no spoiled queen. She was as much a part of the gang as any of the men. How'd he get so lucky?

He checked his watch. Lawson and his wife had returned an hour earlier. They'd made dinner and opened an expensive bottle of wine. Content and relaxed. Perhaps discussing their weekly shopping expedition, or plans for the vacation they'd booked for next week.

Cora drove the van closer to the house. From here, Hades no longer needed the binoculars to see the front door, recessed into a deep and dark porch. On either side were tall windows. The windows upstairs were smaller and squarer, but no less dark.

This was the house owned by a successful doctor who had done well for himself. He'd studied hard and worked long hours. Even better, he had amassed significant wealth. He was even richer than his partner, Donald Warner, had been because of the money they stole from Benny.

Hades would take it all. Before the week was over, Lawson would beg him to do it.

Lawson needed nothing but an incentive, and Hades was a master of persuasion. He hadn't been in his early years. Back then, he had merely mastered violence. In prison, he'd come to understand how violence could lead to consent. He'd learned the hard way, but he had learned well. He planned to demonstrate his skills to Lawson and that bitch he was married to.

Mr. and Mrs. Lawson were eating dinner in the dining room at the back of the house. He had watched their routine. He'd made notes and taken photographs. He knew their movements and actions better than they did. Predicting routines was the easiest thing in the world.

He rapped his knuckles against the metal wall. "Time," he said.

Hades felt the two guys shift their weight, bringing stationary muscles to life. Stretching. Limbering up. They were like athletes; they never played a game unprepared. Hades heard the reverberating noise in the cavernous van as they released safety catches. Pony and Shorty were ready.

Hades pulled a VBR pistol from the holster on his hip. The gun seemed massive. One of the reasons he liked it was that it had a rough surface as if it had been cast from iron and forged in hell. Seemed fitting. A second hand grip and an offset sight added to the gun's presence. Merely brandishing the weapon often encouraged capitulation. Thirty-three 9mm rounds backed up the threat. Hades chambered the first round and placed the gun in his lap.

In his coat, he carried a 12-gauge short-barreled Remington pump action shotgun. He'd removed the superfluous items on the shotgun. No fancy hooks or scrolls, so it slid smoothly out of a loop inside his long coat.

The shells were his own design. Lead shot replaced by chili powder. A single blast disabled an opponent for minutes. Fired into a room full of people, it produced dramatic results. No one died. But they often wished they had.

On his belt, he carried a nine-inch knife. The handle was thick and the blade serrated. Like the VBR, the mere sight of it could paralyze a civilian opponent.

Cora turned the van into the driveway, clicked off the engine, and rolled to a stop. She stayed at the wheel as Shorty slipped on his realistic latex mask. He left the back of the van and walked toward the front door. His shaved head reflected the moon's faint glow until his black clothes melded into the darkness in the corner of the porch.

Hades and Pony put on their masks and headed around the rear of the building. They walked purposefully. The sort of walk that told nosey neighbors they were professionals doing professional work. Which, Hades grinned, they were.

Their clothes were black, too. They made no sound as they walked, the effect of coating the soles of their heavy, steel-toed boots with a layer of spray-on rubber.

The rear of the house sported picture windows that looked out on a full-length concrete patio. In the middle of the patio was a fireplace, open on two sides. On the far side of the fireplace were a pair of sofas, on the near side was a large mosaic table and chairs.

Cypress trees ringed the edge of the concrete, shielding the Lawson home from the prying eyes of distant neighbors. The windows were uncovered. No blinds or drapes. The garden was ringed in thick pine trees. Lawson had planted the trees to ensure privacy.

Fools.

The couple sat across from each other at the oval dining table. The lights were dimmed. A vase of flowers and a bottle of wine served as the table's centerpiece

Lawson stood up, frowning. His wife's eyes went wide.

Hades worked his way between the lawn chairs. His mask was excellent quality. The Lawsons were no doubt surprised to see Babe Ruth walking toward them from the darkness. Or maybe they didn't recognize the slugger at all, which would be even better. He moved smoothly, steadily, smiling all the while.

Keep the targets curious.

There'd be time for fear later.

Pony followed him, pulling an iron battering ram from under his coat. Despite its fifty-pound weight, he swung it with ease.

Five paces from the house, Pony ran headlong into the rear door, planting the flat front of the ram against the door's frame. The combined weight and momentum crushed the door around its lock.

Pony swung the ram back and pounded the door a second time. It sailed open.

Lawson bolted from the dining room. His wife ran into the living room.

Pony, wearing a mask with the likeness of an Australian soccer star they'd probably never seen on television, took off after the wife, his trademark ponytail flying behind him.

Hades went after Lawson, pulling out his shotgun as he ran.

Lawson was already halfway up a wide staircase. Hades knew Lawson kept a pistol in the drawer by his bed. Hades took the stairs two at a time.

Lawson used the banister at the top of the steps to change direction and maintain speed. Hades raised the shotgun. Lawson ducked and kept running the full length of the corridor.

Hades sprinted after him. Lawson darted into the master bedroom and flicked the door closed behind him.

Hades raised his boot and hammered into the door handle. The door whipped open.

Lawson reached for the drawer in his bedside table.

Hades leveled his shotgun. "Simon. Stop it."

Lawson turned, his face screwed up in alarm.

It worked every time. The confusion. He could almost hear Lawson thinking, "I don't know you, but you know me?"

The moment's pause gave Hades all the time he needed.

He pulled the shotgun's trigger.

The charge was small, the impact's force subdued. The chili powder was hot. Painful. Stinging. Immobilizing. But not lethal.

Lawson took the blast in the shoulder. He twisted around, screaming.

Hades held his breath and covered the room in two paces. He swung his boot into Lawson's kidneys.

Lawson groaned once and collapsed.

Hades grabbed him by the collar, dragged him downstairs, and threw him onto the sofa beside his wife.

Pony let Shorty in from the porch shadows through the front entrance. He returned to hold his gun pointed at the couple, in case they hadn't already received the message to cower and be afraid.

Shorty, whose mask was the face of an obscure English footballer, ran to open the garage door.

The van's engine coughed into life and rolled into the garage. Shorty closed the doors. A moment later and they'd all entered the house. Shorty sealed the broken rear door with duct tape.

The only sound in the silent house came from the ticking grandfather clock in the corner of the living room.

Hades dragged a dining room chair into the room and placed it by the coffee table, directly opposite Simon and Natalie Lawson. They pressed closer to each other. They'd lost their snooty arrogance the moment Pony battered their back door. Her lacquered bleached hair was barely disturbed, but her makeup was a mess. His face had aged a decade since he took the chili shot to the shoulder. Perfect.

Hades sat in the chair. He watched the couple huddled in a ball on the sofa.

Seconds ticked by.

Simon shifted his weight. Natalie whimpered and moved closer to him.

Hades eased his knife from the sheath, and dragged the tip across the table, scoring a line through the thick varnish and tearing splinters from the wood underneath. The sound reverberated through the room.

Natalie Lawson gripped Simon harder as if he was half the man she'd believed him to be an hour ago.

Hades smirked and cut another line. The same depth. The same splinters. The same spine-tingling sound.

He made a cross. X marks the spot.

He flipped the knife backward in his hand and swept it down hard, driving the tip deep into the wood.

The couple recoiled into a tighter ball.

This one's for you, Benny. Hades left the knife standing upright, halfway between himself and them, the point buried deep in the expensive wood.

He smiled, revealing his broken front tooth. The one Benny had dinged with a bad bounce of a steely marble when they were kids. "Listen to me. Very carefully. I won't repeat myself."

CHAPTER THREE

Monday, May 22, 7:45 a.m.
Denver, Colorado

JESS KIMBALL WAS EARLY. Her appointment with Carter Pierce, the owner of *Taboo Magazine*, wasn't until eight o'clock. Carter lived and breathed for *Taboo*. He'd have arrived at least two hours ago, even on a Monday morning. Of course, he lived in the penthouse of the building, so his commute was shorter.

She took the elevator to the sixty-sixth floor of the magazine's tower block. A few people exchanged smiles and greetings on the way. Others raised surprised eyebrows because her work rarely brought her to the premises.

She scanned the floor and noticed no decorating changes since she was here last. An open central area dotted with low-walled office cubes. TV monitors on stalks dangled from the ceiling. In one corner was Carter's office. Actually, it was two offices. His personal space, and a large conference room next door where major stories and every issue of *Taboo* was hashed out by the team before publication.

On either side of Carter's office were rows of smaller offices. Jess's was the third door down from his. Though she never flaunted it, she was Carter's go-to reporter. When the story was tough or delicate or likely to make worldwide headlines, he called her. She'd worked hard to earn the position, and she was proud of it, but the legal and contract departments outranked her and filled the offices closest to Carter.

On the opposite side of the floor, her assistant, Mandy Donovan, was busy with an overly complex coffee machine. She juggled a handful of glass and plastic and managed a wave. Jess waved back.

She reached her office and dropped her bag into one of her visitor chairs. Even though the room was spotless, it smelled vacant, the result of her near constant travel schedule.

She flipped through a pile of mail. Mandy had already handled the essentials. She slid the rest into the trash can. Even the special offers that might have interested her were out of date.

At three minutes to eight, she walked to Carter's office.

Carter's assistant, Thelma Baxter, was the epitome of the little old lady in sneakers who truly ran the daily business of the organization. Jess feared *Taboo* would cease to exist when Thelma died. There was no one and nothing the woman didn't know.

Jess had no idea how old Thelma was, but she had seen decades of staff come and go. As a party trick, she could recite the magazine's front page headline for each issue back forty years.

In the early days, Jess had seriously wondered if Thelma was actually the owner of *Taboo* who employed Carter as a decoy. She smiled as Jess approached and held out an envelope.

Jess frowned.

"Ticket and boarding pass, dear," Thelma said.

"Do I need a ticket?"

She nodded toward Carter's office. "I've never heard you turn him down before, so I figured I'd save a few minutes."

"I just got back last night. I've got a couple of appointments scheduled and piles of laundry to do. Does a few minutes make a difference?"

Thelma tapped her watch. "Ten twenty-two. It's the last flight today with a first-class aisle seat." She raised her eyebrows with a mischievous grin. "Or you could go coach tonight. Red eye. Middle seat?"

"Ten twenty-two works. I'll make a couple of calls." Jess took the envelope and stashed it in her pocket.

Carter was talking on the phone. Between sentences, he held up an index finger to indicate she should wait. He spoke a few more moments before punching the phone's off button and waved Jess in with a flourish.

He stood up. "Jess. Long time, no see."

"It's been three weeks."

He laughed. "Ah, yes. But in our business? Half an hour can seem like years."

He walked over to a long table where thin stacks of paper were lined up. He went for the stack closest to him and handed it to Jess. "Remember Dr. Donald Warner? The famous Arizona heart surgeon?"

Jess nodded. "Convicted last year for the kidnap and murder of his wife. And the felony murder of his chauffeur."

Thelma walked in and placed a steaming cup of coffee in front of each of them. "Horrible man," she said.

"Maybe," Carter said, raising his cup and lowering his chin simultaneously. "And maybe not."

Thelma glared at him.

He waved her out and turned his attention to Jess. "There was plenty of evidence to support the jury's felony murder verdict on the driver. But the wife's body was never found, and Warner still swears he didn't kill her."

Jess flipped through the papers, which were copies of short news accounts of the trial, mostly. "Has the wife's body turned up?"

"Maybe. Which is why you're here. It looks like there's more to this story than we knew."

"There always is."

"Right. Stay with me here." He settled into his chair. "A stolen van caused a traffic pile-up in Santa Irene, Arizona, ten days ago. Three fatalities, including a cop. Police were all over the scene in a matter of minutes, but the driver of the stolen van got away on foot."

"They didn't find the driver?"

Carter shook his head. "DNA everywhere, though. Including a lot of blood. Because of the fatalities, and the dead cop, all the trace evidence was fast tracked. When the processing was finished, they realized that among the blood samples they collected was Karen Warner's blood."

"So, Warner's wife is alive after all?" Jess nodded slowly. She covered cases where the wrongfully accused were convicted of murder. Not often did convicts rightfully proclaim innocence, but it happened too frequently to suit Jess because it meant the wrong man was behind bars while the real killer walked free. "Dr. Warner is serving a prison term he doesn't deserve."

"*Maybe*, I said." Carter finished his coffee and plopped the cup onto his desk with a thud. "This is where it gets more complicated. It turns out Karen Warner had a twin sister."

"I remember that from the original case." Jess nodded. "Identical twins, identical DNA."

"Bingo."

"So, was it the allegedly dead wife or the sister driving the stolen van?"

"That's the question. Should have an easy answer. Just ask the sister, right?" Carter shrugged. "No can do because the sister has gone missing."

Jess cocked her head and frowned. "When was the sister last seen?"

"Melissa Green was a recluse, I guess. Not a big socialite. But there are witness reports from a few weeks ago. Nothing since then."

"Absolutely no one has seen her for a *few weeks*? Not the mailman or the paperboy or even the guy who cuts the grass?"

"Seems not. She lived alone. No close neighbors." Carter shook his head. "There is no car in her garage, and her house is closed up."

"Has anyone searched the house?"

"Now that they have a firm report on the DNA from the van, and figured out the connections, local police are searching the sister's house this morning."

Jess rolled her eyes. "Which is why I have a ticket on the very next flight to Arizona."

"It's strange, don't you think? Donald Warner's wife goes missing, and then months after he's found guilty and sentenced to prison for her murder, her identical twin sister goes missing." Carter smiled. "What are the odds?"

Jess couldn't wrap her mind around it. "There's no sign of the sister? No plane tickets? Credit cards? Rental cars?"

Carter picked up his Mont Blanc and twirled it

absentmindedly through his fingers. "No, no, no, and no."

Jess flipped through more of the papers. When she saw photos of the man who called himself Hades, the hideous scars on his face sent a quick spasm up her spine. Below the news reports of the van wreck, she saw witness statements, photographs, and police evidence from Donald Warner's trial. "Does Warner have a motive?"

"For getting rid of his wife?"

"Or his wife's sister."

"Possible, I guess." Carter shook his head. "But not from what I've heard."

"What else have you heard?"

"You don't have a lot of time if you're going to catch that plane." He pointed at the papers with his Mont Blanc. "Everything I know is in there. Call me if you have questions."

Jess leaned back and ticked off options on her fingers, thinking aloud. "Either Warner arranged the sister's disappearance. Or he didn't do the deed, but someone else has a grudge against some combination of him, the wife, and the sister. Or it's all one big coincidence."

"Or something else entirely." Carter smiled and folded his hands on the desk. "I'm not worried. You'll sort it all out."

"If Warner's not guilty of his wife's murder, he doesn't deserve to be doing prison time for that crime." She looked at the sheaf of papers. "And I don't like to leave a killer walking free."

"Who does? But right now, we don't know." He raised his eyebrows. "Could be there's an innocent man behind bars. Or could be there is a killer on the loose, and the last option is...let's call it a human-interest story."

"Only two out of three falls in my wheelhouse."

"As close as we can expect to get in this business." He

smiled and turned his attention to his ringing phone. "I've already got Mandy working on setting up an interview with David Warner after you talk to the cops at the sister's place."

She tapped the first-class ticket in her hand. "Gotta go. Not much time to catch my flight."

On the way out, she grabbed Mandy. "Walk with me."

"Sure. What's up?" Mandy's legs were longer than a sultry summer afternoon. Jess found herself hustling to stay alongside her assistant.

"I had scheduled an appointment with Trent this afternoon to discuss his progress on Peter's case." Jess found herself slightly out of breath and slowed her pace. Mandy seemed to be loping like a giraffe until they reached the elevator and punched the down button. "Can you let him know I'm on my way out of town and I'll catch up with him when I get back?"

"Of course. But I saw Trent last night." Mandy blushed, which was a first. She was straightforward and plain-spoken. Jess had never seen her embarrassed before. Her relationship with Trent Brennan must have heated up a bit since Jess saw them last.

"You really like this guy, don't you?" Jess teased as they entered the elevator.

Mandy cleared her throat. "As I was saying, Trent said he's read all the files, and he's been following up on those leads you sent him, but he hasn't had any luck."

Jess nodded. She wasn't surprised. Her son had been taken more than a dozen years ago. She'd added Trent to her investigative team because fresh eyes could sometimes see things others more jaded did not. Trent hadn't been on the team very long. She breathed in a little patience.

When the elevator doors opened at the garage level, Jess

said, "No need to get out. I'm in a rush anyway. Just pass along the message for me, and I'll call you later, okay?"

"You bet," Mandy replied as Jess hurried into the garage and toward her car.

CHAPTER FOUR

Monday, May 22
Santa Irene, Arizona

HADES OPENED THE BASEMENT door of the Lawson house and descended the steps from inside the garage to the long and narrow storage space underground. Pony and Shorty followed.

The low ceiling was lined with three bare fluorescent lights. There were no windows. Boxes were stacked in the corner and garden tools hung on the walls. The only furniture was an old table flanked by two scarred kitchen chairs.

The basement was only used by the lawn crew. Nothing about it suggested that either Simon or Natalie Lawson had ever set foot in the place.

Hades grinned. He'd waited for the right time to handle the Lawsons. Imprisoning them underground appealed to Hades, god of the underworld.

Even better, Simon and Natalie Lawson weren't simply locked in the basement. Pony had drilled two tie-downs six feet apart in the concrete floor. Each handcuffed wrist had been secured to one tie-down, and each handcuffed ankle secured to the other. Tape sealed their mouths. A small hole cut in the center allowed them to breathe and to swallow small amounts of food and water. Thick black felt was taped over their eyes.

They had been left in the dark overnight. Hades had found this process softened the resolve of the most determined prisoners.

He knelt beside Natalie and removed her blindfold. She blinked and glowered at him.

He gestured to Pony and Shorty. The two men pulled out knives. Short stubby knives with a continuous curve through the handle and blade. Karambits. Compact and versatile, they were designed for close quarter encounters.

"Try anything, and my friends will kill you," Hades said, and he meant the threat literally.

Natalie glowered, but said nothing.

Hades removed Simon's blindfold. He didn't speak, simply stared, his forehead wrinkled with fear.

Hades released their arms from the tie-downs, leaving the cuffs in place on their wrists.

The pair sat up, massaging aching limbs.

Hades drew up a wooden box and sat at eye level. "We need to talk."

Simon Lawson swallowed but kept silent.

"You will give us your money," Hades said. "All of it."

Simon sniffed. "I told you our password last night. You've already emptied our bank account."

Hades shook his head. He hadn't withdrawn the easy money yet. He'd only made a couple of small transfers.

He shrugged. "What is in your bank account is a pittance of your ready cash. You have at least three million in other accounts."

Simon frowned. "But I can't get at it. It's a retirement account. Restricted."

"Don't give me that crap," Hades shouted and noted how his voice reverberated in the enclosed basement. Natalie Lawson's eyes widened, and her body began to tremble. Hades softened his tone. "It's your money, Simon. You can withdraw it at any time."

"But the penalties—"

Hades lifted the big knife and held it between them, the tip just inches from Simon's eyes, rotating the blade so the light glinted off its serrated edge. "You can withdraw the money, Simon. And you will."

Simon's Adam's apple rose and fell as he gulped air through his open mouth. He leaned back, away from the knife. "But…but the bank won't just hand over that much money. They've got rules."

"True." Hades leaned back, returning his knife to its sheath. "But you've made a good number of wire transfers in the past. Including a few international transfers. So a wire transfer of your money to Panama, for example, won't be flagged."

"You want me to transfer the money out of the country? The bank has limits."

Hades inched closer. He could feel the foul stench of Simon Lawson's breath through his mask. "For individuals, yes. Tedious, pedestrian, low limits. I will remove the limits and we will empty your accounts."

"And if we can't?"

Hades leaned back.

Pony and Shorty took a step closer, knives ready.

Snot ran down Natalie's nose, and her eyes leaked tears. "You're going to kill us anyway."

Hades laughed. He turned to Natalie. "Touch my face."

She swallowed.

Seconds passed. Hades' smile faded. He shouted and again the noise bounced off the walls. "Touch my face!"

Both Lawsons jerked backward, as if, being married, they were truly one flesh.

Hades grabbed Natalie's hand. "I said, touch my face."

Natalie grimaced, breathing hard. Even in the cool basement air, beads of sweat formed on her forehead and mingled with the tears and the snot.

Slowly, she lifted her hand. Her fingers hovered two inches from his face. Hades grabbed her wrist in one smooth, brutal snatch.

She fought back. "I… I…"

"I said, touch my face," he snarled.

Natalie whimpered. She lifted her hand to his face. Her fingers hovered an inch away from him.

He nodded.

Her fingers touched his cheek. She pulled back as if she'd touched a hot flame.

He took her hand and wiped it along his jaw. "You know what that is?"

Her eyes were wide. "A mask," she murmured.

"A latex mask. Best quality. Better than Hollywood." He gestured to Pony and Shorty. "And do you know why we wear masks?"

"So you can't be seen."

"Exactly." He let go of Natalie's hand, and she jerked it back to her chest. He resisted the urge to laugh. "As long as you can't identify us, we have no reason to kill you."

Natalie pressed her lips together and swallowed.

"We will take your money and leave. Unless you do something stupid to make me change my mind." Hades covered her eyes with the blindfold and knotted it behind her head. "Trust me."

CHAPTER FIVE

Monday, May 22
Denver, Colorado

JESS DASHED TO HER apartment, threw a handful of clothes into her carry-on, and called FBI Special Agent Henry Morris as she drove as fast as she dared to Denver International Airport.

They had met on a case that started in Dallas and ended in Italy. He was solid and reliable. She had thought him married at the time, but in the months following the case, she discovered he had lost his wife years before.

After that, they'd dated a few times. Hectic work schedules frequently sabotaged their plans, and their relationship had a long way to go, but she liked him. More importantly, she trusted him.

Morris answered on the second ring. "Hello, Jess." His tone suggested he wasn't alone.

"Hey, Henry. I have a favor to ask. I'm on the way to the airport now. I don't have time to get my Glock through the airport red tape. Can you get it sent to me?"

He kept his formal tone. "Certainly. You'll need a Federal Firearms license holder to receive it."

"I'll find a dealer in the area, and send you the address this afternoon."

"Where's the item?" His circumspect question confirmed he wasn't alone.

"Mandy has a key to my apartment. I have a safe. Call me when you get there, and I'll give you the code."

"Right," he said as if making a note. "I'll see that it gets done."

"Thanks, Henry, and…well, just thanks. Very much… You know."

"I know, and I'll see you soon."

Jess ended the call.

The Denver Airport parking garage was almost full. She circled for an annoying ten minutes until she found a sedan backing out. From there she ran a flat-out sprint to security and boarded her flight with barely two minutes to spare.

She buckled in as the plane pushed back from the gate.

The flight was only ninety minutes. Climb, cruise, descend. The cabin crew served snacks and coffee that could have been left over from the previous day. Jess requested a cup of water, no ice, which she sipped while reading through Carter's notes.

The traffic crash had occurred ten days ago. The white panel van had been stolen from a parking lot. A high-speed chase that the police had tried to corner. One of the police cruisers flipped, and the officer died. Eleven other vehicles were damaged, the last being a minivan in which one passenger had died. Passengers in the other vehicles were injured.

The stolen panel van had come to rest with its front end embedded in a flower shop, after hitting several pedestrians. One had died immediately.

The van's driver was responsible for the carnage. Twelve people were hospitalized. A day later, another pedestrian had died.

Jess shuddered as she flipped through the photographs. The stolen van was practically demolished. It was a wonder the driver walked away. The airbag had deployed, which probably made the difference between life and death.

The next report said the entire area was sealed off and crime scene teams had descended on the site the night of the crash. Every shred of evidence had been collected, processed, and investigated.

There were several unexplained details. There always were. Minutiae. Witness statements that didn't quite correspond. Tire marks on the roads that might have been caused by an accomplice, or could have been made by a teenage boy showing off the day before.

Blood evidence was collected from the cars, the streets, and the flower shop. There were so many samples, labs across the state were used to perform DNA tests, and they were painstakingly assigned to those who were injured or deceased.

The stolen van was a petri dish of trace evidence, but the most valuable samples were taken from the cabin on the driver's side. The airbag, the steering wheel, the door handle, and the side window were spattered with trace amounts that matched a small pool of blood on the driver's seat.

There was no question, the crime scene techs said, that the owner of that blood had been driving the van. The driver would be found. And when she was, she'd be charged with at least four counts of vehicular homicide, as well as other crimes related to the wreck. All they had to do was identify her and then arrest her.

A few days later, law enforcement databases had turned up a match for the blood's DNA. Karen Warner. The same Karen Warner who was presumed dead and whose high-profile husband was convicted of her kidnap and murder.

Jess's mouth dried up, even after she drained the water bottle.

It must have been a relief when investigators learned that Karen Warner had an identical twin sister, Melissa Green.

The pendulum would have swung back to incredulity when they were unable to locate Melissa. If Melissa Green drove the stolen van, she was injured in the carnage. But she hadn't turned up at area hospitals for treatment. She might have died, like four others involved in the crash. But her body, like her sister's before her, had not been found.

Jess put the papers down and rubbed her neck. There were a lot of possible answers. Melissa Green's injury might have been relatively minor. She might have left the state, knowing she would certainly be arrested when authorities found her.

Jess put the notes away as the plane touched down with a hard bump that bounced her into the air above her seat until the seatbelt pulled her down again. She deplaned with the other passengers and, forty minutes later, drove away in the Ford Mustang Thelma had rented.

Melissa Green's house was located on the outskirts of a town called Bear Hill, thirty miles from Santa Irene. The police were entering the house in less than an hour, according to Carter's sources. She wanted to be there when they found something.

Jess punched Melissa Green's address into the navigation system and gunned the Mustang's throttle onto the freeway.

CHAPTER SIX

Monday, May 22
Santa Irene, Arizona

PONY SAT IN THE living room. The television was on, but he occupied himself carving crude images into the coffee table with a steak knife. When the blade dulled, he stabbed it into a wingback chair, which he thought too ugly to exist.

The television's volume was turned down, but the mute function displayed the captions.

Some weather reporter was waving his hands around, to say today would be hot, which was a pretty safe bet for Arizona in May.

Pony fetched another steak knife and returned to the coffee table.

The image on the television jolted him. The middle of a small town he recognized. A crossroads he'd passed through many times. A traffic light swinging in a gentle breeze from which he'd waited for permission to proceed.

A blonde reporter in a blue outfit talked into a microphone.

"Cora," Pony called.

She wandered into the room. "What?"

She caught the image on the screen before he answered.

Closed captions about the manhunt for the driver of the stolen white van scrolled across the screen.

"Hades, get in here!"

He burst into the room, stumbling to a stop in front of the television. "What are they doing?"

"Looking for the driver, I'm guessing," Cora said with a smile.

"Why? What's happened?"

Cora shook her head. "Who knows? But we can't go back there."

"You think I don't know that?" He kicked the end table with his heavy boot, and it sailed across the room and crashed into the wall.

"Our cover's blown." She looked at the television and shook her head. "I can't go out in public in the daylight." She waved the back of her hand toward Hades. "Neither can you. Even with our masks."

He ran both hands through his hair and blew an exasperated grunt. "How long have they been searching?"

"Don't know," Pony replied. "But if they're searching, they must have gone in the house."

"They just said they're going inside when they have a warrant, which is on the way." Cora shook her head. "Even if they have been inside the house, they can't have found anything. Otherwise, they wouldn't be asking for help."

Hades shook his head. "They'd ask anyway. They won't be happy until they answer whatever's stirred them up."

"But we don't know what's got them interested," Cora said.

The TV news moved onto another subject.

"Now's the time." Hades pulled a laptop from his backpack.

Pony reached over and yanked the laptop from his grasp. "We can't give them a reason to link this place to our safe house."

"You think I'm that stupid?" Hades shot a withering glower in Pony's general direction. "This is exactly why I set the place up with remote access."

Pony pursed his lips. "Things can always be traced."

Hades replied with exaggerated patience. "The police are going to get their warrant and get inside that house. Then we're hosed. We have to send the command. Now. Not in an hour. Now. Don't you get it?"

Pony nodded.

Hades sat on the couch with a thump and powered up the laptop. "I'll relay it through a server in Latvia. It'll take them months to trace it here."

He hammered on the laptop's keys for a minute before stabbing the mouse button hard. "It's done. Now we wait for the command to work its way through the servers to the house."

"That'll take time," Pony said. "They might find whatever they're looking for in the meanwhile."

"There's nothing else we can do."

"It's a risk."

"No kidding!" Hades stood and paced the room until he calmed himself. He took a deep breath. "That's why you're going over there to make sure the safe house and everything in it is destroyed. Every last scrap."

CHAPTER SEVEN

Monday, May 22
Bear Hill, Arizona

JESS TOOK THE EXIT her navigation system indicated and passed through the town of Bear Hill. The road led into a canyon.

Trees were dotted in clumps along the sides of the road. They seemed to cling together for support in the pulsing heat.

Occasional letterboxes marked driveways. The letterboxes were the rural sort. A wooden post with a box on top, the posts leaning at all angles. Some had numbers, some had the metal outlines of men riding horses, and some were no more than rust and faded paint.

The driveways sloped up the canyon's sides. The houses were invisible behind the trees and the curve of the land.

Jess slowed as the navigation system said she had arrived. The entrance to Melissa Green's property ran over a cattle grate. Barbed wire ran from the gate, left to right, in both directions. The Mustang's stiff suspension took the cattle gate hard, bouncing her phone out of the cup holder. She took it as a warning to slow down.

The dusty driveway twisted and turned as it climbed before depositing her on a broad expanse of almost flat land in front of the house.

In the middle of the driveway's end was a two-story, white painted clapboard home that might have been built in the nineteenth century. The boards bowed up and down, partly from the natural cut of the wood and partly from the movement of the house over the years.

The window frames were outlined in black. Their perfectly rectangular shapes suggested they were replacements for the original wood and constructed of man-made materials.

A porch ran the full width of the house. A swing seat hung crookedly on its chain to one side of the front door.

Cars and SUVs were parked at various angles around the edge of the clearing. She counted two police cars as she worked her way around and parked. She reversed into the space, the car pointing down the hill in case its sports suspension and tires weren't up to the task of starting on the rough ground when she was ready to leave.

She retrieved her phone from the floor, shoved her camera into her crossbody bag, and headed to join a group of people standing near the front porch.

The group consisted of two police officers and four civilians. The civilians all sported DSLRs and handheld recorders on straps around their necks. Reporters. The officers watched her approach. They all stood calmly, as people for whom waiting was an integral part of the occupation do.

"Captain Mitch Jackson." One of the officers stepped forward, extended his hand, and nodded to the officer standing with him. "This is Officer Lester Cook. Who're you with?"

"*Taboo*," she said, shaking his hand.

"The monthly magazine?" Jackson frowned. "You in the right place?"

"Melissa Green?"

He nodded. "We wanted dailies. Get the story out. So she gets to hear it quick."

The other reporters nodded sagely. Jess suspected they were halfway between wondering what had brought her there and hoping the Captain would persuade her to leave.

She gave a flat smile. "I just flew in."

Jackson grunted. "We don't want some big sensation. Melissa Green keeps to herself, but she's a good person. We just need her to know we're looking, and she'll come back."

His words jarred. Did he not know about the crash? "You think she's simply wandered off?"

He handed Jess a sheet of paper. "Leave your name and email, and we'll send you a photograph and description."

An old red truck with a cap on the back labored up the driveway, its diesel engine wheezing and black smoke emerging from the rear. It lurched to a stop, blocking several parked cars. Faded lettering on the side said *Ernest Kettering*. Underneath was the word locksmith, and a phone number.

Ernest Kettering emerged from the truck. He was tall and thin and gray, a hundred and fifty pounds at best. He collected a heavy toolbox from the rear of the truck and struggled to carry it as he joined the group.

"Captain," he nodded toward Jackson.

Jackson smiled. "Good to see ya, Ernie."

Ernie set his toolbox on the grass. "Saw a TV crew in town."

"I gave them an interview. Thought we'd keep them away from here. Don't want a big circus. This isn't reality TV."

Ernie gestured to the house. "Everything ready?"

Jackson nodded and handed Ernie the warrant. Ernie looked it over and handed it back.

"Then let's get started." Ernie lifted his toolbox and struggled up the steps onto the porch. He knelt by the front door, peering at the lock.

Captain Jackson turned to the reporters. "We're going inside to check the place out. When we come back, I'll give you a statement, and you can take pictures of the front of the house."

The four reporters nodded, but they didn't smile.

Jess took a deep breath and kept the questions circling in her mind to herself. She didn't expect them to find Melissa Green inside the house and she got the impression they didn't expect to find her there, either. Let Jackson get on with it. She'd ask questions afterward.

The reporters waited on the lawn. The officers joined Ernie on the porch. In a moment, the front door swung open.

Ernie stepped back and sat in the swing seat.

Jackson led the second officer, Cook, into the house. His muffled voice calling for Melissa reached Jess's ears outside. She heard no reply. No cat meowing. No dog barking. Nothing.

One of the reporters stepped forward, holding out a business card. "Sidney Mackenzie. *Santa Irene Gazette*."

Jess took his card and shook his hand. "Jess Kimball. *Taboo*." She rummaged in her bag and handed him a card, too.

He ran his thumb over the embossed logo. "Let me guess. You're interested because of Melissa Green's relationship to Donald and Karen Warner?"

She shrugged. "We have a lot of different interests."

He smiled. "I'm not fishing. We're a daily. Today it's the Warners, tomorrow I'll be on to something new."

Jess gave him a sympathetic smile. She knew the pressure small newspapers were under to keep turning up the latest news. The constant Internet news cycle had made their jobs much harder. Even so, she wouldn't be manipulated into disclosing *Taboo's* intel.

Mackenzie pointed to the house. "They're upstairs already."

"Probably a good sign," Jess replied.

They stood in silence, watching the two officers move past the windows on the upper floor.

Ernie relaxed in the swing seat. His eyes looked closed. Jess wondered if he knew more about Melissa's disappearance. She made a note to question him before he left.

Captain Jackson walked out of the house and stood on the porch steps. He called the reporters closer.

"As I expected, there's no sign of foul play. Nothing's been disturbed. Bed's been made, and there's food in the pantry. Everything is A-OK normal."

Mackenzie raised his hand. "Any sign of where she might have gone?"

Jackson shook his head. "We're going back in to conduct a more thorough search, but nothing obvious."

"You still want us to report you're concerned about her?"

"I'd say we're interested in talking to her, not that we're concerned. I'm not concerned. These things usually have a simple answer."

The other journalists wrote down Jackson's quote in their notepads. He gave them a moment, but no one asked any more questions.

"Well, if you'll excuse me." He turned back into the house, closing the front door behind him.

A couple of the reporters wandered back to their cars.

Mackenzie walked around the front yard, apparently looking for a good angle to get a picture of the empty house.

Jess walked around to the back. The yard sloped upward behind the house. A second porch ran the width back here, too. Three steps led up from the ground level. Jess guessed that even with Arizona's reputation for blistering heat, the elevation was meant to thwart possible flash floods.

The rear porch had several potted plants, neglected and barely alive. Two large prickly cacti stood guard on either side of a weather-worn table and chairs.

Officer Cook stepped out of the back door, looked up and down the porch, and went back into the house.

A large bright yellow hose was coiled on a reel attached to the rear wall near the door. There was a brass tap beside it, and a dark stain on the porch that suggested the hose had a leak.

Jess climbed the stairs. The back door was half glass. She cupped her hands to keep out the sunlight and looked inside. The window beside the door opened over the kitchen sink. The kitchen had a large pine table in the middle with six chairs. A circular container filled with cutlery rested in the table's center.

Several magazines were strewn over the countertop on the far side of the room. Jess angled her head to read the mastheads. The fonts were too small to read from this distance, so she took a picture with her camera, and enlarged the image. The words were still unreadable in the viewfinder, but the front cover clearly featured a motorbike sliding on a muddy track.

Jess frowned. Melissa Green could be interested in dirt bikes, but it was hard to reconcile with her shy reputation.

Jess tried the backdoor. It clicked open. Cook must have failed to lock it when he poked his head out earlier. She went inside.

She photographed the room as she approached the

magazines. She slid them out into a line, using a knuckle to avoid fingerprints. The last four months' editions of *Dirt and Track*, a motocross magazine, mingled with several women's fashion magazines. Jess snapped pictures of each cover in quick succession and re-stacked the pile.

Captain Jackson called for Ernie from upstairs.

Jess moved to the back door, prepared to dart outside. The last thing she wanted was to get sideways with the local police for unauthorized breaking and entering.

The front door creaked open and slammed shut.

"Bring your tools," Jackson shouted.

The front door creaked and slammed a second time. "What's up?" Ernie said, climbing the stairs.

Jess returned her attention to the kitchen. Coffee maker, toaster, and microwave rested on the countertops. Old mail was piled up in one corner.

The pantry was well stocked. Unsurprising given that the grocery store was a ten-mile drive into town.

Jess rubbed her eyes. Something was making her eyes itch. Probably dust or pollen. She took a tissue from a box on the window ledge and wiped her nose. The last thing she needed was an allergy.

The fridge and freezer were two separate appliances, side-by-side in an alcove. The freezer was three-quarters full. Mostly microwave meals. The door closed with a heavy *thunk*.

Jess listened hard. Ernie and the two officers were talking upstairs, but all she could hear were muffled voices. After a moment, a drill squealed. Jess rolled her shoulders to ward off the screech of metal on metal, and opened the fridge.

The refrigerator was as well stocked as the pantry and freezer. A gallon carton of milk was all but empty, but the orange juice jug was full. She checked the expiration dates on both and saw they'd last a few days longer. Stacked plastic containers were filled with unidentified leftovers. She leaned forward to peer in through the opaque plastic.

The drill motor upstairs ceased its battle and the squealing stopped.

She reached for one of the plastic containers.

Upstairs, someone shouted. Footsteps hammered on the floor. She froze, listening, half in and half out of the fridge, the plastic container in her hand.

After that, everything happened fast.

A deafening explosion tore through the upstairs.

The hallway door snapped off its hinges and whirled past Jess.

A massive pressure wave blasted through the kitchen.

The windows exploded outward.

The back door flew open.

Jess was blown flat on the floor.

The fridge door whipped back, breaking the top hinge and smashing down beside her, inches from her head.

The entire contents of the kitchen took flight.

The pine table rolled over and smashed against the sink.

The chairs tumbled after it.

The mail exploded into envelope confetti.

The coffee maker shot into the corner.

As fast as it came, the pressure wave eased. Almost like a giant sigh. As if the effort had exhausted the explosion itself.

Dust and debris hung in the air.

Followed by something else.

Fire.

CHAPTER EIGHT

Monday, May 22
Bear Hill, Arizona

JESS ROLLED ONTO HER side. She panted hard and wiped her hand across her eyes. Her forehead stung, and her hand came away bloody.

Flames were spilling from the walls and traveling across the work surfaces.

She shook her head, trying to focus.

With the door gone, the hallway was open. Smoke filled the passageway.

Where were Jackson and the others?

She darted through the opening where the back door had been. Beside the hose was a brass tap. She twisted it full on and pulled great loops of hose from the reel.

The spray attachment was set to a fine mist. She twisted it to create a powerful stream and poured water ahead of her as she raced back into the house.

The fire roared. Flames climbed the walls and licked across

the ceiling. Smoke was filling the room from the ceiling down. She soaked a towel by the sink and slapped it across her mouth and nose.

A scream sounded from upstairs.

The hallway burned along one wall.

She soaked the carpet with the hose and ran to the foot of the stairs.

The scream came again.

She dragged the hose up the stairs, flipping it over the banister to lessen the drag of its weight. The height reduced water flow.

The reporter, MacKenzie, appeared at the top of the stairs. "You have to get out!"

"Help!" wailed a voice from a bedroom.

"Get more water!" Jess screamed, working her way along the landing toward the wailing.

"No!" MacKenzie yelled.

"Yes!" She yelled.

The doors and walls were in flames. She waved the spray over the bedroom door, and lunged a hard kick at the handle. The door swept open.

A storm of burning embers swirled out at her. She ducked her face into the crook of her arm, choking on the heat and smoke until the wave passed.

She staggered into what had been a bedroom.

Half of the exterior wall was missing. The furniture was upended in one corner, on fire. Fierce orange flames engulfed the walls and furniture and licked outside the house through the hole in the wall.

"Help!" Jackson screamed.

His voice came from under the furniture. She directed the

hose over the mound of wood and bedclothes crammed against a wall. Smoke filled the air.

She rolled the burning bed away from the wall. Jackson screamed.

His bloody arm appeared through a gap. She pulled a chest of drawers from the pile. He continued to scream.

She trained the hose on him and pulled broken wood and bedclothes from the bonfire until she saw his tortured face.

She threw off the last debris. His legs were twisted at terrible angles. His clothes were torn and burned. Smoke wafted from his hair.

She dropped the hose and fell to her knees to push one arm under his legs and the other around his back. He screamed long and hard.

The heated air burned her throat with every breath. She gritted her teeth and struggled to her feet. Jackson clung to her neck, grunting and groaning to stifle his screams.

The floor buckled. Smoke and glowing embers swirled in the air.

She staggered to the door.

MacKenzie was using a rug to beat back the flames on the landing. She stumbled past. He grabbed Jackson's legs and shared the weight down the stairs.

The front porch was ablaze. MacKenzie guided her to a clear space on the right. He vaulted the railing, and turned, holding up his arms. She handed Jackson over to him and leaped off the porch.

Jess staggered down the slope. Behind her, wood creaked, and one side of the house collapsed inward.

She grabbed one of the reporters. "Where's Ernie? And Cook?"

The reporter shook his head.

She looked back at the house. Flames poured from the doors and windows and escaped through giant holes in the roof. The building was moments from destruction. Anyone who hadn't made it out already, wouldn't survive.

The swing seat on the porch collapsed.

A few yards away, Jackson moaned as he lay on the ground.

Jess's eyes stung and her lungs hurt with every painful breath. Her hands were raw. Her shoes had almost burned through their soles.

Four people were in the house before the explosion. The locksmith, two police officers, and her. Two of them hadn't made it out at all and Jackson seemed barely alive.

She sank to the ground.

It was all she could do not to retch.

There was only one thought in her mind. It was grotesque and abhorrent, as unstoppable as it was unbidden.

The words went around and around in her head.

She was the lucky one.

CHAPTER NINE

Monday, May 22
Santa Irene, Arizona

HADES SAT AT SIMON Lawson's computer, shaking his head. It was remarkable how little people understood computers. Or how easy it was to break in and steal every last piece of information stored on them.

Internet search histories and browser cookies were easy to decode. Security certificates that encrypted financial transactions from a computer to banks and brokerage houses couldn't be decoded, but the names of the firms were available to anyone who cared to look.

And Hades cared. With the names, he could find out anything else he wanted to know.

He gathered everything he needed and made a single phone call. He'd always been a good mimic. He affected the educated, privileged tone of a man who expected his instructions to be carried out immediately and without question.

The banker was comfortable with such men. He had

efficiently recorded the details Hades relayed as if he was Dr. Simon Lawson.

The banker completed the tasks efficiently, too, and twenty minutes later an email notification appeared on Simon Lawson's computer.

Dr. Simon Lawson now owned a new company, incorporated in Panama. The principal business was consumer goods. A token deposit had been made from Simon Lawson's bank into a new account in Panama. The whole transaction was performed by the South American country, with the clear direction that further funds would arrive soon.

Hades picked up a writing pad and a pen and slipped on his Babe Ruth mask. "It's time."

Donning their own masks, Cora and Shorty followed him down the narrow stairs into the dank basement. He flipped on the fluorescent light. The Lawsons were still prone on the concrete floor, arms stretched above their heads, their feet and hands secured to the tie-downs.

Hades pulled up a chair beside Simon Lawson. He nodded, and Shorty unclipped their hands from the tie-down and removed the thick felt blindfolds.

The Lawsons sat up as one. They moved their arms slowly because their muscles had locked into the stretched positions.

Natalie rolled over, easing her rigid back into a new posture, flexing vertebrae and stretching ligaments. She kept her eyes closed against the painfully bright fluorescents.

Simon's hooded gaze darted from his wife to Hades and back. He, too, shuffled his hips and shoulders, using his weight to massage his muscles.

Hades waited while the Lawsons finished physical therapy.

He was patient. Despite the circumstances, he needed a modicum of cooperation a while longer.

Until he extracted what they knew.

Simon Lawson's gaze gradually came to rest on Hades. "What do you want?"

Hades smiled. "I've already told you. We will take your money and leave."

Simon looked down. Natalie watched him from the corner of her eye.

Hades continued the pretext. "You will be poorer, but you're clever. You have a good job, doctor. You'll manage."

He leaned closer. "Most importantly, if you are cooperative, you will be safe. You will survive." He touched his face mask and lowered his voice. "You understand?"

Natalie inched closer to Simon, shoulders touching. Simon lowered his gaze and nodded.

"But only if you cooperate."

Simon nodded.

"Completely."

Simon swallowed and nodded.

Hades stared at him. Seconds passed. Simon kept his gaze down.

Hades took a deep breath and lightened his tone. "Good."

He leaned back in the chair and crossed his legs to rest the pad on his knee. "Very good. We could be out of here in a couple of days. Not long at all. If you cooperate."

He wrote the name of two financial institutions on the pad, one name per line, several lines between each name. He handed it to Simon. "You recognize those names?"

Simon nodded. "My retirement accounts."

Hades held out a pen. "I need the passwords."

Simon hesitated.

Hades kept his hand still, the pen in front of Simon.

Simon studied the pen.

"We will be finished here soon," Hades said, "if you cooperate."

Simon took a deep breath.

Hades waved the pen. Simon took it. He juggled the pad into a stable position. He twisted his cuffed wrists to free his fingers well enough to print.

He wrote small characters. Letters and numbers. Hash marks and semicolons. The full range of symbols that security professionals encouraged him to use. Complex passwords. Difficult to remember, but difficult to break. Supposedly.

Hades smiled to himself.

Simon finished the last password. He held out the pad and pen, his face impassive.

Hades read back the password gibberish, one symbol at a time.

Simon nodded throughout.

Hades stood. "You understand that I will not be happy if these passwords are not correct?"

Simon gave a long slow nod. He wiped his forehead with his forearm.

Hades pushed the chair back under the table. The legs scraped on the bare concrete floor. "Then you both will survive." He paused. "That's all that is important in the end. Isn't it?"

Hades left the basement with Cora. Shorty stayed behind to reattach both Lawsons to the tie-downs.

CHAPTER TEN

Monday, May 22
Bear Hill, Arizona

JESS COLLAPSED ON THE front lawn, breathing deeply. The house burned as she watched. Thick black smoke plumed into the sky.

Jackson's moans drifted across the lawn. Two reporters tried to reassure him as they waited for help, but their words didn't stop his pain.

A siren's wail approached in the distance, and finally, an ambulance arrived. The medics ferried bags of fluid and a stretcher over to Jackson. They cut away his clothes and threaded an intravenous tube into the back of his hand. A few moments later, Jackson's moans subsided.

They hoisted Jackson onto the gurney and rolled him into the ambulance.

One of the medics approached Jess after that. "You okay?"

She nodded.

"Was anyone else hurt?"

Jess pointed to the house. "There were two more inside."

The medic's eyes narrowed. He gazed at the burning home. "Who were they?"

"Another officer and a locksmith."

"Ernie?"

She nodded. "And Lester Cook."

He swore under his breath. "How did all this happen so quickly?"

Before she could answer, a fire engine sped up the driveway. It steered onto the lawn and around the house.

The ambulance driver called to the medic. "Be right there," the medic called back. He patted Jess's shoulder. "Sure you don't want to come along to the hospital? Get checked out?"

She shook her head. The medic jogged back to the ambulance and climbed aboard. Jess watched the ambulance speed away, siren blazing.

The firemen spread out around the house. They ran a thick hose on the far side of the fire engine.

The upper floor of the house collapsed. Flames gushed from the dying building. The firefighters began dousing the ground and vegetation outside. The house was a lost cause now, but the earth was dry. They didn't want the fire to spread.

MacKenzie sat down on the ground beside Jess. "Were you in the building when it happened?"

Jess nodded. "In the kitchen."

"Jackson told us to keep out."

Jess shrugged.

"Maybe he suspected something?"

Jess shook her head. "He called for Ernie. He wouldn't have done that if he'd known the house was dangerous."

MacKenzie nodded. "I'm sure you're right."

Water began running down the slope from the house. Jess pushed herself up and walked to higher ground where she had parked her car.

MacKenzie followed. "Something certainly exploded in that house."

Jess didn't reply.

"I heard a bang all the way out here." MacKenzie took a couple of long strides and walked beside her. "All the windows blew out."

"Whatever exploded, it must have been upstairs."

Mackenzie frowned. "Maybe. But there were flames all over the place. Even the ground floor."

Jess watched as the last standing wall collapsed. It seemed impossible to believe, but in little more than fifteen minutes, the entire building had been reduced to rubble.

MacKenzie said, "Old, dry wood burns quick."

Jess nodded. She found a tissue in her pocket and rubbed her eyes. The sting of smoke still lingered.

Everything had happened so fast. The explosion. The fire. The complete destruction of Melissa Green's home. So fast.

Jess took a deep breath. The fresh air made her eyes feel better, but she remembered how irritated they'd become when she first walked into the kitchen.

She pulled her camera from her pocket and flipped through the pictures she'd shot. The range was electric. Maybe there was a gas furnace in the attic? Which didn't make much sense. Gas space heaters in the bedrooms, maybe? Arizona winters could get chilly. Maybe small gas heaters would have helped.

And gas might explain why the fire spread so quickly. Gas could have irritated her eyes, too. But gas producers added sulfur containing methyl mercaptan. The odor was intentionally distinctive and pervasive. She would have noticed. So would Captain Jackson and Officer Cook.

A white Toyota raced up the lane, screeching to a stop on the edge of the lawn. A woman in jeans leaped out and ran screaming toward the smoldering pile of rubble that had been Melissa Green's house.

Jess swallowed. "One of the wives."

MacKenzie remained silent.

The fire chief caught hold of the woman. She wrestled herself free. He grabbed her again. Her struggle slowed, but her grief-stricken wailing continued to pierce the air.

Jess's stomach churned. The woman's grief was heartbreaking. Jess wanted to comfort her, but she had nothing to say that would help.

A small girl climbed out of the Toyota's back seat holding a tiny doll. She looked around and moved closer to her mom, who was still sobbing in the fire chief's embrace.

Jess took a deep breath and crossed over to kneel beside the girl. She began to speak softly to her. "Hi, I'm Jess. What's your name?"

Gradually she learned the girl's name. And the dolly. And her daddy, the police officer who wouldn't be coming home.

After a while, the fire chief led Mrs. Cook toward Jess and little Emma. He released her with a pained expression. She sank to the ground and Emma dropped into her lap. The fire's smoldering echo was overwhelmed by the sound of a grieving wife's wails.

CHAPTER ELEVEN

Monday, May 22
Bear Hill, Arizona

JESS CIRCLED THE REMAINS of the house, keeping well outside the ring of firemen and the ground they had doused. MacKenzie was right. The house had been old and stick built. Its entire frame consisted of highly flammable wood. The contents were probably just as old and dry. Given the size of the explosion, maybe it wasn't sinister that the fire spread and consumed the house as quickly as it did.

A tent-like structure rose up around where the kitchen had been as if the upstairs floor had been prevented from falling to the ground by the metalwork of the appliances.

Elsewhere, the roof, the walls, and the floors had burned to almost nothing, leaving only small chunks of wood in the ash. Wires and pipes poked through the mess. Most were twisted and bent from the weight of the collapsing structure, but a couple rose ten feet into the air.

Jess took photographs. She zoomed in as close as her lens

would allow. The details would have been clearer if she'd moved in closer, but she didn't want to trample any relevant evidence that might have survived.

Near the rear of the property, an oblong shape was covered in ash. The fridge that Jess had been standing near when the explosion happened. It was remarkably intact. Its strength had certainly helped her survive. She photographed it from both sides.

Across what would have been the hallway was another mound buried in the ash. It looked like a five-foot tall wine bottle. She worked her way around the building for a better angle.

It was a gas cylinder. The type used in hospitals. The surface was rough and blackened with soot. The end with the valve was a jumble of wires and pipes covered in a charred mass.

The more she stared, the more absurd the cylinder looked. No one would want something so crude and ugly in their house without good reason. The pipes and wires indicated it was plumbed into the house in some way. The cylinder looked intact.

Was it bottled oxygen, perhaps? The notes Carter had supplied didn't indicate that Melissa Green had breathing problems, but he might not have known. Or perhaps she had someone else living with her who needed the oxygen?

She took more pictures and then quickly shot video with her phone before a van from a local television station labored into the clearing, and she lost her chance.

Several people jumped out of the van. A technician tended to a satellite dish on the roof. The cameraman donned a bulky jacket and set up his Steadicam. The reporter was last out. She wore a prim blue pantsuit and checked her blonde hair and makeup in the van's wing mirrors.

The cameraman walked the length of the front lawn, getting

his establishing shots. He knelt in front of the fire engine for footage of the vehicle with the smoking remains of the house in the background.

The reporter approached the mother and child. As she talked, she beckoned to the cameraman. He curved around for a sweeping shot of the anchor kneeling beside the little girl with her doll still clutched to her chest.

Jess couldn't hear the words as the reporter spoke into her microphone. The cameraman closed in.

The fire chief started toward the group, dragging a heavy hose behind him.

Jess followed.

The reporter was talking into the camera now. She was kneeling, holding her microphone in front of the mother. The reporter flipped the microphone back and forth, obviously asking the mother questions. Jess couldn't see the mother's face.

"Leave her alone," the fire chief shouted.

The cameraman angled around to block the chief's path to the reporter.

The reporter stood up. "We have every right to—"

The chief twisted the lever on his hose, winding it wide open, then snapping it shut. The force of the water's quick blast jolted him back.

The water hit the cameraman in the back of his knees. His legs collapsed. The weight of his gear pulled him down, and he tumbled backward.

The reporter rushed forward. "What the hell—"

"I'll do the same to you next," the chief said, a bulldog expression on his face to match the threat.

"That's expensive equipment, you crazy—"

"It'll be expensive scrap if you don't get out of here." The chief moved his hand to the lever again, ready to make good on the promise.

The reporter stood still. "We're just doing our job, and you know it."

"You're on private property. Get lost."

"You have no right—"

The chief pulsed the hose again. He aimed to the side of the reporter, but the overspray was enough to douse her clothes and rearrange her perfect hair into a bedraggled mess.

She screamed.

"Leave these people alone and get off this—"

The reporter waved her fist. "You're going to damn well pay for this."

Blue and red lights strobed through the gaps in the trees along the driveway.

The cameraman rolled to his feet and lifting his heavy camera from the wet ground, struggled to stand.

The chief stepped forward, adjusting his grip on the lever that fired the hose to make sure no one doubted his intentions.

Two white and green police cars burst into the clearing. They had different logos from the black and tan cruiser Captain Jackson had arrived in, which suggested a different jurisdiction.

A stocky blond man jumped out of the driver's seat. He raced to the woman and girl and knelt beside them. He wrapped them both in a hug, close to his chest. From the insignia on his shirt, Jess guessed he was a captain, too.

Policemen fanned out around the building, talking to the firemen and corralling the witnesses.

The reporter and cameraman retreated to their van.

Several minutes had passed before the second police captain led the woman back to her Toyota while he carried her daughter.

Once they were settled, he approached the fire chief. The captain's name tag said R. Mercer.

The fire chief waved at the soggy pile that had once been a home. "Some sort of explosion. We heard it all the way down at the fire station."

"How many inside?"

"Jackson and two others, as far as we know. We tried to ask him, but he wasn't very coherent." The fire chief glanced down at the ground and cleared his throat before he said, "I'm not sure whether he'll make it."

"It was Officer Cook. And another man. Captain Jackson called him Ernie. He was a locksmith," Jess said.

Captain Mercer narrowed his eyes to look at Jess. His frown threatened to consume his entire freckled face. "And you are?"

"Jessica Kimball. I was in the kitchen when the explosion happened."

"You live here?"

Jess shook her head. "Melissa Green lives here. She's been missing for several days. We were searching the house."

"You a friend?"

Jess shook her head again. "*Taboo Magazine*."

"If Captain Jackson was here, this was a police investigation. So what were you doing in the house?"

"I saw something and went in to check it out."

Mercer raised his eyebrows, expectantly.

"Melissa Green lived alone. Yet the kitchen was stocked with enough food to feed an army."

"So you broke in."

"The door was open."

Captain Mercer turned away to look at the remains of the house again.

"My eyes were irritated by something before the explosion happened," Jess said.

Mercer grunted.

"At the time, I thought it could have been pollen. Or something harmless."

Mercer glanced back at her. "Probably a gas leak, judging from the amount of damage."

Jess shook her head. "It wasn't a gas leak because I would have smelled it." She pointed into the smoldering remains, toward the charred metal cylinder. "Who has a gas bottle like that in their house?"

Mercer leaned forward and studied the bottle. He nodded and jerked his thumb toward one of his men, who headed off to check out the cylinder. To Jess, Mercer said, "We'll need a full statement from you."

CHAPTER TWELVE

Monday, May 22
Bear Hill, Arizona

JESS GAVE HER STATEMENT to an officer who looked remarkably like a handsome movie star whose name she couldn't quite place. He collected her phone number and verified her status by calling the *Taboo* offices before letting her go.

She walked to the Mustang, rummaged through her bag and found her clean running shoes, and dropped the ruined ballerina flats into the trunk. She used a bottle of water and napkins she had saved from the plane to clean her hands. Nothing she could do about the pervasive smell of smoke that clung to every pore.

There was nothing more she could do here, either. The policeman had suggested she leave and that seemed like a good idea to her. She needed a shower and a meal and about three weeks' sleep. Her strained muscles were already complaining about the day's extraordinary exertion.

As she rolled her Mustang out of the clearing and descended the track to the main road where the air was clearer, she lowered the window and breathed deeply. After half a dozen breaths, she felt better, but she could still smell the fire's reek on her clothes and her body.

Mercer had a job to do, and he was likely dealing with shock and grief himself. He must have known Cook, the second officer. He probably knew Ernie the locksmith, too. And, of course, Captain Jackson. But Mercer should have recognized the demolished house was a potential crime scene from the moment he arrived.

She grunted. There was no innocent way to explain why that explosion occurred, or why fire had consumed the entire house in a matter of minutes, even if the whole thing was a tinder box, like MacKenzie said.

She pulled out onto the main road as a crime scene van turned into the drive.

Arson laws varied by jurisdiction, but Jackson and his men had walked into what seemed more and more like a trap, the longer Jess thought about it.

She worked her way up through the gears.

Donald Warner's chauffeur was murdered. His wife was abducted and was presumed dead. Her sister had disappeared. And now her sister's house had been blown up, killing two more people and leaving another seriously injured.

All these things were connected. Jess didn't know how, but they had to be. And she had only two leads, so it wasn't hard to figure out where to start.

She picked up her phone and sent the pictures she had taken at Melissa Green's house. After the last one was delivered, Jess pushed the speed dial on her speakerphone.

Her assistant, Mandy Donovan, answered immediately. "Jess, how's things?"

Jess watched the road. "Someone blew up Melissa Green's house."

Mandy gasped. "When?"

"An hour ago. I was inside the house at the time." She rounded a curve and passed a bicyclist.

Mandy's voice went up an octave. "Are you okay?"

"Bruised and a bit singed, but otherwise in one piece."

Mandy's voice was shaky. "Glad to hear it."

"Two people were killed in the blast. A police officer and a locksmith."

"Oh, no!" Mandy's second gasp traveled the distance from Denver as if she were sitting in the passenger seat.

"And a police captain was taken by ambulance to the hospital."

Mandy sighed. "Do they know what caused the explosion?"

"Not yet. The police are all over the scene now." She passed a slow-moving station wagon full of Cub Scouts. "They'll figure it out. Explosives leave a lot of evidence behind. It's just a matter of time."

"You sure you're okay?"

"I'm filthy and exhausted, but I'll be okay." She looked down at her clothes. Nothing on her body would ever be worn again. "I sent you some pictures of a gas cylinder. I want to know what was in it."

"I'll have to call around. Can I show people the pictures?"

"Crop them to show the cylinder and nothing else. And don't give anyone any information at all. We don't want to educate the wrong people."

"Who are the wrong people?"

"We don't know yet."

Mandy squeaked and cleared her throat. "Sounds like there's something else?"

"How are you coming along on that meeting Carter asked you to schedule with Donald Warner?"

"The guy in prison, right?" Mandy sighed. "We need his permission, and he's a very bitter man. I had to use every ounce of charm I've got."

Jess grinned. Count on Mandy to call upon her sex appeal whenever she had the chance. "So? Where are we, then?"

"That's why I tried to call you earlier. I sent you some stuff, too." Mandy was a great assistant, and she knew it. "There's an application and a background check and all of that. Usually, takes about sixty days to get any kind of meeting with a prison inmate there."

Jess groaned and swiped a grimy curl away from her face. "I can't wait sixty days, Mandy."

"I know. Carter had to pull some strings, and it sounds like maybe this isn't a good thing now, with that explosion and everything, but your appointment is all set. Warner's expecting you this afternoon." Mandy paused. "And you need to hurry. You've got to be there before five o'clock, local time."

"You're the best, Mandy. Have I told you that before?" Jess heard Mandy laughing when she hung up. Jess glanced at the clock on the dashboard. She'd spent way more time at the Green house than she'd expected to. But Mandy was right. She couldn't be late.

Donald Warner was in prison just on the other side of Santa Irene, Arizona, the city where he had worked as a doctor. Jess pointed the Mustang in the right direction and pressed the accelerator to the floor. Her shower would have to wait.

CHAPTER THIRTEEN

Monday, May 22
Santa Irene, Arizona

HADES IDLY CLICKED THE *buy* button on the computer screen. A picture of the large Swiss watch he'd selected was displayed. Solid gold with diamonds on the face in place of numerals. The price was thirty-eight thousand dollars. Overnight delivery was included, but the tax was extra. He scrolled right and chose a quantity of two.

He'd already maxed out Lawson's credit cards, so he entered Lawson's address and bank account details this time. A big bold button labeled *Confirm* glowed. He clicked it, and the website promised his purchase would arrive first thing in the morning.

Cora was working on a laptop on the sofa.

"What have you got?" he said.

"No worries, here. I'm an excellent shopper." She grinned up at him. "Two rings, two necklaces, two bracelets. A quarter million. You?"

"All watches. A hundred thousand, give or take." He smiled.

"Enough to keep us going a while, even though we only get sixty percent." He'd argued about the terms with his reseller. Everything he planned to dump was new. Never even removed from the package. The sellers had been paid, and Simon Lawson would never complain. This stuff was as free and clear as stolen merchandise could ever be. So he'd negotiated a better than normal deal. But still, he was taking all the risk. Joey had said he was the one with the customers. Sixty percent was the best he could do, and it was a damn shame. Pissed Hades off, but Joey was the best, and Hades needed the cash.

"I found something else." Cora's troubled tone caught his attention. He walked around to the sofa and looked at her screen.

He frowned. "A security certificate. Every website uses them these days."

"It doesn't link to a website." Cora flipped her long hair behind her shoulder and pointed a well-manicured index finger at the link on the screen. "It's not one of the usual financial security certificates we've been seeing on these websites."

Hades leaned over the back of the couch for a closer look. He took a moment to nuzzle her neck first and nibble a little. "How old is it?"

"Eleven years." Cora brought up another screen and pointed to another line of text. "But it was accessed a week ago."

He lifted his head from her neck and peered at the screen. "Movie studios did lots of weird things with encryption. To fight pirates." Hades knew his objections sounded like a Pollyanna, even as he uttered them. He couldn't believe Simon would hold out on him. Not after the rough treatment.

Cora looked up and met his troubled gaze. "This would be weird, even for them."

"Anything in the browser history?" She had his full attention now.

She shook her head. "I checked." But she pushed a couple of keys and brought the history up again to prove her point.

Hades took the laptop from her and carried it back to his seat at the table. He checked the computer's trash, typing furiously to reach the back-end code. Not the graphic icons displayed to ordinary users, but the raw dates and times automatically recorded in obscure log files that controlled the computer. Stuff stored in places people like Simon Lawson didn't know existed.

After a few moments hunched over the keyboard, he laughed and leaned back in his chair. "Well, well. Looks like Lawson emptied the trash on his computer seven seconds after he accessed that security certificate last week."

"Which means what, exactly?" Cora snapped, but he figured she was nervous. This was the first time she'd come across something like this.

"Only good things, Goddess," Hades smiled. "The Lawsons have been holding out on us. Old Simon has been squirreling away his money for quite a while, I'd say. That certificate is eleven years old. He could have built up quite a pile in all this time. This will be an even bigger payday than we'd hoped."

Cora's worried frown turned into a gleeful laugh. "Excellent!"

"Nya ah ah!" Hades laughed, too, and rubbed his hands together, mocking an enthusiastic cartoon villain. "I'm going to enjoy this."

But first, he was going to enjoy her. Lawson would still be there when Hades was ready. No one turned him on like Cora. He lifted her off the sofa and carried her into the bedroom. She giggled all the way.

CHAPTER FOURTEEN

Monday, May 22
Santa Irene, Arizona

MANDY'S WORK WAS, AS always, top notch. Not only had she managed to schedule the interview with Donald Warner at the prison, but she'd also sent a message and a few documents. "Warner said *he would welcome the chance to meet a diligent reporter*. Like all the others got it wrong. Like a convicted killer deserves better or something."

Jess grimaced when she read the message. Warner had been proclaiming his innocence to anyone and everyone since his arrest. Because of its sensational aspects, reporters made sure the Warner case had unfolded in the media, in tedious detail, minute by minute. But Warner had been convicted by a jury and sentenced to life in the Arizona State Prison at Santa Irene by a judge and nothing Jess had seen or heard before today suggested that he didn't deserve to be right where he was.

Mandy had included the prison's address for Jess's GPS. It sat on the west side of Santa Irene, about twelve miles outside the city limits. As she drove, Jess pulled it up on her phone and expanded the map to see the surrounding areas.

The map looked like the place had been plopped down in the middle of nowhere by the hand of God. The high-security prison was accessible by only one road that ran past the entrance, Arizona Highway 297. Given how remote the place was, Jess wondered where prison employees lived. Santa Irene, probably.

The prison buildings were a good half of a mile from the road. She guessed that empty land in the western half of Arizona must have been cheap back when the prison was constructed. An arrow-straight drive ran from the highway, through several rings of barbed wire that surrounded a cluster of broad, two-story buildings the way a moat surrounds a castle.

She glanced at the clock on the dashboard. She'd have one chance today, and she couldn't be late. When she passed Santa Irene, the Mustang's big engine growled as she gunned it on the empty road toward the prison. Cars slowed as they saw the Mustang approach to give her plenty of time to pass them.

She reached her destination with only minutes to spare.

The prison's outer gate was a simple affair. A tall chain link fence and an entrance that looked like two flimsy sections of fence bolted together and set on wheels.

Jess thought the arrangement absurd considering the worst felons in the state were housed here. Until she realized the designers hadn't expected an escaped convict to reach the perimeter. As far as she knew, none of them ever had.

The first guard at the outer gate collected Jess's ID and called to check with another in a control room somewhere inside the giant prison. He must have received a thumbs up. He handed the ID back and rattled off directions like the fine print in a radio ad for pharmaceuticals.

The first part of the route was a straight gravel road that the Mustang turned to a dust cloud behind its wide tires.

The second ring of fences was far more intimidating. The pillars were encircled with razor wire all the way up. No one could climb them without his skin being ripped to shreds. The top of the fence had the same razor wire curled into a broad spiral across from one pillar to the next.

Surveillance cameras enclosed in smoked gray glass dotted the length of this second fence. They were the multispectral kind. They blended visible light with infrared, which meant they could see as clearly in the dark as in daylight.

The gate was an airlock affair. She waited for it to open and she was admitted to an enclosure made from the same razor wire as the rest of the fence. The roof was nothing but layers of razor wire, but the layers were thick enough to block the harsh blue sky.

A second guard checked her ID again. His instructions were slow and clear as if he wanted to ensure she accepted the rules under which she would be admitted.

"Everything inside the prison is valuable," he warned.

Jess nodded. She'd been inside prisons before. Too many times.

"Take nothing inside unless you'll absolutely need it."

Jess pulled a pad and pencil from her bag and held it up for examination.

"Lock everything else in your car." He nodded approval and handed back her ID. "Do not get out of the car until you're told to." He stuck a prison pass on the middle of the windshield and tapped on the Mustang's roof.

The airlock opened, and she drove on.

The final ring of fencing was the same as the second. Same height, same razor wire, same airlock.

Another guard removed the prison pass from the center of the Mustang's windshield. He checked Jess's ID one more time. He directed her through the airlock to a parking area near a door that looked absurdly small for the huge building.

Jess parked and scanned Carter's file on her laptop while she waited for permission to leave the car. Pictures of Warner at his arrest, and on the steps of some courthouse. Photos of his wife. One of his back as he was bundled into a police van after sentencing.

She ran quickly through her limited memories of the trial. She watched bits of the video footage from local TV stations. Warner's voice was deep and confident. His testimony on the witness stand was succinct. Reliable witnesses had testified in his defense.

He had proclaimed his innocence at trial. Forcefully.

The jury disagreed. The trial had lasted a month, but the jury found him guilty on all counts of kidnapping and murder after less than an hour's deliberations.

Jess had been working on another case at the time. Rich, arrogant men who killed their wives and got away with it were of no interest to her. She'd believed Warner guilty then, and she still did.

But now, his sister-in-law was missing, after that big wreck last week, and then the explosion at her house today. Three dead at the stolen van crash, and two more at the house. Dr. Donald Warner was at the center of everything.

Her gut told her there was a lot more to Warner's story and she wanted to know what he was hiding. She planned to let him run his mouth while she listened. Men like Warner loved to hear themselves talk.

Whatever was going on here, Jess intended to find it.

She collected her pad and pencil and locked everything else inside the Mustang. She stashed the key in the tire well. A key, when held inside a hard fist, made a powerful weapon. She hustled along toward the entrance.

She looked up at the looming, sun-bleached concrete prison. A dour existence inside those walls. Harsh. Soul destroying. She wondered how Warner was coping. He was used to much finer living.

If he'd caused that explosion today, killed those two men, destroyed that house, she would make sure he never stepped outside in the sunshine beyond these walls again.

Ever.

CHAPTER FIFTEEN

HADES FINISHED HIS CALL. Lawson had a complex house phone system with buttons, lights, and a colored display. It clicked as he replaced the receiver.

In front of him were several sheets of paper covered in his own handwriting. Addresses. Names. Dates. Numbers. Simon Lawson's secret financial history laid bare. As much as Hades knew of it, anyway.

He tutted. "A foreign brokerage account. Very clever."

"Is there much money in it?" Cora said.

Hades nodded. "It was hidden on his computer and obscured by three investment companies. Like shells within shells. I think we can safely assume he didn't do all that for a few measly thousand."

"Can we get at it?" Cora's eyes lit up like a kid at Christmas. Her appetite for money seemed as insatiable as his. But her needs were fueled by pure avarice and his by revenge. Not that her motives mattered. The only thing that mattered was making sure Simon Lawson was as bankrupt as Benny.

Hades nodded again. "All we need is a little help." He pointed to the basement. "From our friends."

Shorty swung his boots off the coffee table and stood up. Cora followed. Hades followed Cora and closed the door behind them.

A lone night-light glimmered in the underground darkness, but it was more than enough.

Shorty lifted a garden implement from a rack on the wall. It looked like a distorted pair of scissors. The blades were just a few inches long, but the arms that provided leverage extended two feet from the joining screw. It was a lopper for trimming tree branches. When used appropriately, the lopper produced a tidy cut, leaving a tree wound less prone to infection.

Shorty stood directly in front of Natalie Lawson.

Cora switched on the lights. Three large fluorescent tubes pasted a blinding green cast across the room. She pulled off Natalie's blindfold.

Natalie blinked hard. Her eyes slowly adjusted to the glare, and her blinking slowed. Her gaze settled on the shining steel and monstrous curve of the lopper's thick blades in Shorty's hand.

Hades jerked the duct tape from Simon's mouth but left his blindfold in place. Simon whimpered. Hades nudged Simon's sore torso with the same boot he'd used to create the bruise. "I need the password to your brokerage account."

Simon opened and closed his mouth.

As much as he'd like to push Simon as far as Simon had pushed Benny, Hades only pressed a bit harder on Simon's bruise. The skill Hades had perfected was to make his victims fear him without pushing them to a point beyond coherent thought. For now. "Your *foreign* brokerage account."

"I—"

"The one that isn't included on your tax returns. The one you kept secret. Perhaps even from Natalie, here, hmm?" Hades nodded at Shorty, who waved the lopper in front of Natalie's wide eyes. Even with the duct tape still over her mouth, Simon could easily hear the horrified squeals caught in her throat.

Simon's jaw trembled.

"You lied to me," Hades said, calmly.

"I—"

"You said you would cooperate."

Simon swallowed. "I don't know about a foreign—"

"I shouldn't have believed you. I should have known you would do *anything* to avoid paying your debts. Isn't that right, Simon?" Hades gave Simon's bruise a little kick. Not too hard. Just a reminder.

"No. No." Simon shook his head wildly, back and forth. "I don't—"

"I've just talked to them. Their security isn't that strong. Next time, you'll want to use a different firm."

Simon shook his head. He seemed speechless, for the moment.

"I won't order the transfer over the phone. Too many things could go wrong. And we wouldn't want that, would we, Simon?" Hades kicked him again. A little harder. Simon cried out and writhed on the hard concrete. "I'll make the transfer online. Which means I need your authentications."

Hades placed his hand on Simon's forehead. He pulled off the blindfold. Simon recoiled as he took in the sight of the lopper, glinting in the fluorescent light.

Hades unbuckled Simon's hands from the tie-downs in the floor.

Simon sat up. He didn't stretch this time. He didn't work out the pain in his cramped muscles. He just stared up at Hades.

Hades held out the pad and pen. "Write it down. Clearly. Underline uppercase letters."

"I… I can't."

Hades looked at Shorty, who flexed the lopper again and knelt closer to Lawson.

Simon began to whimper. "It's my life's savings."

"Perfect. Your money will save your life."

Simon's mouth hung open. "We'll have nothing. We're not young, anymore."

"You'll find a way to recover." Hades gave a flat smile. "Men like you always do."

Simon took the pen. He heaved and panted. He wiped his brow on his arm. His breathing slowed. "If we give you our money, you'll leave us?"

"Once we are sure the money has transferred. When you write what we need, you will be closer to freedom. You need to focus on that."

Simon took a deep breath. "I… It's everything we've saved."

"You lied to me."

"I can't—"

Hades laid a chair on its side by Simon's legs. He tore a two-foot length of duct tape from a roll on the table. "You can, and you will," he said.

Simon winced, his forehead wrinkled in misery and terror.

Hades grabbed Simon's handcuffed hands and pulled them to the chair. He wrapped the duct tape around Simon's left wrist. Simon squirmed. Hades leaned his forearm on Simon's, pressuring it down onto the chair's leg. Simon fought back.

Natalie made moaning sounds behind the duct tape that covered her mouth.

Shorty leaned down and planted a solid blow across Simon's face. Simon's head jerked back. He grunted and groaned.

For a few moments, the shock and pain stole his mind. His arm went limp. Hades snapped the tape tight, securing Simon's wrists to the chair leg.

Simon fought against the bond. "No, no, no," he whined.

Hades placed his weight on the chair, holding it in place.

Natalie's eyes were wild. She shook her head and tried to scream.

Hades held Simon's hand out.

Shorty handed him the lopper.

"No, no, no, no," repeated Simon. He fought against the tape and the chair. He fought against losing his money most of all. The money he'd taken from Benny, and countless other hard-working men like Benny over the years. Hades felt no sympathy for Simon Lawson and his bitchy wife. Not a bit.

Hades held the lopper's jaws close to Simon's face. He opened and closed the jaws to be sure they were working smoothly. He watched as the long easy travel of the arms was converted into unstoppable power.

Simon watched, too. He panted, his breathing running faster and faster as adrenaline forced his heart rate into the upper limits for a healthy, fifty-five-year-old male.

"No, no, please, no," said Natalie behind the duct tape, her voice choked in her throat.

Simon sucked air. Fear controlled his body. He took air in but barely exhaled. His mind was closing down, preparing itself for the pain to come.

Hades opened the lopper's jaws and slid them around Simon's left pinkie finger. Simon levered his hand sideways, against the tape.

Shorty wrenched the finger straight and eased his weight down on the back of Simon's hand.

Simon made grunting sounds as he swallowed oxygen.

"No, no, no. Tell him." Natalie fought her bonds. Cora ripped the tape off her mouth to let her words escape. "Tell him, Simon! For God's sake! Tell him the goddammed password!"

Shorty pushed two of Simon's fingers into the lopper. Hades didn't want to chop off Simon's fingers down here. The stench of blood and flesh would become intolerable. But he almost admired Simon's fierce commitment to his fortune. Simon had more guts than Hades would have guessed.

Hades nodded to Shorty, who pushed two more of Simon's fingers into the lopper. Hades could cut off all four with one solid push of the lopper's arms. Sometimes, you had to demonstrate that you meant business in this world.

Simon curled his head forward. Finally, he capitulated. "No, no. I'll tell you, I'll tell you, I'll tell you."

Hades inched the lopper's arms together until the blades pressed into Simon's skin. A smaller demonstration. A little bit of blood.

"No, no, please. No," Natalie begged, her voice climbing in octaves.

Simon cried, "I'll tell you! I'll tell you!"

"That's the right choice, Simon." Hades dragged the lopper away from Simon's fingers. He let the blades scrape across the skin. Blood dribbled down Simon's fingers and dripped from the chair leg.

Natalie cried, sobs wracking her body.

Hades dropped the lopper on the table. The clatter of metal on wood joined the tears and panting.

He picked up the pad and pen from the floor, wedged the pad under Simon's wrists, and slid the pen between the fingers of his cuffed right hand.

"Write," he said.

Simon wrote. His hand shook. He scratched out his scribbles three times before he managed to arrange the correct combination of letters and numbers. He looked up at Hades and held out the pen to indicate he was finished.

Hades took the pad and read out the passwords, character by character.

Simon nodded.

"Thank you," Hades said.

Natalie sobbed.

Simon said nothing, a combination of exhaustion, shock, and defeat.

Hades tapped the pad with the pen. "If this isn't correct, when I return, I will take all five fingers. One at a time. Do you understand?"

Simon's lips trembled. He fought back his terror and offered a shaky nod.

"Good," Hades said. "Because if I have to come back down here, I'll take her fingers, too."

Simon's gaze snapped onto Hades. He frowned while Shorty duct-taped Natalie's wrists to the chair leg.

Hades nodded, to show he meant every word of his threat. What an asshole. How could Benny have ever believed Simon Lawson was a man of his word? Benny should have known better. An asshole like Lawson only valued one thing. Himself.

Hades climbed the stairs out of the basement..

CHAPTER SIXTEEN

Monday, May 22
Santa Irene, Arizona

JESS WAITED FOR THE guards to admit her to the prearranged meeting with Warner. She'd arrived on time, but now it was past five o'clock. Visiting hours were long over. But she was inside, and she hoped that meant they'd let her see Warner today. Whether they would probably depended on the power of Carter's connections, which she hoped were as excellent as usual. She didn't want to come back here again tomorrow.

She'd used the toilet in the grimy restroom. She'd dampened a paper towel and wiped the soot from her face and neck. She'd washed her hands with the harsh pink liquid soap. Now, she waited on a hard metal chair.

The waiting room was stark. Sparsely furnished. Green painted walls were glossy with the oil from countless hands, and bright fluorescent lights glared overhead. She was the only person still here. A round schoolhouse clock on the wall marked the seconds with a red hand that jerked every time it moved.

Eventually, she was frisked and walked through a metal detector and finally led to a small visitor's room. Warner, wearing leg and wrist shackles, was already seated at one of two tables. The other table was unoccupied. An armed guard stood near the door.

The inmate across the table was a pale shadow of the handsome and confident physician featured in the photographs and videos she'd seen. This gaunt man was Donald Warner. No mistake. His name was stamped in black letters on the left breast of his white jumpsuit.

She reached out, and they shook hands.

She sat across the table.

"I'm innocent." His voice was weak and reedy. Words he'd repeated endlessly since his wife disappeared, even though no one believed him. "I didn't kidnap my wife. I did not kill anyone. And I certainly did not arrange to have anyone killed."

"So you said at your trial." Jess nodded, watching him carefully.

"Your office told me you were interested in conducting a better investigation."

She cocked her head. "We are looking into some issues."

"So you believe that I'm innocent."

Did she? Not really. "I've heard that before."

"Well in my case, it's true. Someone set me up."

She cleared her throat. "The jury found the evidence against you overwhelming."

Warner shrugged. "They were wrong."

She tapped her fingers on the table. He'd been through a frightening ordeal. Maybe, after the trial and the time he'd spent locked up, he'd reveal something now that she could use to find the truth. "You testified that two years ago, your BMW was sideswiped by a stolen city bus, and your car was attacked by masked men."

He nodded. "We tried to drive off, but the accident caused the fuel switch to cut off. We couldn't move."

"Your wife was with you in the rear seat, directly behind the driver."

He sighed. "Yes."

"And your driver was shot."

He nodded. "I was hit twice myself."

"The police retrieved nineteen bullets from your car." She paused. "And your driver was killed. Shot in the head at point-blank range."

"Yes." He looked down briefly and blinked as if the facts were still hard to bear. He cleared his throat. "Karen was injured, too. A flesh wound, I was told when I woke up in the hospital. But she lost some blood. Police found it in the car. After the gangbangers took her."

"The Devil Kings. Right." She nodded, watching him carefully. "What about the calls? The ones made to the leader of The Devil Kings? They say the calls came from your cell phone."

"Some gangbanger named Hades. I'd only vaguely heard of him at the time."

"He and his gang have been terrorizing people across Arizona and New Mexico for the past decade." She narrowed her eyes. "It's not believable that you'd never heard of him, is it?"

He raised his head and glared at her. "I was a heart surgeon. It's a hard job. When I got home, I was exhausted. I'd crash and sleep until my next shift." His tone was edgy, defensive.

Jess chewed the inside of her lip. "Cell phone calls are automatically logged on computers. You know that."

"Yeah, when the calls are made or received. Which means you've got to have the number to call in the first place."

"Which you did."

He slapped the table and yelled. "How do you think I could get the number of a burner cell phone for some gangbanger I'd never heard of?"

"You tell me." Jess didn't flinch. He was already in prison. She could walk out anytime. He needed her, not the other way around.

"Sorry. It's frustrating." He sighed and laced his fingers behind his neck. "I'm sitting here. They say I hired this Hades to kidnap and kill my wife, and caused the death of a good man in the process." He slammed his open hand on the table and shouted, "All of this is nonsense!" *Slam!* "There seems to be *nothing* I can say that makes a difference to anyone!" *Slam!*

He stopped talking, but his eyes were wild. For the first time, she wondered if Warner was unhinged. If he'd behaved like this at the trial, no wonder the jury had believed he was capable of the violence with which he'd been charged.

"Your computer was used to search references to Hades," she said. "Seems like you did know who he was."

"I told the detectives." He shook his head, and his voice was calmer, almost robotic. "I have no idea how that stuff got there. I never did those searches."

"What about the searches for untraceable methods to kill human beings?"

"Well, sure. Of course. I'm a doctor. So I looked up how to kill people by shooting them with a gun several times in the chest." He practically snarled with sarcasm.

Jess cocked her head. She didn't know quite what to make of

him. The anger made sense. If he was innocent, which was highly unlikely from everything she knew about the case, of course he'd be angry. On the other hand, he might simply be angry because he'd been caught. She'd seen it go both ways.

"Damn it." His face reddened, but his tone remained calm. "I could walk into the hospital pharmacy at any time, and choose any drug I wanted, and never get caught. Why the hell would I need to research murder methods?"

She waited for him to elaborate. She was pretty good at spotting liars, and she watched for the signs.

"You have to believe me." He leaned forward. Slowly, earnestly, enunciating each word. "I did not, I repeat, *not* have my wife kidnapped, or killed. Or anything else."

Jess watched his face and hands. He seemed sincere enough, but sociopaths always came across authentically when they wanted to. "The jury didn't believe you. Why should I?"

"Think about it." He inhaled deeply and steadied his delivery. "Let's say I wasn't all that thrilled with my wife and wanted to get rid of her. Which isn't true, by the way. Have you never heard of divorce? When one wants to stop being married these days, it's really not that hard to accomplish."

He ran splayed fingers through his thick, red hair. He stood and paced the room. "You think I'd have hired the kind of guy who killed our driver? One of the most decent men I've ever known? A man with a wife and two kids? What did I have against him, huh? And then I do the whole thing so damn *stupidly* that I'd get myself *caught*? Just how dumb do you think a Harvard-trained heart surgeon is these days?"

Jess cocked her head. His arguments were logical. Which was not the same thing as being true. "Hades has a string of crimes on his rap sheet, but there are two cases of kidnap for ransom that he might have been involved in. *If* he was the kidnapper in those two cases, he did it for the money. He killed the victims after he collected the ransom. You never paid a ransom for your wife, did you?"

"I tried to pay. The police botched the handoff. They claimed no one appeared at the meeting point. And Karen had money of her own. Maybe he took hers. We've never found any of it."

He threw his hands in the air. "This is my *wife* for God's sake. I *loved* her. Do you get that? She was beautiful. Accomplished. I was the envy of everyone I knew. Why would I kill her? Her body has never been found. So she could be alive, and what are any of you doing to find Karen? Huh?"

Jess wouldn't be led off topic. "What about those phone calls?"

Warner stared at her a moment before he sank back into his chair. His voice was weary now. "All those phone calls with Hades. They were made late at night."

Jess nodded. "Meaning what?"

"I told you. I work long days. I'm tired when I get home. I need sleep. I don't get up in the middle of the night to make phone calls to some guy I don't even know."

"Can you prove you were sleeping when those phone calls were made?"

"We can't exactly ask my wife, can we?" He blew another long puff.

Jess shrugged. "Where do you keep your cell phone at night?"

"The question should be where did I keep my cell phone. Because I don't have the phone anymore. Or my house." He sighed and seemed to give up the fight. "It was in the kitchen. On the counter. We had chargers there."

She frowned. "You didn't get emergency calls at night?"

"I had a work phone for emergency calls. Kept it by the bed. There was a charger built into my alarm clock."

"The calls to Hades were made on your personal cell phone."

"Exactly. And think about that. Everybody who's ever picked up a newspaper knows what you said. Those cell phone calls are logged, maybe even by national security agencies. So, who makes repeated, traceable calls to a murderer on their personal cell phone? Even people who hate me can't think I'm that stupid."

Jess watched him. He wasn't stupid, but maybe he was arrogant enough to think he'd never be suspected in the first place. Enough to be reckless, too.

"What about the surveillance photos? You, Hades, and his gang. Shreds your argument that you didn't know the man, don't you think?"

"You must know I testified about that, too." He hung his head again. His tone was weary now. "I didn't know who they were. They stopped me under a bridge. I was driving home. There's an underpass. They raced past me on motorbikes and blocked the road. I had to stop or run them down."

Jess raised her eyebrows.

He cocked his head. "Oh, come on. What would you have done?"

"The pictures show you outside the car, walking with Hades."

"The bikers had guns pointed at me. You can't see them in the pictures, but they were there."

"What did you talk about?"

"Mainly that they would kill me if I didn't do what they wanted."

"Which was?"

"Walk around under the bridge for five minutes."

Jess raised her eyebrows again.

"Really. That was it." He waved his hand at the door and the world beyond. "I told everyone that."

"But you didn't report the incident at the time, did you?"

"Report what? Nothing really happened. I didn't know who he was. A bunch of bikers made me walk around at gunpoint. I thought they were going to kill me. So, when they let me leave, all I wanted to do was go home and forget about it. And honestly, at the time, it was embarrassing. Nothing happened. I just felt like a fool."

"You didn't tell anyone?"

"I told my wife."

"And what did she say?"

"That I should report it."

"And yet, you still didn't report anything."

"My wife was a worrier. I told her, leaving the situation alone was for the best. Reporting guys like that gives them a grudge against you and makes matters worse. Once I explained that to her, she agreed."

"What about the thumbprint?" She'd saved this question because it was perhaps the most damning piece of evidence presented at the trial.

Warner blanched. He bowed his head. A few moments later, he cleared his throat and looked directly into Jess's unwavering gaze. "Thumbprints can be faked, too."

Jess shook her head. "All the calls made to Hades were done by unlocking your phone with the PIN code. Something that could have been done by someone else. Except for one call. Just once, you unlocked your phone with your thumbprint, and called him."

"I never called him."

"It was a ten-minute call, the night after your meeting at the underpass. Your phone kept perfect records. When it was unlocked, and how. There's no mistake."

He shook his head. "That never happened. I never called Hades. Ever. Not from any phone."

"The prosecution didn't see it that way. They argued you just made a simple mistake. A mistake that proved you were the caller. The jury must have believed you made the calls."

"The whole world can think what they want, but I never called him." Warner folded his hands together and leaned both forearms on the table between them. When she didn't ask another question for a while, he posed his own. "So, what are you doing to find Karen?"

"I'm not looking for Karen."

Warner's face fell. His mouth hung open. "You said—"

"I'm looking for her sister. Melissa. She's disappeared," Jess said. "Same as your wife."

His red-faced anger resurfaced. "Well, obviously I had nothing to do with that! I'm in prison!"

"I find it remarkable that your wife disappears, then—"

"Kidnapped. My wife was kidnapped."

"Her sister has disappeared."

"She's been kidnapped?"

"All we know is that she has been missing for several days."

"Missing?" He snorted and stood up. "You're just looking to sell magazines. You're all alike."

"It's an amazing coincidence," Jess said.

"So what?" He sighed and slumped down into his chair. "Has there been a ransom note?"

"Not so far."

"Then why do you think it's got anything to do with Karen? Or me?"

"Help me find Melissa, and we'll ask her what she knows."

"Nothing much I can say. Karen and Melissa didn't get along. She didn't even come to our wedding." He snorted and shook his head. "Came to the trial, though. Crept in wrapped in a headscarf and thick makeup, but I saw her."

"When was the last time you saw Melissa before Karen was kidnapped?"

He shrugged. "She never wanted to see anyone. A loner. Probably something from her childhood."

Jess leaned forward. "Like what?"

Warner mimicked drinking as if he held a booze glass in his hand. "Karen and Melissa's parents were alcoholics. Wild parties. Died in a car wreck. He was driving drunk and wrapped the car around a tree at ninety miles an hour. Girls were left to fend for themselves. Karen turned out okay, but I think Melissa was emotionally damaged. She's a drinker, too, Karen said. Shame really."

"When was the last time the sisters got together?"

He shook his head. "Never that I know about." He waved his hand. "We might have received a Christmas card sometime, but that was the extent of their relationship."

"Doesn't that seem a bit odd to you?"

"Look, they weren't close. Didn't I say that already? I invited Melissa for the holidays once. Karen damn near bit my head off. Thankfully she didn't turn up. I don't want to sound uncaring, but I was glad Melissa stayed away. Even the mention of her name put Karen in a bad mood. Might have been some sibling rivalry thing, but I never dug into it."

"Has Melissa ever gone missing before?"

He shrugged. "We'd be the last people to know."

Jess closed her pad, pushed her chair back, and stood up.

Warner leaned forward. "I don't belong here, Jess. It was a clever setup, or an understandable mistake. Either way, I'm innocent, and I pray every day that Karen is alive and she'll be found. Can't you look for her? It would make a great story for your magazine. I'd give you an exclusive. Karen would, too."

Jess gave a flat smile.

He put his hands on the table. "Will you help me? Please?"

She took a deep breath. "I'm looking at your case."

"My defense team, the prosecutors, the other reporters. They all *looked at* my case. We see how that turned out. You've got to find out the truth. I'm sorry about Melissa, I really am. But…"

Jess pinched her lips together and kneaded them with her fingers. The guilty verdict made sense to her based on the evidence. Warner had told her nothing new.

The police investigation was solid. The prosecutor presented his best evidence. Excellent lawyers defended Warner. And the jury decided.

But no motive. And no body. Was Jess *sure* Donald Warner was a cold-hearted killer?

And even if he did kill his wife, how would he have arranged Melissa's disappearance and the destruction of her house from behind these thick concrete walls?

"If I find out anything," she nodded once, "I'll be in touch."

She turned and left the room while he was still at the table, hands folded in front of him as if he might begin to pray.

The interview had produced no solid answers, and now she was mired in the case. At least until Melissa Green was found.

CHAPTER SEVENTEEN

Monday, May 22
Santa Irene, Arizona

JESS SAT IN THE Mustang and dictated her notes while the interview was fresh in her mind.

It was almost completely dark by the time she finished. She flipped on her headlights and started the Mustang. She drove out of the prison, through the air locks, past the guards and the rings of razor wire, and out onto the main road. She turned toward Santa Irene and settled into a sixty-mile-an-hour cruise along the two-lane highway, the Mustang's engine barely struggling.

Warner hadn't been what she had expected. His concern for his wife seemed sincere. His protests hadn't once slipped or revealed she was dead. He acted as if he believed they were a couple, even now.

The best liars never gave up the con game. Maybe that was his secret, too.

The evidence against Warner was overwhelming enough, and the jury had found him guilty. Still, the verdict could have gone the other way. Most of what Warner said was true or could have been. Internet searches could have been done by anyone with access to his computer. The phone calls could have been made by anyone with the PIN to unlock his phone. The thumbprint call was problematic, but anyone clever enough to pull off such a charade could have figured out how to fake his thumbprint, too. There were lots of ways it could have been done. He had paid the ransom and, as he said, the drop failed. The kidnappers escaped.

Warner's discussion with Hades under the bridge was harder to explain away. It could have been that Warner wanted to talk to Hades, and thought he was out of sight. That's what the prosecutor had argued at the trial. But Warner claimed Hades forced him, which the jury didn't believe.

The most perplexing question about the whole Karen Warner case was the missing motive. The motive was never an element of the crime that the prosecutor had to prove, but without motive, nothing made sense, and it was hard to get a jury to convict.

Both Donald and Karen Warner had been wealthy. Like he said, they could have divorced without any hardship. They could have been living happy lives at opposite ends of the country right now. Warner was right. He had no obvious motive to kill his wife.

It was full dark by the time Jess reached the outskirts of the town of Bear Hill. A few commercial buildings popped into view, and the traffic slowed.

She passed a gun store and doubled back. After she showed her concealed carry permit and ID, the owner was cooperative. She completed the paperwork, and he was prepared to receive her Glock from Morris.

She was booked at the optimistically named Bear Hill Hotel. A franchise geared toward traveling salesmen, not designed for a lengthy stay. Sterile, everything geared for economy. She lugged her bags to her room on the second floor. It was clean and spacious enough, with a large bathroom. She stripped and stuffed all her smoke-saturated clothes into a laundry bag and stuck them out in the corridor. She eagerly washed off the day's grime and the smell of fire that clung to her entire body. She towel-dried her hair and dressed in pajamas before calling Morris.

"Jess," he said, his voice upbeat.

"I've got an address for you to ship my gun," she said.

He laughed. "No, *Hi Henry?*"

"Well, I—"

"No, *hope you're doing okay? Or, good to hear your voice?*"

"Sorry. I'm dead on my feet." She plopped onto the bed and fell back against the pillows.

He lowered his voice. "You do realize I'm just teasing?"

"I know. But it's been a long, tough day. I got blown up."

"What?" His tone was laced with more alarm than she'd meant to cause. "How? Are you okay?"

"The house we were searching exploded. I'm fine. Exhausted. A little worse for wear, but still in one piece." She paused and took a deep breath. "Two others weren't so lucky."

"What do you mean?" She heard him clicking computer keys, probably looking for details on the explosion.

"Two people died in the blast. And a police captain was in a bad way at the scene. I'm not sure what happened with him." She made a mental note to call the hospital in the morning.

Morris whistled. "You really do have a knack for landing yourself in trouble."

"Says the man who nearly drowned when he spent two

months undercover trying to close down a human trafficking operation."

"I'm an FBI agent. Risky work comes with the job. Reporters, not so much."

"Well, you'd better get used to it. Risky work seems to be the norm for me, too."

He grunted. "You said you had an address for your weapon?"

She read out the gun shop's details. Morris read them back for verification.

"Whose house were you searching?" The clicking keys had stopped, so he'd probably found the reports in a law enforcement database somewhere.

"Melissa Green. She's the twin sister of the doctor's wife that was kidnapped and presumed dead. It was all over the news a while back. We covered it at *Taboo* when it happened, but it wasn't my story."

"Dr. Donald Warner. I remember. They never found the wife's body. You think her sister was involved in the kidnapping?"

"Don't know." Jess closed her eyes, still scratchy and irritated by the smoke from the fire. "But now the sister has disappeared, and today her house blew up."

"So, maybe she's suffered the same fate as her sister." He paused. She heard him sipping something. Coffee, probably. He practically mainlined the stuff.

"Except Dr. Warner is confined in a very secure prison. He can't even *see* outside, let alone organize something like an explosion at his sister-in-law's house." Her throat was parched. She found a bottle of water and took a long swig.

"How long has Dr. Warner been inside?"

"He was sentenced last year, so he's been there a while."

Morris paused to think. "Then he could have set something up from prison, but it's not as easy to do."

"But why? And why destroy the sister's place today?" She sipped the water again. "I mean, if he was going to kill her, why didn't he do it before he was convicted? Makes no sense to blow up her house today, does it?"

"We have a field office out there. I could ask around."

She exhaled. His offer was tempting. "Thanks. But not yet."

"An explosion that leaves people dead probably involves the FBI Explosives Unit, anyway. And I don't want you to get hurt because we knew something you didn't."

"I'm not going to get hurt." Her words carried very little conviction, though. Today's near miss was still too close to ignore. If she hadn't been standing near that refrigerator. She shuddered to think about it.

"I'm not trying to nanny you, Jess."

She couldn't get a reply past the lump in her throat. It had been such a long time since a man, any man, worried about her safety. She wasn't quite sure how she felt about his protectiveness, though, so she said nothing.

"Did you get a sample?" he said.

"Of what?"

"Something near the source of the explosion. A good GC could tell you the explosive."

"GC?"

"Gas Chromatography."

"Crime scene techs were all over the place when I left." Jess raked fingers through her short wet curls. "If I have a chance, I'll try. Meanwhile, you could ask whether your guys are already looking into that issue."

Her phone buzzed. A local number. "I have another call."

"No problem. I'll get your weapon out to you for delivery tomorrow. It sounds like you may need it. Take care, and…keep in touch," Morris said.

Her hotel room suddenly felt a bit warmer, and she was almost sorry he wasn't here. "You, too." She clicked over to the other call. "Jessica Kimball."

"This is Captain Mercer. Santa Irene Police. I need to ask you a few questions. Is now a good time? I'm downstairs."

"Let me throw some clothes on. Meet you in the bar in ten minutes." She slipped off her bathrobe and rummaged through her suitcase.

CHAPTER EIGHTEEN

Monday, May 22
Santa Irene, Arizona

JESS RAN THE BLOW-DRYER for five minutes and slapped a bit of makeup on before she jumped into her jeans and a sweater and made her way downstairs. The lounge was off the lobby and doubled as a breakfast room in the mornings. Mercer was easy to spot. He was the only customer in the place.

She stopped at the bar for a beer and ordered a hamburger before she approached his table. "How's Captain Jackson?" She slid into the chair.

"Holding on. Not good, but stable." Mercer eyed her beer as he raised his coffee mug.

"Buy you one?" She raised the bottle toward him.

He shook his head. "Can't while I'm on duty."

She nodded and took a swig. Her throat felt parched as if she'd breathed in flames instead of the smoke this afternoon. "I'm glad to hear about Jackson. I guess that's as good as we can hope for at the moment."

"Under the circumstances, it probably is." He took a deep breath. "At the scene, I didn't know you were the one who got him out of the fire."

"I wish I could have done more." She looked down at the table.

"I'm sure he'll want to thank you."

"That's not necessary. Not at all. Especially with the other families…"

"Right." He looked away uncomfortably and poured more coffee into his mug from the plastic pot on the table. "It's going to take some time for them to come to terms with what's happened."

"It's never easy to lose a loved one, no matter how it happens." Tears sprang to her eyes, and she blinked them back.

Mercer watched her effort to control herself. "I'm sorry. I must have hit a nerve. I didn't mean to upset you."

"It's okay. My story's no secret." She cleared her throat. "My son, Peter, was taken years ago from my apartment in Denver, when he was an infant. I've been looking for him a long time."

She'd never spent an entire day without missing her little boy, but she didn't say that to people.

"Is that why you work for *Taboo Magazine*? Keeping yourself accessible?" Mercer asked.

"Peter might see me. Or a witness might come forward. You never know." Jess nodded. "I've also got a team of investigators on the payroll and a lot of law enforcement friends to help me."

Mercer cocked his head and studied her a bit before he replied. "I guess you've checked with the boy's father. It's usually the non-custodial parent in those situations."

"His father's deceased." Jess looked away to gather her

composure. Peter's father had never cared enough about her or his son to bother stealing Peter. But she didn't say that to people, either.

The silence lasted a while this time while Mercer wrestled with a situation that he couldn't possibly have words of comfort to resolve. She understood that, too. She'd done her best to comfort others in similar situations, but whatever she had to offer, it was never enough. Nothing but Peter's return would ever comfort her, either.

Mercer was silent for a few moments, and then he cleared his throat. "One thing that will help my daughter is to find out how that explosion happened. I need answers as fast as I can get them."

"Of course." Jess focused on his pudgy face. "How can I help?"

"The other reporters were taking pictures." He leaned toward her. "How about you?"

"Uh-huh. Outside and in."

"I need those pictures."

"No problem." She nodded. "I can email them to you."

"Good. Sooner the better. We're going to be working all night."

He spelled out his police department email address. Jess copied it down on a tiny pad she'd grabbed off the table by her bedside. "I'll send them as soon as I go upstairs."

"Thank you." Mercer was silent for a moment. "You arrived at Melissa Green's house before Jackson went inside, correct?"

"A couple of minutes before, yes."

"And why were you there?"

"She was reported missing. My boss sent me to cover the story."

"A national magazine comes running for a missing person? Forgive me, but that doesn't sound very plausible."

"She is Karen Warner's sister. The woman who was kidnapped over in Santa Irene two years ago and never found." She watched as understanding glimmered in his eyes. "Karen Warner's husband was recently convicted of her murder and the murder of their driver during the kidnapping."

"Two missing sisters. Unusual, but hardly a story big enough for your magazine, surely?"

Jess smiled. "My editor has a sixth sense about these things."

"Meaning?"

"Meaning he suspected there was more to it than coincidence." She sipped the beer and considered how much she should tell him. He had access to law enforcement databases, and she didn't. But was he friend or foe? "He sent me here to find out."

Mercer grunted, and let the connection between Melissa and her sister pass. "And you were inside the house, at the time of the explosion."

"Downstairs. In the kitchen."

"You told one of my officers you were shielded by the refrigerator?"

"That's the only thing I can figure."

"Remarkable."

"Pure luck."

"Maybe."

Jess leaned both forearms on the table and held the beer bottle between both palms. "Have you determined what caused the explosion?"

"Not yet. Your pictures might help with that. After we make some headway, we'll want to talk to you again tomorrow."

Jess straightened her back. "Are you trying to imply something?"

"Only that I intend to get to the bottom of what happened as quickly as possible." He pushed away from the table and stood. "I need those pictures. Come to the station tomorrow morning. We'll see where we are by then."

She nodded. "I can do that."

Mercer turned to leave. "Seven o'clock, Miss Kimball. Don't be late."

Jess exhaled. Her stomach growled. She'd eat her burger and finish her beer before she went upstairs. She walked to the bar and climbed onto one of the stools to wait for her order.

Mercer was probably under a lot of stress. But did he really consider her actions suspect? If he did, she couldn't trust him. She was glad she hadn't told him about the stolen van and the DNA they'd found inside. He'd find out if he bothered to look. But so far, he didn't seem like the sharpest knife in the drawer.

She looked out the window. The moon was a thin waning crescent, barely visible as it disappeared below the horizon, only a day or two from an invisible new moon. Cars were driving with headlights. Street lights had come on more than an hour ago.

The bartender delivered her burger and a second beer. Both were fantastic. Or maybe she was famished. Either way, she gobbled the food and paid the bill and carried her second beer up to her room.

After she'd located and sent Mercer the photos, she leaned back against the pillows and finished her beer. She was more exhausted than she realized. But Morris was right. Good evidence would go bad quickly. She couldn't rely on Mercer to share what he learned. Maybe he would. Maybe he wouldn't. She'd sleep a few hours and then make a plan.

CHAPTER NINETEEN

Tuesday, May 23, 12:05 a.m.
Bear Hill, Arizona

JESS WOKE UP JUST after midnight. She brushed her teeth and slipped into her jeans. In less than twenty minutes, she was behind the wheel of her rental, driving the surface streets out of Bear Hill. She stopped at an all-night gas station and bought a flashlight that advertised itself as "used by the US Secret Army," although she was sure no such outfit existed.

When she reached the canyon that led to Melissa Green's house, the street lights abruptly disappeared. She ran the Mustang's headlights on high beam and slowed as she approached the driveway. The swing gate was closed. Yellow and black police tape wound around the rails. If she removed the tape, Mercer would know.

Jess drove twenty yards past the entrance and parked in a gap in the weeds on the right-hand side of the road.

In the darkness, the road was barely visible. She flipped on her flashlight and immediately shut it off again. It was bright enough to attract attention. Not that there was anyone else around. At least, not anyone she could see. She used the weaker light from her phone to find the easiest way to scale the gate without damaging the police tape.

The driveway slope seemed steeper than she remembered as she moved cautiously forward on foot. When she reached the canopy of trees, the darkness was complete. She heard rustling leaves but saw no movement.

Don't be so jumpy. Just the wind. Or a raccoon. Or something.

She kept the illumination from her phone directed straight down to work her way around the larger potholes. Animals scurried into the undergrowth as she approached.

Halfway up the drive, she judged herself to be far enough from the road and switched to the flashlight. The stronger beam highlighted thin tree trunks and sparse undergrowth, probably the result of low rainfall.

She picked up her pace, and by the time she reached the area where the driveway leveled out into the space where the house had been, she'd worked up a sweat.

She looked at the rubble in the near darkness. "What the hell?" she whispered.

A yellow light flickered toward the rear of the open area. Flames? Her skin tingled. She punched her flashlight off.

Had the fire reignited? Something in the rubble might have remained hot enough to eat through to find something else faster burning.

She jogged along the edges of the rubble toward the flicker. When she was close enough, she saw flames illuminating the pile of stuff that had once been Melissa Green's kitchen. The kitchen might have been the only place where combustibles remained.

She fished her phone out of her pocket and dialed 9-1-1.

As she watched, the flames grew. She imagined she could feel the heat all the way across the open space.

Her phone bleeped. *Call failed* appeared in the display. She punched 9-1-1 again. Again, the call failed to connect, and she gave up when she saw something move behind the flames.

She crept closer, wishing she had her gun. The only weapon in her hand was the flashlight. Beyond the flickering flames she saw a figure. It looked like a man wearing a dark jacket. He was crouched, turning his head back and forth, scanning the ground in Jess's direction.

Did you hear me?

Jess knelt in the shadows. He was closer to the fire. The light from the flames would most likely diminish his night vision.

He stood up. Definitely a man. He was at least six feet tall and muscular. He whipped his head around as if he'd heard an unexpected noise and Jess glimpsed the flick of a ponytail.

She eased backward into the darkness. He had been watching the fire, right up close. Too close. She felt the gooseflesh pop up on her arms. This fire was no secondary ignition from the earlier embers. He had purposely re-ignited what little was left of Melisa Green's house. He'd done it at night when he thought no one would see him.

But why? The place had been reduced to a pile of junk already. She angled for the edge of the clearing.

Her phone buzzed in her hand. An incoming call. She fumbled for the mute switch. The ringer sounded, shrill and loud in the still night air. The display lit up.

The man must have heard. He spun in her direction and half a moment later, a gunshot shattered the silence.

Jess dove for the trees. She ran headlong into the

undergrowth and put a broad tree trunk between her and the man.

A distant voice came from her phone. An emergency operator returning her failed call. Jess whipped the phone to her ear and rattled off a plea for help. The operator urged her to remain still, and stay on the line.

Jess agreed. She left the line open and placed the phone on the ground. She'd locked the display to be sure it continued to glow brightly.

She could hear the rustle of long grass as he came closer.

She moved deeper into the trees, traveling as quietly as possible. She headed up the hill. He was heading downward, toward the visible glow from her phone.

She looked back toward the house. The fire he'd started had found enough fuel to feed itself from a campfire to a raging bonfire. The entire flat space where the home had been was surrounded by a sickly glow. But the flames mesmerized with a vivid blue corona surrounded by the bright yellow heat.

She heard a noise. She dragged her gaze from the flames and saw the man only thirty feet away now. She held her breath and waited behind a tree.

The man's silhouette cast a flickering shadow into the woods. He moved closer with his attention focused on the phone.

A siren sounded in the distance, and its wail echoed down the canyon.

He must have heard the siren at the same time Jess did. He abandoned his careful progress and ran full out for the phone. He held his gun in front and rounded the nearest tree, firing as he ran.

The shots shook the trees. Wildlife took flight. Jess held her arms in front of her face and bounded up the hill in the opposite direction.

She looked over her shoulder as she ran. He was searching the area around her phone with a flashlight.

Only the growing siren's sound filled the air. And, back in the clearing, the fire's voracious roar continued to build.

When she'd put enough distance between them, Jess paused to catch her breath. She crouched down in the shadows.

He loosed off a dozen random shots into the woods before he turned and ran back to the fire. He threw a plastic gas container into the flames and took off into the woods behind where the house had been.

The container ignited with a *whump*. Giant flames washed over the charred remains of the house and spiraled into the air.

The first siren was close. A second siren wailed in the distance.

Jess turned on her flashlight and headed out of the woods. She'd come back for the phone later. If she detoured to pick it up now, she'd lose him. The flames illuminated the area behind the house, and she saw a trail winding up the hill. Jess headed after the man.

She kept her light aimed at the ground. Ahead, his flashlight danced through the trees. He was running. She dashed after him.

At the bottom of the hill, the siren had been switched off and replaced with the heavy engine roar of a fire engine.

She kept going. Following the arsonist.

The trail was nothing but two ruts worn into the undergrowth by passing vehicles. She moved as fast as she could, keeping her light on the path.

He had a head start. He was two hundred yards in front of her and moving fast. She caught occasional glimpses of his flashlight, and she hoped he didn't look back to see hers.

Abruptly, things changed. He shouted, and his light rolled over.

Jess slowed. Maybe someone had set animal traps out here. If he was caught in a trap, he'd be even more dangerous.

She heard grunting, and his flashlight began moving again. He wasn't caught. He'd stumbled for some reason, but he wasn't stopped. His light abruptly disappeared.

Jess kept moving forward, but she was still too far behind. She'd never gotten a good look at him.

An engine started. A deep rumble.

Jess ran toward the vehicle. The trail leveled out. She reached the top of the hill where the trees thinned.

A hundred feet away headlights blazed into the night. She caught the familiar outline of a Jeep as it rocketed forward, twisted along the path to avoid a thick tree, and roared down the slope. The Jeep's headlights bounced wildly, light flicking from side to side down a bumpy trail.

Jess ran after the vehicle as it clawed down the slope, but her effort to catch the Jeep in the dark was hopeless.

In moments, only the red tail lights were visible. The brake lights flared and twisted left before racing away. From there, the headlights advanced smoothly. He had reached the road.

She watched until the tail lights disappeared before she worked her way back along the trail. Spotlights illuminated the blaze and a fire crew dousing the flames. Two police vehicles were parked in the driveway.

She froze when she heard a shotgun ratcheted behind her. She turned her head slowly.

"Miss Kimball." Captain Mercer glowered at her. He didn't lower the shotgun. "What are you doing here?"

CHAPTER TWENTY

Tuesday, May 23
Bear Hill, Arizona

JESS RAISED HER HANDS and turned her body to face
Captain Mercer.

He lowered his shotgun. "This is a crime scene. It's not open
to sightseers."

"I had to look at the house again." She lowered her hands
and nodded toward the remains of the house. "So did the man
who set that fire. I'll show you."

Jess walked toward the destroyed kitchen. Mercer walked
beside her, but she felt his hostility like a palpable thing. She
stopped and pointed. "I first noticed him standing right there,
watching the fire. When he saw me, he started shooting. I ran,
and he chased me. But I think the sirens scared him off."

"Did you see him set the fire?"

"No, but he threw a can of gas into the flames before he ran
away."

Mercer sniffed the air and nodded. "Did you get any

pictures? Video? Anything we can use to identify the arsonist?"

"I didn't have a camera." Jess shook her head. "I used my phone as a decoy when he was looking for me. I left it in the trees."

"Can you describe him?"

She closed her eyes to visualize him clearly. "Tall. Square shoulders. Muscular. Ponytail. Looked like dark hair, but in this light, I can't be sure." She opened her eyes. "I ran after him, but he had a Jeep parked over the top of the hill. Took off down the other side like a scalded cat."

"Did you see the license plates?"

She shook her head. "It was too dark. And I never got close enough."

"Muscular guy with a ponytail," Mercer said, sarcastically. "That narrows it down to no more than half the local male population."

Jess's breath quickened, and she arched her eyebrows. "How do you know he's a local?"

Mercer pointed up the hill. "I know the two-track. He had to leave the blacktop road a couple of miles away and ford a stream on the dirt road to find that trail, even in the daylight. No way to *take off like a scalded cat* unless he was really familiar with its twists and turns. Damn thing's got potholes big enough to stop a Jeep."

"Know any locals with a Jeep and a ponytail?" Jess's appreciation for Mercer had improved a bit. He wasn't as clueless as he'd seemed this afternoon. But something was definitely pushing his buttons about this case.

"At least a dozen." Mercer nodded. "It's a popular *style* around here if you want to call a grown man wearing a ponytail a style."

Mercer looked away when the fire chief called out.

"Stay put. We're not done talking. I'll be right back." Mercer walked away without waiting for her answer. They talked in hushed tones, pointing to the latest fire, and up and down the hill. When they finished, the fire chief called to his men to pack up.

Mercer returned to Jess. "I talked to your editor this afternoon. He didn't seem concerned that you were already in trouble here."

"He's all heart." Jess shrugged. Carter was old school. He thought reporters weren't doing their jobs unless they were ruffling feathers.

"My point is, this situation is not some kind of sensational story for your readers." He frowned. "If you're looking to polish your reputation, Ms. Kimball, this is not the place to do it."

"That's insulting, Mercer. You know nothing about me, or my magazine or my readers." She balled her fists at her side and settled her weight as if she might have cause to throw punches. "Two people died here this afternoon. But another one is still alive, thanks to me. I was damn lucky to get us out when that house exploded. I've got every right to want to know who is responsible."

Mercer looked at her for a long moment. He shifted his weight. "Ernie was well liked around here." He swallowed. "The officer that died has a wife and child."

"I saw them this afternoon." Jess's anger banked a bit. She blinked. "It's heartbreaking."

"So, don't get in my way. And don't keep information from me, or mess with my evidence." Mercer pursed his lips. After a moment, he cleared his throat. His pugilistic expression consumed his features, and his tone was quiet with promised menace. "You mess up this case, and I will personally make sure you go to jail along with the scum who did this."

"Not likely, Mercer." She stuck out her chin. "Who do you think you're talking to?"

"I don't actually care who you think you are." Mercer scowled. "Because the officer who died in that house this afternoon was my son-in-law."

Her indignation deflated. Jess bit her lip and blinked. "Mrs. Cook is your daughter?"

"That's right." Mercer nodded. "And this is a murder investigation now. Don't break the rules again unless you're ready to face the consequences."

CHAPTER TWENTY-ONE

Tuesday, May 23
Santa Irene, Arizona

HADES AND CORA LAY on the bed. It was late, but he couldn't sleep. Not until Pony came back from the house. Maybe not even then. He hadn't slept much since Sunday. He loved home invasions like this one. Invasions were a buzz better than any other. The planning, the execution, everything about them spiked his energy and excited his senses like a non-stop electric charge to his nervous system.

His mind was racing. Partly because this invasion was special. This one was for Benny.

Lawson didn't know why they were here. Not yet. Right now, Lawson believed the invasion was random. That he was simply unlucky. He was right, in a way. He should never have done what he did to Benny. That's when Lawson became unlucky. More unlucky than he could have ever imagined.

Hades laughed. Cora whimpered in her sleep. She was so friggin' beautiful. He marveled at how perfect she was. Very soon, they'd find themselves a beach somewhere. Just the two of them. The thought of it made him hard, and he almost woke her. But she only had another hour to sleep, so he left her alone.

He thought about Lawson's secret account. An offshore brokerage account. Puzzling. Hades appreciated a good puzzle. Lawson was more clever than most. It appeared he'd set up one account that invested money in the next one in the chain. Kind of like a scavenger hunt. But a chain of how many before Hades found the pot of gold at the end of the rainbow?

Yet, the online services of each company were restricted. Each provided a phone number and an email address. Nothing else. No account details, no balance, and no hint of the nature of the transactions.

So Lawson had gone to a lot of trouble. Which meant he was hiding something, probably big. Otherwise, why all that secrecy? The last company in the chain was Robertson & Robertson. Hades had never heard of them. Pretending to be Lawson, Hades had sent them an email a few hours ago. So far, no response. Which could be a time zone thing, perhaps.

He took a deep breath. Patience.

He glanced at the windows. The house was completely silent. The drapes were closed over the big windows. Behind the heavy fabric, Shorty had taped sheets of black plastic to keep light from spilling outside. As a result, the room was pitch black. The only illumination came from the master bathroom night light.

Shorty was on watch. He was in the bedroom down the hall. He sat in the dark, watching the street through a thin slit in the plastic. It was dull and tedious work, so the four of them took three-hour shifts around the clock.

Hades had done his stint. In another hour, it would be Cora's turn. She was an equal member of the crew. She shared the same duty watch as the others, and she served without complaint. He'd chosen his queen well, indeed.

Shorty whistled. Hades rolled off the bed and sprinted to his side in less than two seconds.

"Pony's back," Shorty said.

Hades looked through the slit in the plastic. In the dim glow of the streetlights, he saw Pony in shadow. He was alone, but Hades searched the length of the street from every window as he headed downstairs to let him enter through the locked steel garage door in the back.

Pony locked the door behind him and placed a hand on Hades' arm.

Hades' senses prickled. "What's wrong?"

Pony lowered his voice. "The house was mostly destroyed already, but I burned the remainder."

"Good."

"There were two cops in the house when it exploded."

Hades swore. He paced back and forth on the garage carpet. "What did they find?"

"From what I heard when I asked around, nothing. They'd barely got inside when the explosion started the fire. They were upstairs and couldn't get out."

"But the place is completely gone now. Everything reduced to ashes. Yes?"

Pony nodded. "Yeah, yeah. It was a big explosion and a hot fire. Mostly burned to the ground before the fire department could get out there. Then I finished it off tonight."

"So, we've got nothing to worry about." Hades wished he felt as secure as he sounded.

Pony took a deep breath. "One of the cops got out. The other one died. You know how cops are when they lose one of their own. They'll never give up."

"If it's all burned, they've got nothing to find." He only needed a couple more days, but Pony didn't know that and Hades didn't plan to tell him. He turned and led the way into the kitchen.

Pony drew a glass of water from the tap and leaned against the counter to drink it. "There was a woman there when I burned the last part of the house."

Hades' anger flared, and he tamped it back. "And?"

"She might have seen me. She had a flashlight and there was light from the fire."

He knew what was coming before Pony said anything more. "You weren't wearing your mask."

Pony shifted his weight.

Hades hammered his fist into the refrigerator's stainless steel door. "Damnit! What have I…" He paused to breathe and get himself under control. "What have I told you about wearing your mask every single time?"

"I know, I know." Pony waved his hands in front of him. "But it was hot, and there was no one around to see me. I was in the woods, late at night. It's totally black out there tonight. Zero moonlight. There was—"

"I don't give a damn about what there was, Pony!" Hades' temper erupted like a volcano from deep in his gut. "*Someone saw you.*"

"Might have seen me. I can't be sure—"

There was a long silence while Hades struggled to control himself. He didn't want to kill Pony if he didn't have to. For Benny's sake. This could be okay. Pony could be right. But even as he tried to persuade himself, he knew the truth.

"Okay. She probably didn't see you, like you said. But why the hell didn't you kill her?"

"I went after her. But she ran into the woods, and by the time I was closing in, I heard sirens. I had to go." Pony ducked his head. He didn't like to admit he'd screwed up, Hades could tell. Not that it mattered what he liked and didn't. Not anymore.

Hades looked at the floor and shook his head. "What an absolute—"

"She probably won't—"

Hades snapped. He ripped his VBR pistol from its holster and pointed it at Pony's head. "Don't you dare tell me what she will or won't do!"

Pony raised his hands in front of him. "I didn't mean—"

Hades shook the gun. "Shut up!"

Pony kept his hands up, in front of him. His gaze was locked on Hades, as if he hoped by ignoring the two-pound chunk of lethal metal between them, it would vanish.

Hades adjusted his grip on the VBR. He breathed heavily. Pony kept staring.

Hades calmed himself. He lowered the gun. His tone was quiet, measured. "I'm the one with the experience here, Pony. I make the decisions. I organize the jobs. Do you understand me?"

Pony nodded miserably.

"The fire killed two people. One was a cop. So they'll dig into every angle, and you've just been seen."

"That wasn't my—"

"I know. But with a cop down, they won't give up. What if that woman gives them a good description of you? Or a picture? Maybe she took a picture." Hayes patted Pony's shoulder. "You'll have to stay here with us until we're done. We can't risk them finding you."

Pony lowered his eyes and shook his head.

"It'll be okay. Everything will work out. We just need to keep you out of sight for a while." Hades pointed to Simon Lawson's computer. "Check the Internet. News sites, gossip, police, anything that might have any reports about that damn house. We'll only be here a couple of days. Everything will work out, Pony. It wasn't your fault."

But of course, it was Pony's fault. After a cop had died when Cora stole the first van, the last thing they needed was another cop dead. Two jurisdictions. Plus the feds now, probably. Pony had put the entire operation at serious risk tonight, and he had to know it. Hades would be the one to deal with the problem. But he had to think about the best thing to do. For now, he walked back upstairs and returned to bed.

CHAPTER TWENTY-TWO

Tuesday, May 23
Bear Hill, Arizona

JESS ROSE EARLY THE next morning after a few hours of fitful tossing. She showered, breakfasted, and drove into town before seven o'clock.

The building was easy to find. A large, illuminated sign perched out front proclaimed *Bear Hill Police Department* in front of a single-story block construction, L-shaped, with a red brick facade and smoked glass windows. The parking lot nestled in the crook of the L. Three parking spaces were reserved for police vehicles. Only one was occupied, and the cruiser wasn't Mercer's.

Jess parked the Mustang in guest parking and walked into the station. The large, open reception area was filled with three rows of molded plastic chairs facing a counter. A woman behind the counter typed on a keyboard. She looked up when Jess entered. "You looking for Captain Mercer?"

"Jess Kimball. He asked me to meet him here at seven o'clock."

"He's out. Should be back soon." She gestured to the rows of chairs. "Take a seat."

Jess sat and waited. Minutes ticked by. The woman behind the counter finished her typing and walked deeper into the building.

Jess poured herself a drink from a small coffee maker on the counter. The carafe looked like it had been there for years. The coffee tasted the same.

Mandy called. Jess stepped outside to answer. She poured the thick sludge into the bushes and dropped the paper cup into a trash can perched on the sidewalk.

"I've found the information you wanted on that cylinder." When Mandy launched right into her purpose, that usually meant she'd found something useful. Jess smiled. "It's from one of the big chemical companies. I called. Talked to a rep and sent you an email about it. The cylinder is an old-style bottle. They identified it from the engraving. It holds methane."

"You mean like natural gas?"

"Close, but not quite. The rep said that's different. Apparently, they put something in natural gas called a tertbutyl—something-ithol to make it smell. The full name is in the email. Anyway, the methane in that cylinder was the stuff they use in chemical labs. Very pure. It's colorless and odorless."

Jess whistled. "So the house could have been full of it. Which would explain why the fire spread so fast after the explosion, I guess?"

"Could be. I don't know. But the rep said you might be able to notice it in the air."

"Let me guess, it causes itchy eyes?"

"Yep. And breathing gets difficult, he said."

Jess nodded, even though Mandy couldn't see her. "Can they tell who bought this particular canister?"

"I thought you'd ask that." Mandy sounded pleased. She wanted to move up to reporting, and she was always trying to prove herself. The problem was, she was a beautiful woman and Carter seemed to doubt such a gorgeous head could also hold a fine brain. "They recycle the cylinders, I guess. So they keep good records. But they need the serial number on the bottle to trace it."

"Where do I find the serial number?"

"On the bottom of the cylinder. But wait a second." Mandy clicked a couple of keys. "Okay. The number is printed on there. The man I talked to said the numbers often don't survive if there's a fire."

Jess frowned. "You're saying a highly flammable material is stored in a bottle with a label that burns?"

"Yeah. I guess they didn't expect them to burn. Or maybe they thought no one would want to know the serial number after a fire." Mandy stopped a moment to breathe. "Whatever the reason back in the day, the rep said the new cylinders have the number engraved on the bottom."

"Okay. I'll try and get the number. Maybe we'll get lucky." Jess hung up and went back into the station.

She passed the time reading her email. Mandy had collected a lot of information about the gas cylinder from the manufacturer. She'd included pictures that confirmed the identification of the cylinder. And a formal looking document called a "Material Safety Data Sheet" that identified the gas, explained the dangers, and repeated side effects and other warnings.

After thirty minutes, Jess grew tired of waiting, and the woman had returned to her desk.

"Captain Mercer asked me to be here at seven, prompt." She tapped her watch. "Could you check on him? If he's going to be much longer, I'll come back this afternoon."

"I'll check." She turned to a compact radio set on the rear wall, donned a headset, and hailed Mercer. She listened for a few moments, nodded, then switched off the radio. "Captain Mercer would like you to join him at Melissa Green's place. I'll get directions for you."

"Thanks," Jess said on her way out the door. "I know where it is."

She drove within the speed limits until she reached the driveway where the gate was open. She eased the Mustang up the drive. Three police cars and a crime scene van were parked in front of the home's charred remains. Jess parked at the end of the row.

Mercer appeared from the woods behind the house. He pointed to the police cruiser at the front of the row, and Jess joined him there.

"Get in," he said, gesturing to the driver's seat.

She slid inside amid the odor of stale fried food. The passenger's seat was hemmed in by a large computer mounted on a stalk, and a mass of wires that filled the foot well. An extension cord was duct-taped to the transmission tunnel with what looked like mobile phone chargers plugged into it.

Mercer struggled into the passenger seat and stuffed a large notepad into a broad plastic bin behind the console. "I need the full story."

Jess frowned. "I told you. Karen Warner went missing, presumed kidnapped and murdered, and then her sister goes missing."

"You said your editor has a sixth sense about these things. What did you mean?"

Jess shrugged. "Two sisters go missing within two years of each other. I mean, that's not exactly an everyday thing."

Mercer scowled. "You've interviewed Donald Warner."

"I talked to him yesterday, after the fire." She pulled her phone from her pocket and brought up her notes from the meeting. "I can send you my notes if you like?"

Mercer held out his hand. She passed her phone, and he skimmed through the file. "Why did you go out there to talk to him?"

She shook her head. "I don't know what you're looking for. Two sisters went missing. One was his wife."

"I talked to him, too. He claims you're working to get him released." He returned her phone. "If you have exculpatory evidence, let's see it."

She frowned. "I have nothing, and I didn't tell him otherwise. I said I would look into the case."

"Why?"

"Because this doesn't make sense, does it? He says he's innocent. Not likely, of course. But that could be true. People have been wrongfully convicted before." She paused. "You surprise me, Mercer. If he didn't kill his wife, don't you want to know who did? Could be the same person who killed your son-in-law yesterday, couldn't it?"

Mercer frowned and said nothing.

"Before I nearly died yesterday, I didn't care that much about David Warner. Truthfully, I still don't. But something's going on here, Mercer." Jess kneaded her forehead where a headache had started between her brows. "Look, I want to know. For sure. Don't you?"

Mercer nodded. Quietly, he said, "Yes. I do."

"Okay. Did you see that cylinder that was left after they put out the fire in the kitchen yesterday?" Jess waited until he nodded again. "Turns out it contained pure methane. Odorless and colorless. When I was in the house, my eyes were itching. Today, I've got a slight headache. Those are symptoms of exposure to methane. I think someone filled the house with the gas and set it off somehow."

"We agree there." Mercer nodded, and he seemed to be slightly less hostile.

Jess kept going. "There is a serial number on the bottom of the cylinder. We…you could trace who bought it."

"We did. It came from the university in Santa Irene. Stolen eighteen months ago." Mercer paused, and then seemed to make a decision to tell her more. "There was a device on the valve that released the gas through the walls and filled the house. The kind of thing you can buy at the store to turn your lights on remotely, over the Internet."

Jess's headache suddenly spiked pain into her eyes. "The place was rigged."

"Methane is lighter than air, so it rose to the top of the house and would have filled the place from the top down." Mercer swallowed hard. "And the team found a large rectangular lump of metal. A transformer. It was mixed with a mess of cables. Wired up properly, it would have generated a storm of high voltage sparks when it was told to."

Jess sighed. "So Jackson and Ernie and…"

Mercer gestured at the house. "And my son-in-law."

"Assuming the arsonist knew they were inside—" Jess's breath caught.

"The transformer was connected to the Internet. Same as the gas. The whole thing was remote controlled, and someone knew exactly when to trigger it all. It was cold blooded murder.

Nothing less." Mercer's breathing was loud and rapid while he fought his feelings. He stared at the empty space where Melissa Green's house had been.

She gave him a few moments, letting him work through his pain until he leaned back in his seat.

"We'll get them, Roy. We will. We'll find out who did this." Jess laid a hand on his shoulder.

CHAPTER TWENTY-THREE

Tuesday, May 23
Bear Hill, Arizona

"I'M AFRAID THAT'S NOT how these things work, Jess." Mercer glanced at the road in the distance beyond the driveway. "Santa Irene PD, Arizona State Police, the FBI, ATF, Homeland. Maybe more. They're on the way. This isn't my jurisdiction. I'm filling in for now because Jackson is in the hospital. But I'm Collingwood." He pointed with his thumb. "Ten miles down the road."

Jess looked down the road, too. She didn't see anyone headed this way, but she believed him. She was a bit surprised that the feds weren't here already.

Warner was already on the watch lists because of his connection to The Devil Kings and their multi-state criminal activities over the past decade. Kidnapping Karen Warner for ransom was a federal offense. These days, explosions also brought out the federal agencies, as Morris had said when they talked. The way this explosion was rigged and the deaths that resulted were matters best left to the experts with the resources to do the job.

"My daughter and granddaughter. My son-in-law. Captain Jackson. Ernie. I knew the ones who survived and the ones who didn't." He pressed his lips together and breathed hard through his nose. "But now, another department will take the lead."

"And you don't feel you can let them do that," Jess stated flatly.

"In twenty-two years on the job, I've never led a murder investigation. Never had to." He waved his hand at the pile of rubble that had been Melissa Green's house. "Now, we have three murders and arson."

Jess gazed at the rubble and shook her head. Yesterday, when Mercer had arrived at the scene, he'd been on automatic pilot. His years of experience had kicked in. Process and procedure had kept him focused and on track. But his feelings were controlling him now, undermining his confidence and tangling his rational mind with boiling emotions.

And then Jess realized what he'd said. "*Three* murders? What do you mean?"

Mercer nodded and clicked his door open. "Come with me."

Jess followed Mercer around the wreckage to the trail that led into the woods and over the hill. Several electrical cables ran from the crime scene van along the trail, too.

"Have you found out something about the Jeep?" She watched the rough ground, glad she'd worn her running shoes again.

"You could say that." He stopped and pointed to the dirt. "What do you see?"

The track was nothing but two ruts on either side of some

weeds. The ground was hard. The weeds were the lightest shade of green, leaves barely hanging on until the next rainfall.

She knelt for a better look. Tire treads had marked the earth during a rain storm some time ago. The Arizona sun had baked the evidence hard in its place. The marks were worn around the high spots, although the pattern was visible and edges weren't well defined.

"Looks like the trail's been used repeatedly," she said.

Mercer nodded as if she was a star pupil. "Do you remember what I said about this trail?"

"Yeah." She stood. "Not easy to find or navigate."

"Right. On the other side of the hill, the trail is positively dangerous. Very easy to get into a bad accident along there," Mercer waved along the track and over the hill.

"Who made these tracks? Melissa Green?"

"Not likely. She didn't own an off-road vehicle. Or a Jeep." Mercer's eyes scanned the area and jerked his thumb back toward the road. "And if a friend came out here to visit, why wouldn't they take the road and use the driveway?"

"You're thinking either she had a boyfriend into off-roading, or this had nothing to do with her." Jess would have mentioned the dirt bike magazines she'd seen in Melissa's kitchen if she trusted Mercer. Which she didn't.

He nodded and continued making his way up the hill.

Ahead, bright lights were hung from trees. Two uniformed police officers and several people wearing blue disposable coveralls were clustered together in the edge of the woods.

"Crime scene techs?" Jess said.

"Yes."

As she approached, Jess saw three technicians kneeling around a dark hole in the ground. Their blue coveralls were smeared with mud. Behind them, two shovels were sticking out of the ground.

Jess sighed. "A grave? How did you find it?"

"No idea whose yet." Mercer nodded slowly. "I sent one of my guys up here to look for evidence that might identify that Jeep. He's an experienced hunter, too. He found it."

Jess shivered. She looked around. She couldn't see the house from here. They were enveloped in the trees. The barely marked trail continued its upward climb for another hundred feet before reaching the peak of the hill.

The grave's location was carefully chosen. A hidden spot in an isolated place. She shivered as she realized she'd stood not twenty feet away the night before.

Mercer introduced Jess to the officer who had found the site. Sampson was six-six with biceps thicker than some of the surrounding trees. His ears led down a curve of solid muscle along his neck and into his shoulders.

"How did you find the grave?" Jess watched his dark eyes.

"There was a depression in the soil. You often get that around here. People dig something up while the ground's dry, then when they put it back, there's air pockets. Soon as it rains." He made a sinking gesture with his hands. "Could have been anything buried there. People hunt out here and bury their kills if they aren't fit to eat. I had a shovel, and it didn't take a minute to look."

Mercer led her to one of the crime techs standing by a wide hole in the ground. "This is Arthur."

Jess shook the technician's hand and leaned over to look in the hole.

At the bottom, a half-covered body in a ripped floral print dress lay on its back. The flowers were darker than the background, and the dress was stained dark brown from time and the soil. The face was unrecognizably decomposed. Several items poked out of the ground that looked like the contents of a handbag. Jess identified a shiny gold lipstick case and a matching gold compact.

Only the upper half of her body had been cleared so far. The other techs were bending into the grave, brushing the soil away and collecting it in small dustpans. They worked slowly, leaning into the grave to sweep soil, and leaning out to empty their dustpans and stretch their backs.

"Tell us what you've got," Mercer said.

Arthur cleared his throat. "White female. Been in the ground for a while. The body has been damaged. Both arms are broken and several of the fingers. There is a lot of material evidence to process before we have cause, time, or manner of death." He held up his hand. "And don't get too excited by this, but we found a driver's license in the handbag. The height, weight, and photo roughly match the deceased. The name on the license is Karen Warner."

Jess exhaled a breath she hadn't realized she was holding.

"Show me," Mercer said.

Arthur held up a clear plastic evidence bag with a mud covered plastic card inside. Mercer didn't have gloves on, so he gestured, and Arthur turned it around to show both sides.

Jess leaned in for a better look. The Arizona driver's license had expired a year ago and the birth date and address matched Karen Warner. The license was too soiled to see clearly, but the picture showed a long-haired female who could have been Dr. Donald Warner's wife. On the back, a magnetic swipe strip and a bar code were the first things Jess noticed. She read that the license had no restrictions or endorsements, which was normal.

"Find anything else notable so far?" Mercer said.

"Lipsticks, powder, a plastic case with some melted breath mints inside. Usual stuff."

"A phone? Diary? Papers?" Jess asked.

Arthur shook his head. "Bits of paper, but nothing intelligible yet. They look like a few restaurant receipts, maybe."

"When will you have the full results?" Mercer said.

"Weeks, usually, if all goes well." Arthur nodded. "But we'll have a preliminary postmortem tomorrow, and maybe some unconfirmed results at the end of the day."

"Another twenty-four hours, at least." Mercer sighed. "We need it as quick as you can." Mercer took out a notebook and scrawled on it. He tore the page out and handed it to Arthur. "And copy it to this address." He shook his phone, "So I can get it while I'm out of the office."

"Okay. But if this is Karen Warner, I don't see what the rush is." Arthur pushed the paper into a zippered pocket in his coveralls. He gestured to the grave. "I'd better get back to it."

Jess walked down the hill with Mercer. "Karen Warner was abducted by a gang called The Devil Kings."

"Yeah. I remember." He glanced at Jess. "The press loves those guys. Romanticizes them, if you ask me."

She ignored the barb and pointed toward the ashes. "Arson is one of their preferred methods of operation."

"Like everyone else in Arizona law enforcement, I'm aware." Mercer pushed aside a tree branch and held it for Jess to pass. "But our town has never been bothered by The Devil Kings. Not enough money around here to attract them, I guess."

"The leader, who calls himself Hades, is a sociopath with grandiose ideas named Norman Kemp. He's served time in the Arizona prison system. You have access to fingerprints and DNA."

Mercer gestured to the house. "There's nothing left of that house to compare to Hades so far. Even if we had forensic evidence, Hades hasn't been seen for a couple of years."

Jess ducked under another tree branch and emerged on the other side of the woods. "Maybe The Devil Kings have moved on to a different part of the country. Or maybe Hades learned some new tricks in prison and is now involved in less obvious crimes."

Mercer opened his mouth to speak, but a single *whoop* of a police siren echoed through the air. He sighed. "They're here."

"Who?"

"Santa Irene PD. When I tell them it's Karen Warner up there, they'll take over."

"You don't think they'll do a good job?" Jess frowned.

"That's not it." He shook his head. "They'll do a great job. They have the resources and manpower. Everything they need."

"Except you," Jess said.

"They won't want me. My resources are limited, and I'm covering two jurisdictions until Jackson gets back to work. And I'm connected to the case. Because of Lester and the others."

Jess nodded. He was right. "What are you going to do?"

"I can't go back home and say I did nothing. Not to my daughter. I couldn't face her and say that." He angled his head down and looked at her through narrowed eyes. He jerked his thumb up the hill. "If I'm right about you, I expect you'll keep digging, and I'd very much appreciate it if you repaid the courtesy and kept me informed."

"I see." Jess gave a slow nod.

"We understand each other, then." He took a deep breath. "I'll do the same for you."

Jess nodded again and walked away from him, toward the new crew.

CHAPTER TWENTY-FOUR

Tuesday, May 23
Santa Irene, Arizona

HADES SLAPPED THE CLOCK to silence its buzzing alarm. He rolled off the bed fully dressed, as usual. He remained prepared to tackle whatever came up.

Cora had come to bed after her watch less than an hour ago. She turned her head and edged one eye open.

"Get some sleep." He patted her ass. "I need to get them on it as soon as possible."

He ran a toothbrush over his teeth and checked the next room. Pony had replaced Cora on watch duty. They grunted to acknowledge each other.

"Find anything?" Hades said, nodding toward the laptop.

"Nothing. They can't find Melissa, and don't know squat else."

"Check every hour. TV stations want to impress people before they go to work. They'll be reporting as soon as they find out. I need to know as soon as they know."

He walked downstairs. Shorty was asleep on the couch.

Hades tapped the keyboard on Simon Lawson's computer. The screen came to life. A small icon indicated there was unread mail.

Hades flipped through the emails, a long string of junk and special offers. Way down in the queue, he found an email from Robertson & Robertson and opened it.

The language was formal, dry, canned. Blah, blah, blah. At the end, the email said Robertson & Robertson did not conduct transactions online and listed the phone number of the first company in Simon Lawson's chain of brokers for this account.

Cora came down the stairs a few minutes later and started the coffee machine. The noise woke Shorty. He rummaged in the refrigerator and found a bagel.

Hades eyeballed the email. Robertson & Robertson's phone number was the same as one of the other companies Hades found in Lawson's paperwork earlier. Otherwise, the email was practically anonymous. Or would have been, to the average person.

Hades opened a tool to examine the email's header information, the data that routed the message through a long string of servers before it arrived at Simon Lawson's computer. He noted the details.

The message had come from downtown Atlanta. He found the building, but Robertson & Robertson was not registered at that address.

"Coffee?" Cora called.

"Yeah." Hades nodded without looking away from the computer screen. The header also contained the bare Internet Protocol address of the server that had originated the message.

He sent the server a basic Internet request to verify. The

server responded immediately. He inched closer to the computer screen and typed furiously.

The server responded to each command he sent. Simple commands. Basic Internet stuff. He grinned with each response. By the time Cora had filled a mug of coffee and placed it in front of him, he had compiled contact details for every employee at the mythical Robertson & Robertson, including email addresses, phone numbers, and job titles.

He sorted through the job titles until he found Gordon Ferrari, the vice president of accounts.

He took a swig of coffee. Robertson & Robertson's standard form reply to last night's email made clear that they weren't concerned about customer relations unless that customer was willing to call on the phone.

Cora pushed between Hades and the computer and straddled his lap. He stared at her with his mouth clamped shut.

She turned to the computer screen. "Either the account is empty, or Lawson lied and now the account is locked?"

"Neither." Hades relaxed his jaw. "The company doesn't deal on the Internet."

She frowned. "What financial company doesn't have a website these days?"

"Robertson & Robertson sends form emails and has a poorly secured server, but no online trading." He pointed to the screen. "They're the end of the chain. They referred me back to the first company in the chain."

She cocked her head, trying to make sense of what he'd showed her. "So they're laundering the money?"

He shrugged. "Laundering, exporting, hiding. Hard to say. But it's illegal, I suspect."

"Woo hoo!" Cora jumped up, a big, toothy smile on her face.

She danced around the computer, waving her hands in the air. "Money, money, money."

Hades grabbed her as she passed by. "Maybe, maybe not. Just chill. I need to think."

She lowered her arms. "What is there to think about? We get simple Simon up here and do the garden tool thing until he tells us everything."

"This is complex. Not an everyday set up." Hades stood, pacing as he drank the coffee. "Lawson went to a lot of trouble here."

"It's still just account numbers and passwords. After the last session, he'll piss his pants at the sight of a garden implement."

"I don't trust him. One wrong word from him, and we could be shut out."

Cora sighed and sat on the arm of the sofa. "What if they use voice recognition?"

"Because they do their dealing over the phone?"

She shrugged. "They have to have some security to protect their customers' money, and themselves. You said their server isn't secure. What else could it be?"

"My bet is they protect themselves first," Hades replied. "That's what I would do."

"Can we get him up here? And her? Put them on the phone?"

Hades shook his head. "We keep them secured. And we never, ever, let them talk to anyone." He thumped his chest. "My golden rule for a happy home invasion hasn't failed me yet."

"And we don't break the rules," Shorty said.

"Exactly." Hades looked back at the computer, the email still on the screen. "We have no choice. I have to talk to them. If it goes to hell, we cut our losses, and hang up."

He picked up a pencil and made a list of numbers and names

as he finished the coffee. His notes covered three sheets. Names, dates of birth, and addresses. A family tree from grandparents to the Lawson's daughter. He laid everything out beside the phone. He listed every account Lawson owned, along with the passwords.

He completed the list with the names, addresses, and numbers for the firms involved with the foreign brokerage account. Finally, he listed the top people at Robertson & Robertson.

He looked over the lists. These were all the details he knew. If someone threw him a curve, like a simple identification question, the lists would give him a good chance of finding the answer quickly enough.

He underlined the number for Gordon Ferrari, Accounts Vice President. The man who, in most organizations, would have the final word. The guy at the top of the pyramid.

He held his mug out for more coffee. Cora refilled it and sat back on the arm of the sofa, silent.

Hades steadied his nerves with several lungfuls of air. He picked up Lawson's telephone handset. The coiled cord bounced and vibrated in the air and tethered Hades to the connection.

He dialed Gordon Ferrari's direct line. Exchanges clicked and buzzed as the call was routed halfway across the country.

The phone rang twice before it was answered in Atlanta.

"Yes." A young woman's voice.

"Gordon Ferrari," Hades said.

"Do you have a number?"

Hades looked at his notes. He had masses of numbers. If she required a security code that he didn't have, it was going to be a short call.

He stabbed his finger by the account number. The woman

sounded young. Lawson was sixty-three, ancient to her. Hades guessed she wouldn't be surprised if Lawson were slow to catch on.

"You mean my account number?" Hades said, feigning confusion.

The woman gave a bored uh-huh.

Hades read out the number carefully in six lots, four digits at a time. Twenty-four numbers. No mistakes.

The girl remained silent, but he could hear her keyboard clicking with each digit.

He reached the end of the account number. "Anything else?"

"I'll put you through," she replied.

He heard two clicks, and a man's voice came on the line. "Ferrari here."

"Lawson," Hades said. "Simon Lawson."

"Forgive me, Mr. Lawson. I recognize the number, but not the name."

Perfect. Ferrari had no idea what Lawson sounded like. Hades relaxed slightly and he scanned down the chain of brokers Lawson used to funnel his money into Robertson & Robertson. "I usually go through McDonald."

"Right," Ferrari said. "Good company."

"Too many middle men in my investments, Ferrari," Hades said. "I'm going to take a more hands-on approach."

Ferrari cleared his throat. "Most of our clients prefer to work through advisors."

"My plans have changed."

"You're not unsatisfied with our service, I hope?"

"On the contrary. The arrangement has worked well."

"I am glad to hear it."

"So well, that I believe I'm going to adjust my plans. Going forward, so to speak."

"I see."

"I would like to cash out my accounts."

"Cash out?"

"In full. Everything."

"Everything?"

"Precisely."

Ferrari's various strangled groans came across clearly. "Well…you ought to give us time to advise you. To help you manage the tax implications. That sort of thing."

Hades grinned. "I don't think that will be a problem."

Ferrari remained silent.

Hades said, "Please liquidate my investments effective immediately. I have a bank account ready to receive the money."

"Mr. Lawson. I'm sure you realize, these things can't be done quickly—"

"You've been well compensated for your services. As has everyone else involved. Let's get this moving."

"I can arrange for the sale of your investments. Not all the markets are open at the same time. Different time zones and so on." Ferrari sighed. He pounded a keyboard. After a few moments, he cleared his throat. "There are currency exchanges to be made. We will look for the best spot rates. Then the monies will have to be collected. In one location."

"I have an account in Panama," Hades said.

Ferrari grunted. "We will have to prepare closure statements."

"Thank you."

"And if expediting fees are required?"

"Pay them."

More typing. Ferrari cleared his throat again as if the words he uttered were painful. "Then I believe the money could be available to transfer to your bank account tomorrow evening."

"Then do it. I'll be waiting."

"All we require is your signature."

Hades smiled. He'd found examples of Simon Lawson's signature. He wasn't a forger, but he could perfect a passable copy. "I'll fax it to you."

Ferrari gave a short laugh. "I'm afraid your signature must be made in person and witnessed appropriately." He clicked a few keys. "We have a representative in…er…Tucson. Is that close enough?"

Hades shuffled in his seat. "You can't be serious. I have to drive to Tucson just to sign a piece of paper?"

"I'm afraid—"

Hades gripped the phone harder. "It's just a signature."

"We can make exceptions for smaller amounts, but I'm sure you understand. Even we have limits."

"What is your limit?" Hades said, his jaw hardly moving.

"Twenty million."

Hades took a long slow breath and let it out. The tension drained from his muscles, and his mouth split open into a wide smile. "Then I guess I'll just have to drive to Tucson. Send me the details by email."

He hung up before he burst out laughing.

CHAPTER TWENTY-FIVE

Tuesday, May 23
Bear Hill, Arizona

AFTER SHE HAD INTRODUCED herself to Mercer's replacements, Jess drove back into Bear Hill and parked in a small lot in the center of town. Melissa Green had lived outside of Bear Hill for a couple of years, according to the property records. Although she was a recluse, surely she came into town for occasional supplies.

A no-name gas station stood on a corner. Melissa probably bought plenty of gas, but the teen working the register was unlikely to know details.

Further down the road was a tiny grocery market. Jess went inside. The shelves were packed to the ceiling. An older woman sat at the register reading a magazine. Jess collected several bottles of fruit flavored water and a bunch of bananas.

The woman looked up from her reading when Jess approached. "Got everything?" she said, waving the first bottle of water across a price scanner.

"Yes, thanks." Jess placed her shopping on the counter. "I was wondering if you're a local resident?"

The woman nodded. "Bear Hill, born and bred." She put her hand on her heart and, with a grin, spoke in a falsetto voice, "My whole twenty-one years."

Jess smiled back. The woman was over seventy if she was a day. "I was hoping you might know Melissa Green?"

The woman stopped. "You family? Friend?"

Jess shook her head. "I know Melissa's missing."

The woman looked relieved to know Jess was already aware of Melissa's circumstances. "Police have been looking for her for a while."

"Did you know her?"

"Well…she didn't shop here much. Probably not for a good year or so. I hardly ever saw her out and about." She gestured down the road. "You know about her house?"

Jess nodded.

The woman grimaced. "Terrible situation."

"Where did she do her shopping, if not here?"

The woman shrugged. "Who knows? She was an odd duck. Never seemed to mix with anyone. Really attractive, though, even without makeup."

Jess held out a picture of Karen Walker. "Like this?"

"That's her." The woman nodded. "I think the only place I saw her was over at the post office."

"Did she go there regularly?"

"You'd have to ask Dawn. She runs the place." She winked. "She's twenty-one as well."

Jess paid her bill and walked to the small post office. Inside was a counter with two cash registers. There was an island in the middle of the room for completing postal labels and packaging.

Seven people were in line. A sign on the counter identified the woman behind the counter as Dawn.

Jess waited her turn. By the time she reached the pole position in line, only one man was behind her. Jess waved him forward and waited until the lobby was empty to approach the counter.

Jess moved closer and spoke quietly. "I understand you knew Melissa Green?"

"Knew?" Dawn said. "I know her, yes. People shouldn't be so quick to write her off."

"Like who?"

"You, for starters."

"Touché." Jess straightened up. "Actually, I'm trying to find her. I heard she used to come in here regularly."

Dawn shook her head. "Not regularly, but every few weeks. Just to mail stuff. A letter or a parcel. Bought a book of stamps sometimes. So I guess she used to have a lot of correspondence."

"I thought you said she posted her letters here."

"Yeah, but certainly not as many as the stamps she bought."

Jess looked out through the windows. "Is there a mailbox nearby?"

"Five. All in town. Nothing down her way. We pick up from everyone's mailbox, though."

"Who delivered mail out to Melissa's place?"

"I'm not sure. She hasn't had any mail for a while." She paused and thought a moment as if Bear Hill had a lot of delivery people to sort through. "Bill was the regular carrier, but he's gone up north. His sister's sick."

"Did Melissa pay with a credit card or a check?"

Dawn cocked her head and closed her eyes. "Um, cash, I think. But it was only ten, maybe twenty dollars tops."

"Did she ever mention her sister?"

Eyes wide open now, Dawn pursed her lips and shook her head. "Never. I never brought her up either. She wasn't the sort of person you get close to. There was always… I don't know. A barrier?"

"You know who her sister was?"

"Sure. That doctor's wife. He killed her."

Jess was about to say that they never found the body, and thought better of it. "Did she ever talk about the case to anyone in town that you know of?"

"You mean, did I hear any rumors?" She shook her head again. "Few of us, older ones, wanted to offer her some support, but we were scared of how she might react if we brought it up. Far as I know, no one ever did. Better to talk about those sort of things, I always say. But she wasn't approachable like that, you know?"

"Did you ever see her sister or her husband here in town?"

"Dr. Warner? Don't think so." Dawn frowned. "But I would have noticed her sister. They were twins, you know. I would have noticed that."

Jess thanked Dawn and left. She carried the heavy groceries to the Mustang and stashed them in the trunk. Two women who knew Melissa both said she rarely came into town and they hadn't seen her in quite a while.

Briefly, she considered trying a couple more of the shops, and then she shrugged. *No reason to keep hitting my head against this brick wall.*

On the other hand, Melissa Green must have known someone in this town. Jess looked down the main street. Where might she have made a friend?

CHAPTER TWENTY-SIX

CORA GAWKED AT HADES, mouth agape. "Twenty million?"

Hades picked her up and twirled her around. She giggled, and he pulled her close for a long, hard kiss. When he set her down, he said, "Maybe even more. Can you believe it?"

"Hot damn!" She stamped her bare foot on the floor and fist-pumped the air.

"I heard all the shouting" Pony walked down the stairs, his heavy boots thumping on the treads. "What's going on?"

"Looks like Lawson was hiding a hell of a lot more money than we thought." Cora laughed. A long, rippling sound.

"Let's not get ahead of ourselves." Hades scowled. "We don't know for sure yet. All we know is that Lawson has a foreign account with some money in it."

Cora shook her head. "You said they want a signature because it's over twenty mil."

Pony whistled. "Twenty million?"

Hades held up his hands to stop the conversation. "They did say that. But maybe they were testing us, knowing that there is nowhere near that amount there. Maybe we just triggered some alarm, and don't know it yet."

Cora sighed and sank onto the arm of the sofa.

Hades waved at Pony. "Get back up there. I need to think, and we still need a lookout."

Pony looked at Cora and back to Hades on his way up the stairs to his post. "That's a lot of money."

"I know."

"We have to get it," Cora said.

"If we can," Hades said.

"If it's real," Shorty said.

"It is a lot of money. We can get it. And it's real." Cora walked around the sofa. "I can feel it. I can taste it." She spread her arms out to encompass the luxury surrounding her. "Look at this place. Lawson is a doctor. Sure, he makes good money. But the electric bill alone must be more than most people earn in a year."

"Maybe, but we don't know anything yet. We all just need to—"

Shorty threw his arms up. "Twenty-frigging-million!"

Hades stabbed his finger at him. "Shut it! We won't have anything if I can't figure out how to get this signature done."

Cora waved to the desk. "There's lots of examples of his signature around here. You could practice."

Hades sighed. "But can I do it in an office in Tucson? Under pressure? And it could be a setup."

"Why?" Cora shook her head.

"People there could know Lawson. Personally. Or what if they have a photo on file?"

"We could make a mask," Cora said.

"It wouldn't look exactly like him. Not up close." Hades sat silently. Minutes ticked by.

Cora refilled her coffee and returned to the sofa. "We have to do something."

"We're going to." Hades stared into space. "For twenty million, we could get out of this game forever."

CHAPTER TWENTY-SEVEN

Tuesday, May 23
Bear Hill, Arizona

JESS WANDERED ALONG THE main street through Bear
Hill. She passed two banks. They would be ideal places to find
information about Melissa Green, but they were also the last
places that would talk to a merely curious reporter.

She saw two diners and a coffee shop. Not franchises or
chains. The coffee shop was on one side of a bakery. The
intoxicating aromas made her stomach growl. Jess lingered in
front of the fresh bread and pastries displayed in the window.

Bear Hill was a small, but self-sufficient, town. If Melissa
Green had wanted to leave the public glare after her sister
was kidnapped in Santa Irene, Bear Hill had been a great
choice.

Okay. So Melissa didn't come into town much. But her
kitchen had been fully stocked when Jess was there before the
explosion. Her food and supplies had to come from somewhere.

Jess looked up and down the street. It would be hard to visit this town without being seen. She had the feeling that no one walked the street that Dawn failed to see.

Jess returned to the Mustang and drove the length of Main Street. She turned a couple of times and found herself headed north on a parallel road. There were a few stores mingled between older homes here.

She passed an antique store, a Presbyterian church, and the Bear Hill fire station. The houses she saw were settled on large lots, but they were old and tired-looking. The residents she'd seen were mostly seniors, too. A gray-haired couple sitting on a porch waved as she passed.

She was heading into a fully residential area. There was one last building that looked larger than most. It was the back side of a warehouse. All manner of lumber and pipes were stacked and protected behind a fence bearing warnings about video cameras recording twenty-four-seven.

She circled the block. The front of the warehouse sat back on an unpaved parking lot large enough to hold a couple of dozen vehicles. A large pull-in loading dock was reserved for trucks to load purchases and then pull straight through. *Bartlet's Building Supplies* had been painted over the main doors long ago. Like everything else she could see, the paint also looked in need of TLC.

Three men were unloading an eighteen-wheeler. Two of them worked as a team, picking up the larger lumber and boxes and moving them inside. They kept a steady pace, carrying the load into the warehouse and returning for the next without a break.

The third man cherry-picked what he lifted, and placed the boxes on a bright red dolly. When the dolly was three-quarters full, he wheeled it into the building.

A horn beeped. Jess pulled into the parking lot, clearing the edge of the sidewalk and moving out of the way as a truck with the words *Don's Electrical* on the side entered, bumping over the rough ground. A man in heavy boots got out of the truck, gave her a wave. He disappeared into the warehouse.

Jess frowned. Building supply stores were typically the preserve of men. But every new place she'd ever moved into had needed a million little things to make it a home. A single woman like Melissa would have had no choice but to shop here at least a few times and probably more frequently.

Jess parked and followed the man from the electrical supply truck inside. Building supplies always had the same smell. Not unpleasant, just a reminder of the components that go to make up a home. The basic mixture of wood, plaster, and concrete had barely changed in a couple of centuries.

There was no one behind the checkout counter.

The men unloading the big truck carried in a shower cubicle. They avoided eye contact with her and returned to the eighteen-wheeler in the loading dock.

The building was densely packed with merchandise. Jess wandered through the aisles. Commonplace tools rested beside peculiar electric saws for which she couldn't imagine a need. Another aisle displayed bathroom fixtures, waste disposal units, and big wide pipe for venting residential clothes dryers.

She met the man from the supply truck in the electrical section. His work shirt was embroidered with his name over the pocket. Don uncoiled a thick cable on the floor, paced out a section, and cut off the length he wanted. He smiled as she passed.

The remainder of the store was filled with lawnmowers and garden tools of all kinds.

She returned to the checkout counter, but the register was still unmanned.

Don arrived behind Jess, his coil of cable over his shoulder and several boxes of electrical supplies in his large hands.

The man with the dolly wandered in from the loading dock with another half-load. He steered away from the checkout.

Don whistled. Loud. "Hey, Steven! Come on. Customers are waiting here."

The man with the dolly looked over. Steven flashed a half smile, half grimace, and sighed. He let go of the dolly. It rolled to a stop of its own accord.

Don nodded to Jess. "This lady's first."

Steven ambled to the checkout. He looked Jess up and down. She had the feeling he wasn't looking for what she was going to purchase.

"What you got?" he said.

Jess looked at Don. "Actually, I just wanted some information. If you want to go first…"

Don put down his armful of switches and hefted the cable onto the counter with a thud. "No problem. Steven here needs to work on his customer service skills."

Jess took a deep breath and looked at Steven. "Do you know Melissa Green?"

Steven screwed up his face. "Who?"

"Melissa Green." Jess pointed in the direction of Melissa's house. "She lives up the road."

Don laughed. "Well, this is good."

Jess frowned.

"You remember Melissa, Steven."

Steven shifted his weight and shrugged his shoulders.

Don grinned. "She slapped Steven once."

Steven scowled.

"Pretty hard, so I heard," Don said.

Steven glared at Jess. "Are you going to buy anything?"

"Why did she slap you?"

"The usual reason a woman slaps a man," Don said.

"She been in here lately?"

Steven sighed. "Who are you, again? What do you want?"

"My name's Jessica Kimball with *Taboo Magazine*. I'm looking for Melissa Green."

Steven took a half step back. "I didn't have nothing to do with that fire."

"I didn't say you did. I'm just trying to get an idea of what Melissa is like. So I can find her." Jess paused. "You know she's missing, I assume."

Steven nodded and shifted his weight from foot to foot.

"Tell her what you know," Don said. "Bad situation up at her place. Least you can do is help when you're asked."

Steven opened and closed his mouth a couple of times before speaking. "I don't know nothing. She used to come in here. Sometimes. A while ago."

"How long ago?"

Steven shrugged. "A year? Maybe two?"

"Closer to two, maybe," Don said. "When she first moved in. You know how it is, setting up a new place."

"Maybe closer to two years than one, yeah," Steven said.

"What did she buy?"

Steven screwed up his face. "I don't know. Stuff. Things." He waved toward the warehouse. "We sell tons of stuff."

"Plumbing things," said Don. "I saw her buying pipe and joints. A torch as well."

"Torch?"

"Blowtorch." Don mimed welding. "To join copper fittings."

"She did her own plumbing?" Jess arched her eyebrows.

Don shrugged and smiled. "I heard she had a man helping out. But that might have been a rumor. Never know around here. Not much to do except gossip about the neighbors in a town like Bear Hill."

"What kind of gossip did you hear about Melissa?"

"She was a looker. Really pretty. Hence Steven's…" He patted the side of his face and turned his head with the push. "Anyway, I think she wanted to be left alone. Stayed out there in her place, mostly. Some people didn't like that and weren't above telling tales."

"Like what?"

He shrugged. "It was just speculation. No substance to it. Gossip about men around her place. Stuff like that."

"What men?"

"I don't know." Don shook his head. "I figure she had a plumber out there to do some work, and after that people just made up stories to have something to talk about. You know. After her sister, and all. I doubt there was any truth to any of it. I figure she moved here to get away from all that circus in Santa Irene. Stands to reason she wasn't going to go out of her way to look for attention when she got here."

"That makes sense," Jess replied and thanked Don for his candor. She walked back to the Mustang thinking that the rumors could easily have been true, too.

CHAPTER TWENTY-EIGHT

Tuesday, May 23
Santa Irene, Arizona

HADES SAT AT THE computer. Cora sat across from him with her coffee. Shorty had gone upstairs to shower. Pony was still on lookout and searching the Internet for news about Melissa Green.

Hades hadn't spoken in a long time. His coffee mug was empty, and his mouth was dry. He licked his lips and cleared his throat. "We can't trust Simon Lawson."

Cora frowned. "To do what?"

"Go to the broker's office and sign over his money. You saw him downstairs. He's falling apart. Desperate." He shook his head. "No. Lawson would do anything to save his own skin."

Cora frowned. "What about his wife? Would he do the right thing to save her?"

"I don't think he cares. At least, he doesn't care enough." Hades shrugged. "His own skin is more important."

"We could try threatening her. See how it goes."

He shook his head. "I saw the look on his face when Shorty

taped her arm to the chair. He didn't look alarmed. More like relieved, I'd say."

Cora snorted. "He's pond scum."

"We already know that."

"But we can't ignore twenty million, baby." Cora collected both coffee mugs and refilled them.

"Or possibly more." He tapped the computer screen. "Which is why I've been searching through Lawson's email."

Cora handed him the coffee and looked over his shoulder. He pointed to a string of emails. She chuckled. "Well, well."

"Exactly." Hades sipped the coffee. It felt good going down. His throat was parched ever since he'd heard about the twenty million. He wanted it. Wanted it bad. But he didn't want to die to get it. "What do you think he would do for her?"

She smiled. "He's not complete scum then."

"Close enough. But she's our best chance." He'd made up his mind. He patted her ass. "Get Pony and Shorty."

A minute later, all four stood around the kitchen island.

"We have a new plan," Hades said.

"The brokerage account?" Pony's eyes grew as wide as the rim of a shot glass.

"I'm not sugar coating this. It's a big risk. And if we get the money, we have to leave the country. No ifs, ands, or buts. We'll be burning bridges. Thousand ways things could go south quick. And if they do, there's no turning back." He took a deep breath. "So if anybody wants out, now's the time to jump ship."

"Twenty million dollars?" Pony glanced at Shorty and Cora, then back at Hades. "Who the hell wants out?"

Shorty nodded.

Cora's decision was never in doubt.

Hades looked carefully into their eyes. To each member of

his crew individually. Each one nodded. He nodded in return. "Then we're going to get it. All of it."

"But we're going to finish what we started, too, right?" Pony said.

"Hell, yes. And we're not leaving anyone or anything behind. Which means we're going to have to split up." He pointed at Pony and Shorty. "You have to clean out the safe house. Everything. Take a truck, empty the place. Sterilize it. Then drive the truck off a cliff."

Shorty said, "Why not just torch it all?"

"Look at what happened to Green's place when we did that," Pony said. "We don't need any more heat."

"Driving a truck off a cliff doesn't attract attention?" Shorty said.

"A stolen truck in the middle of nowhere. Plenty of gas in the tank, so it explodes and burns." Cora purred. "It'll take days before they even figure out what model it was."

"Torching the house would be easier," Shorty grumbled.

Hades leaned in and lowered his voice to make them all pay close attention. "Everything we do leaves some evidence. I'll be damned if I'm giving anyone any more than we have to. Not when we're this close to getting out of here with twenty million dollars in our pockets."

"You clean the place out, leave the keys for the owner. An ordinary bunch of people doing ordinary things." Cora said, smoothly. "We'll be a distant memory out at the lake house even before you're safely back here with us."

"What will you two be doing?" Shorty said.

"In Tucson. Signing for the money."

"Clearing the house is going to be a big job. Shorty's right. We could use the help," Pony said.

Hades held his fingers like a pistol and mimicked a gunshot. "After that's done, we're finishing what we started."

"You going to put the squeeze on them?"

Hades shook his head. "Not worth it."

"We didn't think Lawson was hiding twenty mil."

Hades kept shaking his head. "We need to focus. We risk it all if we're too greedy."

There was silence around the island.

"The money will transfer tomorrow night. Once it's gone, we're gone."

"What about…" Pony looked around the island. "We're not all here."

Hades glowered. "And that's the way it'll stay until tomorrow. No contact with anyone else. No surfing the Internet looking at Ferraris. Nothing. We keep the lowest of low profiles. Absolutely nothing to attract attention."

"You better not be thinking of taking his share of this money."

Hades grabbed Pony's shirt. He dragged him close, and whipped his knife into his hand and shoved it against Pony's abdomen. "Don't you dare accuse me—"

Pony twisted, but Hades kept a tight grip on his shirt and the knife close.

"Then why don't you want to collect—"

Hades shoved Pony back. "We're not leaving anyone."

"But—"

"But nothing. We're not leaving anyone behind. We collect Benny's family tomorrow. We clear out his stuff and pay his bills. Just like the safe house. We just don't need anyone getting interested at the last minute. Got it?"

Pony glowered. "If you say so."

"I damn well do. If we keep our wits, we're all going to be rich. Very rich."

Shorty pointed at the floor. "This is all great. But what about the weasel downstairs? How do you plan to get him to cooperate?"

"That's the difficult part." Hades smiled. "But it starts with something right up your alley."

CHAPTER TWENTY-NINE

Tuesday, May 23
Bear Hill, Arizona

JESS RETURNED TO HER car and started the engine. Had Melissa Green done her own plumbing? Did that explain the methane gas booby trap at her house?

There was really only one reason for the booby trap, and whatever she wanted to hide had probably been successfully destroyed in the explosion and fire.

Did she have a man helping her? If she did, he had to be an accomplice. No legitimate plumber would have installed plumbing that spread highly flammable gas throughout her house.

The accomplice must have known what she was doing, and presumably why.

Jess flipped through the photographs she had taken in Melissa's kitchen. The well-stocked kitchen was way too much for one person. And the four months of *Dirt and Track* magazines practically shouted a male resident.

But if Melissa had done her own plumbing, maybe she was into dirt bike riding, too.

Jess ran a search of the county records yesterday. Melissa Green had purchased the property two months after her brother-in-law, Donald Warner, was arrested. He'd been behind bars since then, either in the Santa Irene county jail or in the prison where she'd seen him yesterday. Unless Melissa Green had access to the property before she actually closed the sale and paid for it, Warner could not have been the plumbing accomplice.

Jess sent a message to Mandy requesting Melissa Green's previous address. While she waited, she drove to the gun shop to collect her weapon. The shop didn't open until noon, but the owner answered the rear door when she rang the bell.

Her Glock and holster had arrived in an oversized box because Morris had added plenty of padding. The owner confirmed the paperwork was in order and handed her the gun. She bought a box of ammunition and loaded the gun before she left.

Her phone chimed as she walked to her car. Mandy had texted Melissa Green's previous address. A house on the north side of Santa Irene in the art district. From what Jess remembered the area was like a mini-Santa Fe on the edge of a metropolis.

The more she learned about Melissa Green, the more perplexing the woman became. She was the beautiful, identical twin sister to a socialite who had been kidnapped and murdered by her famous husband, a heart surgeon. After she'd moved away from Santa Irene's art district, fleeing the fallout from overwhelming negative media attention, she'd lived in the middle of nowhere and did her own plumbing or had a male accomplice who helped her to booby trap her own house with a remotely triggered firebomb.

No matter how she studied the pieces, nothing Jess knew about Melissa Green could be reconciled into a cohesive picture of a normal woman.

Jess plugged her phone into a power outlet to recharge it and started the Mustang. The engine growled to life as if it were unhappy to have been left cooling for so long. She eased out of the lot and headed north.

If there was an answer to Melissa's odd behavior, maybe it would come from her life in Santa Irene before her sister had been taken.

CHAPTER THIRTY

Tuesday, May 23
Santa Irene, Arizona

CORA DROVE THE WHITE panel van expertly, as she always did. She was a remarkable driver. Much better than he was, even when they were kids. Hades felt the adrenaline throbbing in his veins as if he was the one behind the wheel. It tingled the ends of his fingers, and goaded his right foot, imploring it to press harder on an accelerator he didn't control.

Cora kept pace with the traffic flow. Never the fastest and never the slowest on the road. It was the best way to avoid suspicion, she'd said.

Santa Irene had grown from nothing over a century's time, in a state with few limits on open space. That single feature had broadly defined its zoning and the roads, too. Rush hour congestion was non-existent here on the affluent west side of the city.

Cora turned off the freeway onto a major road, and then into a new housing development.

Hades marveled that she didn't consult a map or wait for a navigation system to announce turnings because she had committed the journey to memory, as she always did. He'd watched her play through the roads in and out of the target zone. She had assessed parking lots as viable escape routes, and open ground in the event that roads weren't an option. If anything went south, as occasionally things did, she was always fully prepared.

The development was less than half built. Large blocks of house plots were marked out, but empty. Lone houses stood surrounded by spaces that would soon be filled in.

Hades wore a dark jacket that he had taken from Simon Lawson's closet. He'd ripped the pockets and the collar to disguise the jacket, in case she recognized it as Simon's. He was larger than Simon, more muscular. He'd removed the cord that cinched up the waist, and still, the jacket would not button around his hard abs.

Shorty had similarly grunged up a bright yellow plastic workman's jacket he'd found in the garage. He sat quietly in the rear of the van, waiting.

Cora turned onto another street. A pair of new houses perched on one side, and three rested on the other side. Cora slowed as they approached.

"We're here," Hades said, knocking once on the metal partition.

He heard Shorty pick up a garden fork and two shovels, and shuffle to the rear doors.

Cora turned into the driveway of the first house. Hades and Shorty had jumped out of the van before she turned the engine off.

Hades led the way around the side of the house. He moved

fast, but he placed his heavy boots on the flagstones with care, keeping noise to a minimum.

Wooden fence panels separated the house from its only neighbor. An eight-foot wooden gate opened into the enclosed rear garden. Shorty lifted the crude metal latch and closed the gate silently behind them.

A small porch was set into the rear of the house. Hades stood with his back to the porch and drove the spade into the recently sodded grass. He levered a large clod from the ground. Shorty did the same.

They built up a rhythm, heaving their shovels into the air, pounding them into the soil, and levering out a mound of earth. In a few minutes, they had a five-foot length of the garden excavated and a growing mass of earth by the edge of the porch.

The rear door burst open.

"What the hell are you doing?" A woman's voice demanded.

Hades turned. "Hello."

The woman looked exactly like the pictures she'd emailed Simon Lawson. She was in her mid-twenties. Almost six-feet tall. Long dark hair and flawless tanned skin. She wore yoga pants and a sports bra. Hades doubted there was an ounce of fat on her.

"I said, what are you doing?"

Hades frowned. "Digging."

"Digging what?"

"A hole," he said.

She pointed at Shorty as he levered up another shovelful of earth.

"Stop him," she said.

Shorty dug his shovel into the ground.

She stepped to the edge of the porch. "Stop it!"

Shorty looked at her, his foot resting on the edge of his shovel, ready to drive it into the ground.

She waved a finger at Shorty. "Don't. Don't you dare."

Shorty shrugged.

She turned to Hades. "Why are you digging up my grass?"

Hades pulled a crumpled piece of paper from his pocket. "You ordered a French drain."

The woman shook her head. "No, I didn't."

Hades checked the piece of paper then held it out in front of the woman. He pointed to a name. "This you?"

She studied it. "Yes, that's me. But I did not order a drain."

"French drain," Hades said. "It has holes along the length—"

"I don't care if it has a Gallic accent." She pointed to the mound of earth. "Put that back, and get out of here."

"Amanda, right?" Hades gave a bemused shake of his head. He surveyed the paper. "It has this address." He read out a phone number.

"That's my number, but I'm telling you, I did not order a French drain."

"Someone must have. Our computer records the number. Your husband, perhaps?"

She shook her head. "I'm not married."

"Boyfriend? Anyone else at this address?"

She kept shaking her head.

Having confirmed all the information he needed, Hades handed over the piece of paper. "Well, call our office and talk to the boss. Number's at the top of the page."

Amanda snatched the paper and headed back inside. As she kicked the door closed with her heel, Hades barged through.

The door slammed back against the wall.

Amanda leaped sideways, astonished. "What the hell—"

Hades brought his shotgun to bear. Amanda swung a kick at the gun. It twisted in his hands, crushing the trigger against his finger. The gun fired. A muted double-boom. Chili powder exploded across the living room. He was out of shots.

He rotated the gun and swung the stock like a club. She jerked back, her right leg flicked up and punched his thigh. She was strong. Her kick was full of power. He felt a momentary numbness in his leg.

She grabbed a kitchen chair and hurled it at him.

He deflected the chair with the shotgun as she ran through the kitchen shouting.

Shorty raced in through the rear door and straight into the living room on a path to intercept the woman on the other side of the kitchen wall.

Amanda saw Shorty and turned for a wide L-shaped staircase with a balcony above. She took the steps three at a time.

A man appeared at the balcony, tying the belt around a robe. Amanda screamed at him. He frowned before turning to run back the way he had come.

Shorty took the stairs with the same three-at-a-time gait as Amanda. He didn't bother slowing for the L-shaped corner. He let his shoulder blunt his speed against the wall before bounding up the second half of the stairs.

Hades dumped his shotgun, and followed Shorty, drawing his VBR as he moved.

Amanda darted through a bedroom door, slamming it behind her.

Shorty went after the man.

Hades went after Amanda. He used his momentum to slam his boot onto the door by the handle.

The door shook, but the latch didn't give. It might have

opened with a simple twist of the door handle, but the king of the underworld cared nothing for what governed ordinary lives. He pounded the latch with his boot. The door swung open after the third blow.

Hades jumped into the room. He saw a bed with side tables and a chest of drawers. No sign of the woman. He knelt to look under the bed, letting the gun be visible to her first if she was hiding there. She wasn't.

Two doors led from the room, one on the left, one on the right. He heard shouting from the left. Shorty and the mystery man. The door led to a Jack-and-Jill bathroom. Hades raced in, leading with his gun. The shower curtain was already back, and the tub was empty.

He heard the sound of fighting from the second bedroom attached to the shared bathroom.

He crouched low as he entered. The man held a pistol in his hand. Shorty was holding the man's hand and pointing the pistol at the ceiling.

No sign of Amanda.

Shorty punched the man under the arm, straight into the least protected area of his ribs. The man collapsed.

The closet door shifted. Hades lunged forward, shoving the gun into the dimly lit space. He wrenched the clothes back and forth, opening up the spaces where a person might hide, but found no one.

He ran back through the bedroom. The man was on his knees. Shorty had a lamp cord around his neck.

Through the door, Hades saw Amanda on the landing. He ran after her.

She leaped down the stairs and turned for the dining room.

He jumped onto the half-landing at the turn in the stairs.

He had to catch her. The dining room led to the front door, and then it would be all over.

He vaulted over the banister, swinging his legs in an arc. She was within range. Close enough. His right boot caught her a glancing blow.

She stumbled and wrapped her arms around her head.

He landed on his left foot, curling and rolling to absorb the impact.

Amanda was moving before he had rolled to his feet. She swung a dining room chair around and launched it at him. He rotated, letting it hit him on the back, then he picked it up and hurled it back at the front door.

She diverted around the table, pulling the chairs out as she ran.

He took the opposite direction around the table. She ran for the kitchen.

He threw the chairs out of his way as he gave chase.

She was working her way around a breakfast counter. He grabbed a red coffee maker, yanking the plug from the wall, and threw it across the room. It hit the woman in the middle of her back, just below her neck. She stumbled as she twisted to relieve the pain.

He grabbed an ornate teapot as he ran, and hurled it at her.

She grabbed the back door handle. The teapot hit the wall above her head. She closed her eyes and wrapped an arm over her head to protect her eyes from the shattered pottery.

He reached her quickly. He curled his fingers, and slammed his fist into the side of her head.

She fell against the wall.

He punched her in the ribs. She collapsed to her knees, gasping. He waited for her to turn to look at him. Her eyes were wide, and her mouth was open. Her cheeks were flushed from her exertion. She was beautiful, even in her pain.

He delivered a single punch to her temple. Not fast, but solid. Measured. Plenty of follow through. Not enough force to kill her. He hoped.

She rolled forward, and slumped, face down on the kitchen floor.

Shorty descended the stairs. "We're going to have to take them both." He took out a box knife and pushed out the gleaming blade. It was new. As sharp as they get. Ideal for what he had in mind.

Hades nodded as he duct-taped the woman's arms and legs together. He taped across her mouth. Her broken nose required him to leave a small hole for her to breathe. He didn't want her to suffocate just yet.

Shorty knelt in the middle of the living room. The knife was unstoppable. The mixture of natural and man-made fibers was no match for its cutting edge. In a couple of minutes, he had two eight-foot-wide swaths of carpet.

The woman was regaining consciousness. They wrapped her first. Rolling her inside the heavy carpet from the neck down. They carried her out to the van.

The man was heavier, but easier to carry. He was long past the point where he could object to his treatment.

Ever.

CHAPTER THIRTY-ONE

Tuesday, May 23
Santa Irene, Arizona

JESS DROVE TO SANTA Irene. Traffic was light. The Mustang ate up the miles with its powerful engine barely breaking a sweat.

Her phone provided directions to Melissa Green's prior address. She left the freeway and followed a long string of left and right commands.

The houses on the north side had paintwork that complemented their mid-century look. Window frames and wooden beams were picked out in striking, but not garish, colors. Picket fences lined the gardens and cars were parked in long driveways, leaving the roads free.

Melissa Green's old home was one-half of a tiny single-story duplex. The facade was not quite white. Blue drapes adorned the windows which, along with the doors, were accented in a rich tan. The house was small but very charming.

Jess parked on the side of the road. She took her notepad and recorder. Melissa's house and the houses on either side were empty. She crossed the street. The curtains twitched in the residence directly opposite.

She took the pathway to the house and rang the doorbell. Someone reached the door and peered through a spy hole. "I'm not buying anything," a man's voice said.

"I'm not selling anything. I'm looking for Melissa Green."

"You press?"

"I'm Jessica Kimball with *Taboo Magazine*."

"I'm not interested."

She heard the sound of metal scraping. Jess guessed the man had closed a shutter behind the spy hole. She heard footsteps receding.

She went back to her car. According to Carter's notes, Melissa Green had made a living selling arts and crafts. Jess skimmed a map of the area.

There were numerous shops that sold art of various types, but the one that interested her the most was a building called The Art Market. According to its website, artists could rent space on a daily, weekly, or monthly basis. Given the size of Melissa Green's home, Jess guessed this was a more likely outlet for her work than the big-name art shops.

She found the building easily. It's square and boxy shape had been partly masked behind murals on the walls. The parking lot was optimistically large. There were only three cars in the lot.

Jess parked by the front door. Inside, the building was one continuous open space. The rented spaces were twelve-foot squares arranged in rows. Most had covers drawn down over their fronts.

A man approached her. "Help yer, love?"

"I'm looking for Melissa Green. Does she have a space here?"

The man frowned. "I…er…that doesn't sound familiar."

"She was here a couple of years ago." Jess smiled. "Do you know where she sells her work now?"

"Right. Well," He pointed down the row. "I have an office. Might have some details."

He walked off without waiting for an answer. Jess followed. A handful of the booths were occupied. People looked out, smiling as she passed.

They reached the man's office. He sat at a dust-covered computer. After a few moments, he looked up. "Green, you say?"

"Melissa."

He pointed to the screen. "Yeah. She had a booth here. Looks like she moved out a couple of years ago." He scanned a column of numbers. "Always paid on time, which is good. You know, for artists."

"Can you tell me anything about her?"

He looked at his screen. "Looks like she kept in touch for a few weeks after she left here. Mostly to say she was still interested, but couldn't return to The Art Market anytime soon."

He shrugged. "We like to keep up with our clients. There's always the chance they'll come back."

"But she didn't?"

He shook his head. "She stopped responding to our emails about two months after she moved out." He scrolled up and down a list on his screen. "Looks like we never heard from her again."

"Thanks for your help." She returned to the parking lot and started the Mustang. With the air conditioning running, she looked through the calls on her phone and found Mercer's number.

"Mercer here."

"It's Jess. Are you off the case?"

"I'm assisting. Not that it means much. But they have been drip feeding me some information."

"Like what?"

He hummed. "What have you been doing?"

"Looking into Melissa Green's life before she moved to Bear Hill. She was an artist."

"I heard that said."

"Did you ever see any of her art?"

"No, but the closest I get to art is painting the house."

Jess grinned. She told him what she'd learned from her morning of poking into Melissa's life, which was not much. "That's all of my news. What have you been *drip fed*?"

"Nothing really new that we didn't know already. We knew she had no landline telephone. If she had a cell phone, we can't find a record of it. Before she moved, she announced on social media that she was taking a break. Then nothing after."

Jess coughed. "Ties up with what I've heard, but it's kind of unusual for someone who was making a living."

"Yeah," Mercer said. "And I don't know what she did for work once she moved out here, but she paid her bills on time. Gas, electric, and water."

"What about credit cards?" Jess hadn't found any credit card history for Melissa Green, but Mandy was still checking.

"One. Used sparingly. Last time was about a month ago." Mercer paused. "The curious thing is, she used it to buy gas at the station here in Bear Hill."

Jess frowned. "Why is that significant?"

"Did you look in her garage?"

Jess remembered the separate structure which hadn't burned down. "No."

"She had no car. At least not on the property, and nothing registered in her name has turned up, so far."

"Maybe buying gas for a friend? Someone giving her a lift. Like maybe her plumbing friend?"

"I know old man Bartlett over at the DIY store. I'll see what I can get out of him about the mysterious plumber's helper. But even if I find out, it doesn't explain why she'd booby trap her house like that. What was she trying to hide?"

Good question. Jess pulled the Mustang onto the main road and headed back to Bear Hill, not much wiser about Melissa Green than she had been yesterday.

CHAPTER THIRTY-TWO

Tuesday, May 23
Santa Irene, Arizona

HADES TOOK THE STEPS into the basement rapidly and switched on the fluorescent lights at the bottom of the narrow stairs. Pony followed behind. Hades leaned down and pulled the felt blindfold from Simon Lawson's eyes.

Simon blinked, attempting to clear the spotlights from his night vision.

Hades touched his face. "I still have my mask on. You will survive. You understand, yes?"

Lawson gave a single nod.

Hades smiled. "Good. You have to do something for us."

"What?" Lawson said through the tape across his mouth.

Hades reached down and ripped off the tape. "Your international broker is insisting on a signature."

Lawson groaned. "You're never going to let us live."

Hades grunted. "This mask is itchy and unpleasant. It's hot. I could happily take it off, but I haven't."

Lawson looked away.

Hades nudged Lawson with his boot. "I have no desire to kill either of you. You are going to survive."

Lawson breathed hard. It was a good thirty seconds before he spoke. "All right. Get me a pen."

"Good." Hades pursed his lips and nodded. "We have to sign the document in Tucson."

Lawson looked up at Hades. He struggled to keep his facial muscles in check. His lips still curled down at the ends, but his eyes had widened a fraction. Not much. But enough to betray a change in his internal state. Not fully formed hope yet, Hades was sure. Not yet.

"You will need to shave and dress," Hades said.

Lawson gave the barest of nods. "I understand."

Natalie's eyes were flicking between Hades and her husband behind the blindfold. Lines wrinkled her forehead. She was almost hyperventilating.

Hades smiled to himself. She knew her husband well. She should. They had been married for years. But over the past few hours, she had realized, finally, something she hadn't admitted before.

He put himself first. No doubt. No hesitation. The flicker of hope that he had accepted was no opportunity for her. It was a death warrant. Even if her husband tried and failed to escape, she would be the hostage. She would be the one sealed in their basement. The money was all in her husband's name. There would be no reason to keep her alive.

They would dispose of her quickly. No doubt or hesitation about that, either.

Hades smiled again. He'd wondered how long she would remain willfully ignorant of these facts. Longer than he'd expected.

Pony cut Lawson free from the tie-downs. Simon groaned as he rolled over into a fetal position.

Hades waited.

Lawson flexed his limbs, restoring the blood flow and reviving his muscles. After a while, he rolled into a sitting position.

Pony cut the tape around his wrists and ankles.

"You're going to Tucson to sign and transfer the money this afternoon. I will be with you. We will have a guard outside the building."

Lawson nodded.

"You try anything, and you'll be shot. And the news will come back here."

Natalie swallowed.

Lawson took a deep breath and nodded again.

"Do this right, and we will be gone tomorrow. Do it wrong, and there will be no mercy."

"Simon," Natalie murmured behind the duct tape.

He didn't look at her. "It'll be okay."

"Just…"

He shook his head. "We'll just do exactly as they say." He stood up. "We will be okay."

Hades smiled. "That's the idea."

Lawson looked at his clothes. "I need to clean up."

"In a moment." He reached down and removed Natalie's blindfold and waited for her eyes to adjust.

The door bumped open. Shorty slid a roll of carpet down the stairs. A loud grunt was forced out when it came to a thudding halt on the concrete floor.

Shorty cut the tape holding the carpet roll in shape.

Simon frowned.

From her place on the floor, Natalie strained to see.

Shorty unrolled the carpet with his boot. The last of the bundle's spirals flipped over with a jaunty kick, leaving Amanda lying face up.

Her hair was matted around her face, and her eyes were crunched up, shielding her from the light. Her arms were taped to her sides, and her feet were bound at the ankles.

Natalie burst into tears.

Lawson swallowed. His lower lip trembled. "No."

"You bastards," Natalie sobbed, behind the duct tape that covered her mouth.

Amanda's eyes widened, adjusting to the fluorescent lights. She forced herself up to a seated position.

Pony dragged her to the tie-downs.

Shorty took Lawson by the arm and pushed him toward the stairs. He stumbled, his bare feet dragging on the concrete.

Hades pointed upstairs. "You can get cleaned up. Wear a suit."

Shorty shoved Lawson. He didn't lift his feet, and he fell onto the stairs. Shorty kicked him.

Lawson's head hung down. He barely looked able to support his own weight. He climbed the steps on his hands and knees.

Hades waited until he was halfway up. "You're a strange one, Lawson. We go to all this trouble, and you don't even say hello to your daughter."

A strangled noise escaped from Lawson's throat.

"Don't worry. She'll be here when you get back," Hades said. "Assuming you do a good job."

CHAPTER THIRTY-THREE

Tuesday, May 23
Santa Irene, Arizona

JESS FOUND A DINER. She ordered coffee and a cranberry bagel. The waiter returned with her order a moment later.

She pulled out Carter's notes and reread everything. Nothing significant jumped out, and there was nothing she'd missed when she'd read the file earlier.

She ran back through the pages again until she found the statement she wanted. Dr. Warner had worked at Santa Irene General Hospital. He had a medical staff and assistants working for him.

Several of his colleagues had testified at his trial. They'd all been supportive, of course. Otherwise, they wouldn't have been called to testify in his defense. One of his assistants on the stand had worked for him for a number of years. Her testimony was overwhelmingly positive.

It was often assumed that the people at the top knew what was happening in a hospital, but in Jess's experience, those at the opposite end of the power spectrum were the ones who really knew what was going on.

Jess finished her food, paid her bill, and left the diner. She drove through downtown Santa Irene to the medical district and parked in a multi-story garage outside Santa Irene General.

The hospital was a modern five-story building with mirrored windows. The wide entrance deposited visitors inside where colored lines on the floor led to different departments.

Jess took a business card from her bag and approached the front desk. A large man sat behind the counter. He examined her through thick eyeglasses.

She held out her card. "I wonder if I might talk to Melanie Franklin?"

The receptionist's gaze flitted over the card, and back to Jess. "Appointment?"

Jess shook her head.

The man huffed and turned his back on Jess.

He dialed a number. "Franklin?" he said.

Jess couldn't hear the reply.

The man uh-huh'd. "Got another one for you."

Another uh-huh. "Not local. Magazine."

He was quiet a few beats.

"Uh-huh. Okay, I'll tell them."

Jess leaned over the counter and whispered. "Tell her the police might have found Karen."

He rotated his head to look at Jess from the corner of his eye and raised his eyebrows. "Karen who?"

"She'll know," Jess said.

He grunted and turned back to the phone. "Woman says the police might have found Karen. Says you'll know who she means."

He hung up a moment later. He pointed to a group of worn beige armchairs in one corner of the lobby. "She'll be out soon."

Jess took a seat. Five minutes later, a woman arrived dressed in the kind of impeccable, classic nurse's uniform, complete with white shoes and stockings, that Jess hadn't seen in a couple of decades. She held out her hand. "Nurse Melanie Franklin."

Jess gestured to the chair beside her. Nurse Franklin sat, her back straight, and smoothed out her uniform. "You asked to speak to me."

"You worked for Dr. Warner until he was arrested?"

She nodded. "Five years, but I've been with Irene General for twenty."

"That's a long time to work as a nurse."

"Started as a secretary. But I liked to help. I wanted to do more than just take names and such." She cleared her throat. "It was Dr. Warner who encouraged me to take night school classes, and, well…"

"Was that when you worked for him?"

"I only started working for him after I qualified." She rubbed her hands together. "I wasn't the quickest at school. Took a while, but," she shrugged, "it worked out in the end."

Nurse Franklin checked her watch. "I've only got five minutes."

"Were you surprised by his arrest?"

"Completely shocked. We all were. First he, and we were trying to come to terms with what had happened to Karen, and then he's arrested."

"At his trial, you testified in his defense."

Nurse Franklin nodded and swallowed. "You said…the police have found Karen."

"Might have."

Nurse Franklin frowned. Slowly, she closed her eyes. "She's dead, isn't she?"

"Nothing is definite yet."

Her eyes snapped open. "But you thought you'd come here and try and get some headline—"

"Did you hear that Karen Warner's sister is missing?" Jess said.

Nurse Franklin's glower softened a fraction.

"It's a big coincidence that two sisters should vanish two years apart. The two situations may be connected, and in the second case, Dr. Warner was in jail. So…"

Nurse Franklin took a deep breath. "You think he's innocent?"

Jess shook her head. "I don't know. I keep an open mind. Which is why I'm here."

Nurse Franklin curled up one side of her lips, but it wasn't quite a smile.

"I'm wondering whether you felt something wasn't right between him and his wife?" Jess said.

"Absolutely not." Franklin scowled. "He was an attentive husband. They talked a couple of times every day." She mimicked typing on a phone. "And text messages. He took good care of her. Looked after her. He'd buy her presents. We all knew because he'd come back from lunch with a bag, or smelling of some perfume. You don't do that if you're not…well, he was a good husband. I'm certain."

"You sure he wasn't trying to cover something up?"

"Like what?"

"An affair?"

Franklin scoffed. "He wasn't like that."

"He might have been trying to apologize. Or to distract her from what was really going on."

Nurse Franklin shook her head. "Definitely not. He wasn't into all that stuff. He didn't mess around with the secretaries or join gambling rings or…anything."

"Is there a lot of gambling here?"

"It happens, but it's a hospital. Lots of things happen."

"Like what?"

"Everything. The place is full of doctors. They have God complexes, or get-rich-quick schemes, or any number of things. But he wasn't that sort. He had his head on straight."

"Who was he most friendly with in the hospital?"

Nurse Franklin shrugged. "He was a hard worker. Didn't socialize much. Dr. Palmer and Dr. Lawson some. They would go out to eat fairly regularly. But that fell apart. The pressure of work, I guess."

"Dr. Palmer testified for his defense."

"I should think so. Dr. Warner had an excellent reputation. Dr. Palmer definitely knew all about his work."

"So, they were still friends?"

"I guess. They weren't close or anything. I always thought their relationship was mostly professional respect."

"You make him out to be something of a loner."

"Not really. Just very intense. Dedicated to his patients. The staff had to arrive at work ready to go. No drinking coffee to wake up. He worked one hundred percent from the moment he walked in through those doors to the moment he left in the evening. He expected all of us to do the same."

"Long hours?"

"Always. Seven-till-seven. He'd leave here dead on his feet and come back the next day to do it all again. The poor man must have passed out the minute he made it home and slept like the dead."

"You're thinking about the late-night phone calls to The Devil Kings?"

She shrugged. "That never made sense to me. Really, if a doctor wants to get rid of someone," she held her hands out to gesture to the whole hospital, "the place is full of ways."

Jess nodded. "Did he work weekends?"

"Not usually. Except for emergency surgeries. And he was on call once a month."

"An all-round dedicated guy, then?" Jess lifted her voice at the end of the sentence, giving Nurse Franklin another chance to open up if she was so inclined.

Nurse Franklin nodded. "Certainly seemed so to me. It's what I've always said. I can't explain what happened, but the prosecution's theory didn't line up with the Dr. Warner I knew."

CHAPTER THIRTY-FOUR

Tuesday, May 23
Santa Irene, Arizona

THE MUSTANG'S ENGINE RUMBLED impatiently while Jess waited in line to exit the hospital's parking garage. She dialed her assistant.

Mandy answered on the second ring. "What's up?"

Men thought Mandy's greatest attribute was her runway model looks, but really it was her straightforward demeanor that made her everyone's friend. She and Jess had formed a bond that allowed them to go months without direct contact, and instantly pick up where they'd left off.

"I need everything we have on an Arizona gang called The Devil Kings. And their leader, a guy who calls himself Hades, but his real name is Norman Kemp. I'm looking for gossip. Stuff we have that the cops don't. And I'm also interested in places he's lived, prisons he's been in, and every crime he's committed."

"Sure. Won't take long."

Taboo's archives were legendary. If Hades or The Devil Kings had ever been noticed, even once, *Taboo* would have access to the information. Mandy was a genius at searching and sorting.

"That it?" She said.

Jess rolled forward in the exit line. "I also want to know where Mrs. Karen Warner spent her spare time. She didn't work, and her husband was a workaholic. So what did she do with herself all day every day?"

Mandy released a strangled groan.

"What?" Jess rolled up to the barrier and rummaged in her bag for singles.

"She could have done anything, gone anywhere. Where do I start?"

Jess slipped bills into a slot in the parking machine. "I don't know. She was financially well off. She must have done something besides read trashy magazines and eat bonbons."

The barrier rose, and she drove out, easing the Mustang onto the side of the road out of the flow of traffic. "Did she go anywhere unusual? Any changes in her routines?"

"What do you expect to find that the cops didn't?" Mandy was already clicking away at the computer keys.

"I wish I knew." Jess ran her hands through her hair. "Her husband's life was scrutinized down to his underwear preferences. Hers, not so much."

"Why not try her neighbors? Or her friends?"

"I need all the help I can get. Try a few high-end restaurants. Or bars, manicure places, fashion boutiques, or—"

"Santa Irene has three-quarters of a million people, but I'll do what I can."

"Thanks, Mandy. This situation just doesn't make sense, and

I'm getting nowhere. I need a fresh approach." Jess pulled out into traffic. "I owe you."

Mandy laughed. "You know how I love a challenge."

Jess fed Dr. Warner's home address into the Mustang's navigation system and set off toward the outskirts of the city.

The area was filled with million dollar homes inside the city. Trees lined the streets, giving shelter to the sidewalks from the blazing Arizona sun.

His was a modern property on the side of a hill, toward the top of a long gradual slope. A wide single-story building set well back from the road. Large windows dominated the front, presumably to take advantage of the view, which Jess had to admit was pretty good. A long rolling swath of well-watered green lawn separated the estate from the concrete jungle.

The skyline rose as the buildings marched toward the center of the city. She guessed she could see more than half the population from the front of Warner's house.

Not that it was his house anymore. He no longer owned the property, having sold it before he went to trial to pay for his legal representation. He had the best, and he paid for it. For all the good those pricey lawyers did for him.

Whoever had purchased Warner's house probably knew nothing of the habits of the previous owners, so she parked in front of Warner's neighbors.

She collected her bag and walked up a long pathway to the front entrance. The door looked as if it were made for a giant, maybe five feet taller than Jess. The door handle was equally large, but it was placed at a height normal human beings could reach.

She pushed the doorbell but heard no noise. Above the button was a dark glass circle. A camera. She smiled.

"Help you?" said a woman's voice from a speaker above her head.

She looked up. "I'm Jessica Kimball, *Taboo Magazine.* I'd like to talk with you for a few minutes."

"Could you look at the camera, and say that again?"

Jess had to force herself to look into the camera, and not turn toward the speaker. "I'm Jessica Kimball, *Taboo Magazine.* I'd like to talk to you about Karen Warner if you've got the time."

"Now I get it." The speaker clicked off.

She waited. People were busy. They couldn't drop everything when a stranger knocked on the door. Jess told herself the same thing every time she made a cold call. It was true, but also served to encourage patience.

The lock clicked, and the door swung open. A plump woman smiled at her. She was maybe mid-fifties with thick glasses. She wore a fashionable dress and flat shoes. She beamed as she held out her hand. "Charlotte Hapsburg."

Jess shook hands. "Jessica Kimball."

"You said you were interested in Karen?"

Jess smiled. Bingo. Someone on a first name basis with Karen Warner on the first try. "You knew her?"

Charlotte waved Jess into the house. "Come in, come in."

She walked into a large entrance hall. A staircase spiraled up one side. Jess's shoes clicked on a marble floor. "You have a beautiful home."

Charlotte closed the door and pointed through a wall of glass at the rear of the house. "I'm just having tea. Would you like some?"

"That would be nice."

Jess followed Charlotte to a massive wooden table and four

cushioned chairs on a large outside deck. A large striped awning sheltered the deck from the sun.

There were two pitchers of tea on the table and a single glass. Charlotte sat down in front of the glass. Jess took the seat beside her.

Charlotte pushed a button on a remote control, and a woman stepped outside. Charlotte made an elaborate hand gesture, and the woman disappeared. A moment later she returned with a glass and placed it in front of Jess.

Jess smiled. "Thanks."

The woman smiled, nodded, and returned to the house.

"Rachel is deaf," Charlotte said.

"You're fluent in sign language?"

Charlotte tapped her own ear. "I'm almost deaf, too. So we get along well."

"Is that why you asked me to look at the camera when I rang the bell?"

Charlotte nodded. "I can hear some, but mainly I lip read."

She tapped the tea pitchers. "One is jasmine, the other ginger-mint. Though…" she rubbed her forehead. "I don't remember which is which."

"No problem." Jess didn't expect to enjoy either, so she poured a half-glass from the pitcher closer to her, and lifted it with a smile. "Thanks."

"You're interested in Karen," Charlotte said.

The tea tasted terrible. "You knew her?"

"Oh yes. She would visit sometimes. We would have a laugh." She nodded to her garden. "We'd sit out here when it wasn't too hot."

Jess lifted her glass. "And drink tea?"

Charlotte laughed. "Sometimes she'd go for drinks with a

little more kick. Her thing was red wine. She would bring a bottle of something she liked. She wasn't a drunk or anything. Nothing like that. Don't get that impression."

Jess nodded and smiled to encourage her. "Did you testify at the trial?"

"No, dear. The police took a statement, and lawyers for both sides talked to me. Here," she waved an open palm around the deck, "but they didn't ask me to testify." Charlotte looked at her garden.

Jess sat up in her chair. "Did you—"

"She was a nice girl. Always well dressed. Dr. Warner saw to that. He was always buying her things. He was a heart surgeon. I guess they're pretty well paid."

She looked at Jess. "And they had a driver. Poor man. He was very nice. Helped me in with my luggage one time. When I returned from Europe."

"I was—"

"She could drive, of course." Charlotte leaned close to Jess. "She told me once that she used to go to the race track. Drive cars like that one you've got."

"Really?"

Charlotte stared Jess in the eye. "Apparently, you can hire cars to drive around on some tracks."

"But she didn't drive at home?"

Charlotte shook her head. "That's why they had the driver."

"Did she have a driver's license?"

"I'm not sure." Charlotte shrugged. "That's not the sort of question you ask, but I guess I got the impression she didn't have a license."

"Did you think that was strange?"

"Not really. Like I said, they had a driver. And I don't think Dr. Warner liked her to go out on her own."

"Were they having problems in their marriage?"

Charlotte shook her head. "Not that she ever told me. And he was always buying her…oh."

Jess remained silent.

Charlotte leaned forward. "You don't think he was having an affair, do you? I don't want to spread rumors, but that is the sort of thing men do, isn't it?"

"It's not out of the question. Did she wear a lot of makeup?"

"Nothing excessive. Why?"

"It covers up bruises."

Charlotte shook her head. "She wasn't trying to cover up anything like that. We talked about a lot of things. I would have known."

"Abuse is not always—"

"In fact, she was always well turned out. Her hair, nails, clothes. She was naturally very attractive. She didn't have to cover herself in makeup. Sometimes she would wear jeans and a T-shirt and still look like a million dollars."

"I have an assistant like that."

"But she would never wear jeans while he was around."

"Dr. Warner?"

Charlotte nodded. "He was always, well, formal. Very rigid. Never seemed to know how to relax."

"Were you surprised when she was abducted?"

Charlotte's eyes widened. "Shocked. Absolutely. I mean…who wouldn't be? She was a fun girl. Maybe she was kind of in a straightjacket with Donald, but she knew how to laugh. She was outrageously funny when he wasn't around, but she seemed to settle down around him." She took a deep breath. "Perhaps that was a good thing, you know? She seemed like maybe she could be a wild child." She raised her eyebrows.

"Which I think she was in her early years. She gave that impression."

"Did she ever mention The Devil Kings? Or Hades?"

"Nothing like that. We would talk about all sorts of things, but never that. Most of the things we talked about was just fun stuff. What would you do with a million dollars, which movie star would you want to be marooned with, and so on."

"Did she ever mention other friends?"

"Most of their friends were his friends. Doctor friends. I don't think she had many girl friends."

"Did she have places she would go? Restaurants, bars?"

"He used to take her to Milo's once a month. Expensive place in the city. I think he liked to show her off. It's a nice place. You should try it. But she didn't go out on her own. Or perhaps I should say, she never went without him."

"She didn't go anywhere on her own?"

"Well…things like shopping and hairdressers."

"Where did she get her hair done?"

Charlotte screwed up one side of her face in concentration. She shook her head slowly. "I can't remember. She said once. I didn't pay attention. I think it was somewhere on the west side." She frowned. "I'm sorry."

"Did you notice any change in her behavior in the months before her disappearance?"

Charlotte shook her head. "Can't say I did."

"And what about Dr. Warner? Did he seem different at all?"

"I can't really say. I didn't see him much. Mostly just driving to and from work. It seemed like that was all he did. No golf or anything."

"Would you say they were suited for each other?"

"You mean, did they have a good marriage? I think so, but

it's hard to tell, isn't it? No matter how much you think you know someone, they can always surprise you. It's what makes life interesting."

"You can say that again." Jess smiled. "What about Karen's sister, Melissa? Did you know her, too?"

Charlotte shook her head. "Goodness no. Karen never mentioned a sister. Not even once."

CHAPTER THIRTY-FIVE

Tuesday, May 23
Santa Irene, Arizona

WHEN JESS LEFT CHARLOTTE'S house, she tried a few more neighbors but found no one home. Her phone rang as she drove out of the area. Jess pressed the button to answer the call. "Mandy. Got news?"

"Hades and The Devil Kings were easy. I have a ton of stuff, which I've just sent your way. Most of it is crime reports. Very few photographs. Norman Kemp has been in jail several times and did a stint in Arizona state prison, but I don't think the police even know the names of the other members of The Devil Kings."

"Okay, great. I'll look at it as soon as I can. Anything on Karen Warner?"

"A whopping great big whole lot more difficult, Jess. Santa Irene isn't Beverly Hills, but it's a fairly wealthy community. Which means there's a ton of places women like Karen Warner can spend money."

Mandy rarely objected to any request, no matter how

difficult it might seem to mere mortals. She must be hitting a brick wall on this one.

Jess thought about it and made a choice. "Let's focus on fashion boutiques. There are fewer of them, and they pay better attention to their high-end customers. She might have had a personal shopper. She was beautiful, and her neighbor said she was always well dressed."

Mandy sighed. "I can do that."

"And check the best hair stylists," Jess said. "Her hair looked amazing in every photo I saw. Her neighbor thought she went to a place on the west side of the city."

Mandy hummed. "Yeah, she was a looker for sure, and that sun-bleached look would have to be a once a month thing, at least."

"Which means she probably had a regular stylist. And stylists are part therapist, anyway. Like a bartender without the alcohol."

Mandy snorted. "You obviously haven't been to my place. Their red wine isn't a spectacular vintage, but it sure makes waiting more pleasant."

Jess grinned. "Throw *Taboo Magazine*'s name around. Salons love the chance for publicity. And let me know what you find ASAP."

"I'm on it."

Jess found a chain restaurant she knew would have Wi-Fi. There was no way she would be able to read the *ton of stuff* that Mandy had sent on her phone. She took her laptop with her and headed inside.

A boy who barely looked out of middle school showed Jess to a table. He was halfway through struggling to recite the specials when Jess put him out of his misery and ordered a burger.

The restaurant Wi-Fi was slow. Mandy's email consumed the waiting time for her food to download. She nudged her laptop to one side when the boy returned with her burger.

The fries were crunchy, and the burger had the fresh, tangy pickles she liked. She nudged the laptop and continued reading the email as she ate.

Hades had a short list of minor crimes on his rap sheet, but a far longer string of suspected crimes reported on the gossip sites that weren't as concerned with truth as sensation.

The Arizona and New Mexico police forces had been trying to pin crimes on Hades for the better part of ten years. The FBI had been in on the action more than once. He had been inside twice. The first time for a minor offense, and the second time, a three-year robbery sentence.

There was a two-year gap where his crimes, or at least crimes attributed to him, stopped without explanation.

The gap had ended with the Karen Warner kidnapping for ransom and the death of the Warners' driver during the commission of the felony. Police had traced Hades' mobile number to a burner phone. The phone went dark again after Karen Warner was taken.

Jess scrolled on through, scanning the email.

Hades and The Devil Kings were suspected of more serious crimes, involving kidnapping and home invasions, but those cases were never proved. Occasionally, he demanded a ransom, but most times, he emptied the victim's bank account through a string of purchases of easily disposable merchandise.

There were a couple of small, untraceable foreign transactions and speculation that he had a foreign connection. But the sums of money he took didn't seem to be large enough to attract an international crime ring.

The home invasions always ended the same way. The homeowners were killed, and their houses burned to the ground. Neither Hades nor The Devil Kings were prosecuted for murder. Lack of evidence.

The similarity to Melissa Green's situation was obvious.

Jess's laptop chimed. She had a new email from Mandy titled *KW salons*.

Mandy had included a map with several hair salons, and a place called The Crystal was ringed in red.

A note at the bottom of the page said Mrs. Warner had been a client, and her stylist, Luca, was working today. Mandy had included directions.

Jess put the address in her phone, left the waiter a good tip, and headed out to the Mustang.

CHAPTER THIRTY-SIX

Tuesday, May 23
Santa Irene, Arizona

TRAFFIC WAS HEAVY, BUT moving. Mandy's directions were perfect. Jess arrived at the salon without a single wrong turn.

The Crystal was a standalone structure built to serve wealthy clients. It practically oozed money. Everything about it was high-end, edgy. From the rustic stonework to the glass and stainless steel, nothing was ordinary.

Jess surveyed the pictures of models in the windows. Unlike the building, these women sported distinctly traditional hairstyles. Jess smiled. The Crystal's owners didn't expect their customers to be cutting the same edges as their architect.

The foyer resembled a large serpentine bend. A low counter arced around the curves. The floor was stained concrete in subdued but pleasing yellows and greens. Spotlights picked out locations along the counter, but there was no sign of anything as gauche as a cash register or even a computer.

A young woman who introduced herself as Ginger appeared magically behind the counter. Jess realized the curved wall hid the entrance to a considerably less stylish staff room.

"Welcome to The Crystal." Ginger smiled. "Do you have a reservation this morning?"

Jess shook her head. "I'd like to talk to Luca."

"For a consultation? That's always a good idea for a new stylist, isn't it?" Ginger glanced down the serpentine bend. "When would you like to come back? He won't be able to give you his full attention right now. I think he has a client arriving any moment."

Jess took out a card and handed it to the girl. "Jess Kimball. I'd like to talk to him about Karen Warner."

Ginger's gaze crossed the card twice as if she couldn't believe what she'd seen the first time. "*Taboo*?"

Jess nodded.

Ginger tossed her hair over one ear. "We get your magazine here. Several copies. Every month. Our clients read it cover to cover."

"Thank you. We're always happy to be in the best places," Jess said with a smile.

Ginger wriggled as if cold water had run down her back. "We try."

"So, could I have a word with Luca?"

"Of course, you can. Luca would be thrilled to talk to you, I'm sure." Ginger started down the serpentine bend, gesturing for Jess to follow.

The foyer curled around into a large room with pod-like booths inset like futuristic caverns. Steel and glass were everywhere. Mirrors surrounded the booths. Recessed spotlights glittered like jewels in the ceiling. Jess imagined a single three-hundred-and-sixty-degree turn would disorient her enough to make her fall over. At the rear of the room was a bar with an ornate espresso machine and several rows of bottles.

The booths were devoid of customers, but staff members were checking and cleaning and stocking. Ginger pointed to one of the largest booths and left.

A thin young man with olive skin, black slicked hair and huge brown eyes defined by long, black lashes sat in a molded chair. He stood as Jess entered the booth, and towered over her by a good six inches.

The salon's uniform left little doubt to his physique. In a word, Luca was cut as sharply as the decor demanded. He flashed a confident smile as he held out his hand.

"Luca." He bowed slightly in a way that could have seemed theatrical, but he somehow pulled it off.

Jess handed over another of her cards. Luca glanced at it and gestured toward the rear of the room. "We take your magazine."

"So Ginger said."

He pulled out two stools from under the counter. Jess sat on one, he sat opposite her, his back straight and eyes wide.

"You created Karen Warner's hairstyle."

He smiled. "I'm her stylist." He shrugged. "Well, I was." He held up crossed fingers. "Hopefully I will be again one day."

Jess saw the hope in his face. His subconscious hadn't accepted the jury's decision that Karen Warner was dead. He really wanted to believe she would be coming back. Hell, Jess wanted to believe that, too.

"How long have you been Karen's stylist?"

"Six years. Thereabouts." Luca rubbed his temple with two

fingers. "Trim every two weeks, highlights every four. Tuesdays at ten. Her husband scheduled and paid for a recurring appointment, whether she needed it or not."

"Meaning?"

He grinned. "Sometimes we'd just sit here and chat for an hour." He nodded toward the bar. "She liked a Mimosa or a Bloody Mary. Or two." His eyebrows bounced up. "Would you like…?"

Jess shook her head. "A little early for me."

Luca nodded, sagely.

"Did you notice any change in her routine in the last few months before she was kidnapped?"

Luca twitched his lips and shook his head.

"Did she pay with a different credit card? Was she worried about anything? Did she seem preoccupied?"

Luca shook his head again. "Do you think she had anything to worry about?"

"She was kidnapped. Maybe she knew she was in danger."

Luca scoffed. "She wasn't worried about that. She wasn't worried about much it seemed. She just liked to talk. Give her a drink, and she could really talk."

"Did she drink a lot?"

"She would have liked to, but she wouldn't have dared go home smelling of alcohol."

Jess frowned. "Dared?"

Luca shrugged. "Well, just saying. But she wouldn't have done it. Her husband wouldn't have approved. You only had to listen to her to know it took all her effort to keep him happy."

"You think she was worried about her marriage?"

"I didn't get that impression." Luca shook his head. "She

just had more life in her than him. But she once said that nothing would make Donald divorce her. I think she just acted like he was always there with her, even when he wasn't."

"Did he ever come here?"

"Not to my knowledge, but I don't do the bookings. Might want to check with the front desk. I can say for sure that I never met the guy."

"Did she have a phone?"

Luca nodded. "She had a ten-year-old thing. Big buttons. Black and white display. No touch screen. We used to laugh about it."

"Isn't that a bit odd?"

"She had it before they were married. She liked to keep it because it reminded her of her single life."

Jess frowned. "Was her single life very different?"

"She told me some stuff. Different things. She was young. No responsibilities." He smiled and winked. "We're all a little bit crazy when we're young."

"You're still young."

He grinned. "And still crazy."

"So, tell me. How crazy was she?"

He shook his head. "Stupid stuff. No big deal. She rode a motorcycle and things. Nothing."

Jess again remembered the *Dirt and Track* magazines she'd seen at Melissa Green's house. "Riding a motorcycle doesn't sound that crazy."

"Doesn't, does it?" Luca closed his mouth, pressing his lips together.

Jess smiled. "Tell me what crazy things she did before she was married. It might help me find her."

"No."

"What about her behavior? Was there any change before she disappeared?"

He shook his head.

"Please, Luca. I'm trying to find her."

He sighed. "She didn't change her behavior, her credit cards, her drinks, nothing. She was a friend. We shared an hour or two twice a month for years. I don't know what's happened to her, but what we shared won't be publicized by me just because she's not here."

"I'm not looking for a story, Luca. I'm looking for Karen. Anything at all could be helpful."

Luca pursed his lips. He took a deep breath.

"Please, Luca."

He sighed. "I *think* she might have been seeing someone."

Jess leaned forward. "Who?"

Luca shrugged. "She never said anything. It was just a feeling. She was… I don't…happy."

"She wasn't happy before?"

"It was just…she was just a little different. But she wasn't worried. Definitely."

"Did you tell anyone?"

"You mean the cops? I talked to them. But…like…it was just a feeling. It was probably nothing."

Jess sighed. "If I find something that might be related to her background, can I ask you about it?"

"You mean like to confirm something? Course. If it helps find her. I'd do anything to bring Karen back. Or anybody else who'd gone missing like that. Course, course."

Jess rose. Her phone buzzed in her pocket. She pulled it out. The buzzing stopped. A moment later the display showed *Dropped Call.*

Luca shook his head. "Bad reception in here." He pointed to the walls. "Too much metal and stuff."

Jess pushed her phone back in her pocket. "Did Karen's phone work in here?"

"Are you kidding? Her phone was so old it barely worked when she stood under a cell tower. When she wanted to call someone, she'd use the one in the staff room."

"Really?" Her skin tingled. "Can I see it? The phone in the staff room?"

"Believe me, it's not that exciting."

"I'd still like to see it.

"It's just a phone…but okay."

Luca led her through the serpentine bends to the foyer, and through the gap Ginger had slipped through earlier. A few people were lounging on chairs playing cards. They sat up nervously when Jess entered.

"Chill," Luca said to the gamblers.

He pointed to an ordinary wired landline phone. "Nothing special. Can't dial international, but US is okay."

Jess looked at the card players. "Were people in here when she made a call?"

Luca shook his head. "When clients use the phone, we leave the room."

Jess looked at the card players. "Did anyone ever hear Karen Warner talking on the phone?"

The crowd gave her glum looks.

"Raised voices? Anything?" Jess said.

The crowd shook their heads as one.

Jess picked up the receiver and dialed her own phone. It rang and a number appeared in the display before the call was dropped.

Luca shrugged. "Told you. Bad reception."

"But she used this phone?"

He nodded. "Most times. Just a few minutes. Usually at the end of her session. No big deal."

"And no change in the pattern before she disappeared?"

He took several breaths, concentrating before replying. "No. No change."

Jess thanked Luca, left The Crystal, and sat in her car with the air-conditioning running. She forwarded the staff room phone number to Mandy with a request to trace calls for the past three years, which would cover the period before Karen Warner was kidnapped. Mandy's reply was typically flip, but she'd do the work. She always did.

CHAPTER THIRTY-SEVEN

Tuesday, May 23
Santa Irene, Arizona

MANDY FORWARDED THE PHONE log from the service the magazine used for such work. It spanned three years and almost ten thousand entries. Each call was listed with the number dialed, time and date, and duration of the call.

Jess downloaded the list to her laptop's spreadsheet program. She filtered out incoming calls and narrowed her search to calls on Tuesdays from ten in the morning until noon. There were eleven outgoing numbers. A couple of local numbers appeared frequently. When she checked online, she found they were pizza places.

She used a spreadsheet to generate a table of the most frequently called numbers. After the pizza places, nothing stood out. She pulled out her notebook and found the number Dr. Warner had dialed from his phone, the number for the burner cell phone that had once been used by Hades. The number wasn't on the list. Jess leaned back in her seat. When she exhaled, she realized she'd been holding her breath.

She manipulated the spreadsheet data again. She looked for regular incoming calls, the same number every time Karen visited the salon, but there was no match.

She hovered her finger over the spreadsheet's exit button and stopped. There was one more possibility.

She opened up the original list of numbers and filtered on Tuesdays from ten to twelve, but this time she included incoming calls.

A grin stole across Jess's lips and vanished as quickly as it came. One phone number showed during Karen's appointment time. Ten-fifty a.m. Two minutes' duration. Jess scrolled down the list. There was no other occurrence of the number on any other day. The calls came in consistently every two weeks for several months and then stopped.

Jess shivered. The calls had stopped the day before Karen Warner was kidnapped. She scrolled up and down the list, eyeballing the dates and times and numbers. She ran her search again, to be sure, but there was no doubt. Someone had called the salon for two minutes every Tuesday when Karen Warner was there. Once Karen had been kidnapped, the calls stopped.

Jess sent the number to Mandy with a request to locate the number. A few minutes later the details came back. It was a landline. A fixed location. The number had an address, and an owner: Fred Wilson.

Should she call the police? Santa Irene PD had closed the Warner case. They were hardly likely to rush to open it up again.

Mercer seemed like he would jump at any information, but what did she have, exactly? A phone number with a physical address that might or might not belong to someone who called Karen Warner at the hair salon?

She could be wasting his time. Worse, he was strung out

enough already. If it turned out to be a school friend or an old roommate, he would be crushed.

She needed more information, and there was only one way to get it. She punched Fred Wilson's address into the Mustang's GPS and raced out of The Crystal's parking lot.

CHAPTER THIRTY-EIGHT

Tuesday, May 23
Santa Irene, Arizona

JESS FOLLOWED THE GPS'S instructions south, out of Santa Irene, toward the mountains.

The route showed a hundred and fifty miles to a town fancifully named Death and Taxes before it speared off into the Yuma National Forest. She settled into a fast cruise and reached the mountain road in less than two hours.

The Mustang's engine struggled to find the right combination of gear and revs as the slope climbed. She locked the transmission in manual.

The rock formations were spectacular. They were different than the mountains around her home in Colorado. These had a regularity that seemed unreal. As she gained altitude, she couldn't help but feel the arrangements had been carved by a giant.

The woods were thick in some places, thin in others. Occasionally, houses were visible between the firs and pines. The road narrowed.

Her cell signal was showing one flickering bar. She was unlikely to find reception as she traveled further into the mountains, so she pulled over, and checked the address on the map on her phone.

There was no developed land reflected on the street map, but the satellite view showed a log cabin in a clearing. The layout looked simple enough, but she snapped a quick screenshot and saved it to the phone before resuming her drive into the mountains.

The road twisted and turned, following the contours of the land and weaving around outcrops of rock. Pavement gave way to well-worn ruts in the hard-packed ground. She stopped a half mile short of the log cabin and stepped out of the rental.

The air was crisp. Chilling after the heat in Santa Irene. Jess pulled her jacket closer.

The silence was shocking. Her ears took a few moments to adjust from the city sounds they were accustomed to. It seemed that every single sound she heard was separated by long silences as if everything in the forest loathed to break the tranquility.

She collected her Glock from the trunk of her car and confirmed the magazine was full. She slipped a second clip into her pocket.

She only intended to recon the area. Get an impression of whether the landline and Fred Wilson might lead to more information about Karen Warner, or useless data that had deceived her instincts.

But nature could be more dangerous than any city street. Preparation had kept her alive more than once.

She walked along the road, looking to the right, for any sign of a driveway to the log cabin. She glimpsed a roof behind the trees.

She crouched down as she continued along the road. Nestled into a natural clearing was the cabin. A few feet closer and she saw it was constructed in two sections joined by a continuous roof, creating a covered breezeway between them.

In front of the clearing was a hitching post, but no horse. It looked straight out of an old western movie, lacking only John Wayne to make the wild west come alive.

The woods around the clearing were thick with undergrowth. A mixed blessing. Good cover, but daunting for progress. Why didn't she bring binoculars? She'd only be observing from afar. From what she now knew of Hades, she had no desire to get close enough for physical contact.

She knelt low by the trees around the cabin's driveway, drew her Glock, and waited. After a couple of minutes, she was satisfied that nothing was moving.

She tucked her jeans into her shoes. She really wasn't prepared for what she had in mind, but she wasn't going to turn around now.

An unmistakable metallic click sounded behind her.

A man spoke. His voice rough and slow. "Don't. Move." His enunciation made it clear it wasn't a suggestion.

Jess's heart thumped. Her skin tingled. She remained stationary, her hands on her Glock, but her Glock pointed forward.

"Nothing stupid," said the man. His voice was gravelly, rich with harmonics. He was old. His words were easy. Jess hoped whoever he was, he was as calm with his trigger finger.

He approached her, his steps making the barest crunch on the thick vegetation. "Put that gun on the ground," he said.

"Who are you?"

"We'll talk after you're disarmed, missy."

She took a deep breath and placed the Glock down in front of her.

"Now stand up, and turn around."

She did as she was told.

The man was tall and thin, maybe about sixty-five. He wore light green digital camo and sported a full beard. He was pointing a revolver at her. And not just any revolver. A Smith and Wesson Model 29. A long barrel .44 Magnum. Dirty Harry's weapon of choice.

Despite the threatening potential of the gun he wielded, there was one thing in his appearance that was cause for relief. He was way too old to be Hades.

"What you here for?"

Jess glanced left and right. The man was alone. She took a deep breath. "I'm lost."

He eyed her gun. "With a Glock? You're going to have to do better than that."

"I'm a lone female, wandering around the wild." She nodded at the man's revolver. "You never know who…or what you might meet."

He snorted a laugh. "Could say that. You from the city?"

Jess frowned.

"City council? Big government? Tax office? Any of that crap?"

Jess shook her head. "I'm a reporter. With a magazine."

"Don't suppose it's *Guns and Ammo*?" He grinned. Either he had surprisingly white teeth, or he wore dentures. Jess put money on the latter.

Jess gave a flat smile. "*Taboo*."

The man sneered. "Well. I don't need it. Can't remember the last time I wore a tuxedo and gambled in Monte Carlo."

Jess ignored the sarcasm. "Do you have a telephone?"

A smile grew wider across his face. "Just 'cause I live in the woods, doesn't mean I don't talk to folks from time to time."

Jess nodded toward the log cabin. "You live alone here?"

"Twenty years. Built it from nothing."

"Nice place." She looked at his gun. "Could you put that away?"

He lowered his Smith and Wesson a fraction.

She smiled.

He lowered the gun all the way. "Put your Glock in your bag."

She did as he instructed. He kept his small cannon in his hand.

"Dirty Harry's," she said.

He grinned again. "Yes and no. His had the full ten-inch barrel." He pointed the gun at the sky. "Eight inch is easier to handle in the woods." He nodded toward her bag. "Your Glock. That good?"

She smiled. "One of the best. Good control on the recoil. Helps with multiple shots."

He arched his eyebrows and widened his eyes. "Does a reporter need to fire multiple shots very often?"

"You'd be surprised."

He laughed. A hearty, genuine mirth. "Is it accurate?"

"Very. For a handgun, of course." She looked at the man, his beard, and the camos. "What's your name?"

"Wilson. Fred Wilson."

Jess smiled. He wasn't trying to hide anything. All she needed him to do was get talking, but she had the feeling he'd never done that in his life.

"I've never fired a twenty-nine," she lied.

He grinned. "Ditto with a Glock."

She looked around the clearing. "There somewhere here we could use to try these guns out?"

Wilson grinned. He walked past Jess and down the rough track leading to his cabin. She followed.

They rounded the cabin, and she almost laughed aloud. Behind the cabin was a shooting range. A boarded walkway ran from a deck to three trestle targets. Wilson disappeared into the cabin and returned with two large sheets of white butcher's paper. He handed one to her. They pinned them to the targets. He drew two bull's-eye rings on each target with a black marker, and they returned to the deck.

She took a deep breath and handed her Glock to Wilson. He studied the surface and tested the balance. "No safety. No problem. My safety is my finger and my head."

Jess smiled, she was starting to like the guy. "Old school."

"Like me." He grinned and waved the Glock. "Let's see how old school does with new school."

He took safety glasses and ear muffs from a box on the deck and handed a pair of each to Jess.

"Not completely old school, then," she said as she donned the glasses.

He shook his head. "No sense being blind and deaf to prove a point, is there?"

He lined up the Glock. A solid stance. His feet braced. His head angled forward. All his concentration on the rings he'd drawn.

The Glock sounded oddly quiet in the wide-open space. Not at all like the ranges she used. Wilson's first shot was high. He licked his lips, aimed, and fired again. His second shot was an inch high. His third hit the dead center of the bull's-eye. "Nice," he said.

"And a dozen rounds left to go," she said.

He fired three more shots. A close group. The paper flapped as all three bullets went through the same hole.

He lowered the Glock. "Very nice. Now let's see how new school handles old school."

Jess had fired a Model 29 before. Once. On a range. It had been the shorter-barreled one, too. She'd binge-watched Clint Eastwood movies over a holiday weekend and caught the bug to try his cannon.

The balance wasn't bad, but the kick was strong on the short barrel. The longer barrel would probably be worse, and the extra time spent in the barrel would deflect the bullet upward.

She lined up. Feet a natural distance apart. Leaning forward a fraction. Bracing for the recoil. She leveled the gun's sight a couple of inches below the target's center and squeezed the trigger.

The action was heavy. She felt the mechanical actions of the revolver. The firing pin, the barrel. But most of all she felt the bullet's kick. The magnum exploded from the chamber with the force of a mule.

The sound struck her like a physical blow. She kept her eyes on the target, kept her muscles taut, kept the barrel down.

The target whipped open. A tear in the middle snapped the paper to life. The two halves flapped in the breeze.

Wilson laughed and slapped Jess on the back. "That's old school for you."

Jess laughed, too. The man's simple pleasure and honesty were refreshing. She lowered the gun. No point in firing again. There was no paper left to shoot.

They swapped guns. Wilson put his down on a table on the deck. He took a deep breath. "So, break it to me. You're not trying to sell me a magazine subscription. Why did you really come here?"

The smile faded from Jess's face. She tightened her grip on her Glock. "Do you know a place called The Crystal?"

He shook his head. "Where is that?"

"Santa Irene."

He grunted. "Haven't been there in years."

"The Crystal is a salon."

He frowned like the word was foreign to him.

"Hair styles, facials, and such."

He laughed. "Do I look like the sort of person that goes to a," he waved his hands mockingly, "salon?"

"And yet calls were made from this property to a salon in Santa Irene."

"Not by me."

"I have records. There's no doubt."

He frowned. "Really. I would know if I'd called a hair salon."

"This was two years ago. Maybe more."

Wilson frowned. "Oh, that might be…" He looked at the woods behind his property.

Jess followed his gaze. "Be what?"

He nodded toward the woods. "A guy moved into Parker's old place a couple of years ago. Keeps to himself, mostly. I hear him and his friends, but I never see him go out."

Jess angled her head forward, encouraging him to continue.

"When he moved in, he had a lot of trouble with his electrics. The place was old. Needed lots of work."

"And your new neighbor used your phone?"

Wilson nodded. "He'd come by every couple of weeks."

"Tuesdays? Around eleven?"

He shrugged. "Can't say. One day is like another up here. But it was morning time."

"Has he stopped coming over to use the phone?"

Wilson nodded. "Got his electrics sorted out, I guess."

"Does he have any scars?"

Wilson's forehead wrinkled as he thought about the question. "No. Can't say he does."

"On his face? Several scars?" She pointed with her fingers to the locations.

Wilson shook his head. "Nope. When I saw him last, he was clean shaven. No scars."

Jess breathed out. She felt relieved. Sorry, too. And glad she hadn't tried to get law enforcement to come out here with her when she learned about the phone number. She'd have looked like a fool now.

Maybe he wasn't Hades. But he could still know something about Karen Warner. "He used your phone, every two weeks?"

He nodded. "Lives a couple of miles that way. Other side of the lake." He pointed to the rear of his property. "There's a trail through the woods."

CHAPTER THIRTY-NINE

Tuesday, May 23
Santa Irene, Arizona

JESS THANKED WILSON AND headed in the direction he'd pointed. As she approached the woods, the trail became visible. She tucked her jeans into her socks and headed into the darkness. Once she was inside the edge of the woods, the undergrowth thinned. She found it easier to walk along the trail and covered ground quickly.

After about two hundred yards, the trail turned left and worked its way along the banks of a mountain lake. The water was mirror smooth, and the blue sky was reflected in the deep blue water. She guessed the other side was maybe a mile away. Which meant the perimeter was more than three miles. A big lake.

At the edge of Wilson's property was a boat dock and a silver and black, fourteen-foot aluminum fishing boat with a huge outboard engine. A thick chain and padlock secured it to the dock.

Jess grinned again. It seemed like Wilson didn't trust anyone. Not an entirely bad policy when you lived in the middle of nowhere and had to look out for yourself.

The neighbor's house was on an upslope, maybe a quarter of the way around the lake. Jess wondered who owned the lake, but there were no signs of a fence, so she walked on, keeping to the inside edge of the trees, checking behind her. Wilson had sneaked up on her. She wasn't going to let that happen again.

She stopped a quarter of a mile from the house. It was rustic, rising four floors. A large balcony hung from the top floor, facing the lake. The other floors had picture windows with lake views, too.

Jess moved closer, working her way around to the side of the house. The windows facing away from the lake were smaller. The ground was steep. The structure was built into the slope. On the left side of the house, was a door on what was technically the second floor.

A driveway circled the house, dropping away fast from the road level at the front to the lake at the rear.

A garage structure was halfway down the drive. It had two double doors and looked long enough for several cars. There were windows on the second floor. She watched for a few minutes. Nothing moved. She surmised the garage was empty. At least, she hoped so.

She moved further around the building. A white panel van with a decorator's name on the side was parked in front of the house. Jess figured visitors arriving by road would only see the two stories when they entered the house.

Jess knelt beside a pine. The undergrowth had thickened and provided good cover to shield her from discovery. There was occasional movement at the windows inside the house. The daylight was bright, and inside the house was dark. With the backlighting, she could see little more than blurred shapes inside.

She'd come this far. She wanted to know who was inside that house. She wanted to know who had called Karen Warner every Tuesday for months before she disappeared.

She shuffled back to sit on a fallen log. Maybe she could wait until nighttime. The house lights would come on, and the outside would be dark. A much better situation for observing the occupants.

Or they might close the drapes, and she wouldn't see anything. Then she'd be stuck until morning. No way could she find her way back to her rental in the dark.

She heard two voices. Male. Swearing. Laughing. Doors slammed, and silence returned.

She waited a while. She was going to get no better view until the sun moved toward twilight, and then she'd be in danger of becoming lost. She'd have to give up for now. When she was back in cell phone coverage, she could research the house's owners, and come back again.

She moved back the way she had come. Back down the slope. Passing the door on the second floor, and coming within a hundred feet of the garage.

This time, the rear door to the garage was open. Inside, something glinted in the blackness. She inched forward until she saw the light reflected off a motorcycle. She moved closer still. It was a big motorcycle. Not a Harley. Something Japanese. Something fast.

She listened for a minute. She heard nothing inside. She stepped out of the trees and to one side of the open door. There was no sound and no movement inside. She took a deep breath and peered around the corner into the garage.

The first thing she noticed was a huge, cavernous space. Four motorbikes were lined up, side-by-side. All were big, powerful machines, glinting in the sunshine that found its way through the windows and the open door.

She saw no one inside, and the windows on the far side of the garage offered her a clear view of the house.

Jess crouched and worked her way across the garage floor to a window. Her proximity to the house was better, but the contrast of sunshine and the dark interior was still too strong. She could barely see inside.

One of the men appeared at the lake's edge. He was far away, and the glass distorted her view, but she saw he was bald.

He held a large black trash bag and started picking up debris around the rear of the house.

She pulled out her phone and took a few pictures. The man finished collecting litter and disappeared into the house.

She'd done all she could. She was probably outnumbered, and definitely out of her depth. She'd seen no one who looked like Hades and picking up litter didn't exactly fit the MO of a hardened criminal gang. These people might not even have lived in the house when the phone calls were made.

She checked her cell phone, but there was no signal. She pushed it into her pocket. She would have to return to Wilson's and take her car back to civilization.

She took one last look at the house.

The back of a man's head was framed by one of the small side windows. The floor above Jess. The window was open. The glass no longer obstructed her view. When he turned around, he had a clear view of her, too.

His face contorted into an expression between a frown and a scowl.

She was an intruder. Any homeowner would be vexed.

But this man wasn't just vexed.

A split second too late, she realized where she'd seen him before.

He was the man she had seen at Melissa Green's.

Jess gasped, and she slapped a palm over her mouth to silence the sound.

Too late again.

The man with the ponytail raised his right arm, holding a pistol.

And then he opened fire.

CHAPTER FORTY

Tuesday, May 23
Santa Irene, Arizona

THE FIRST BULLET DISINTEGRATED the windows in front
of Jess. Wood and glass splinters exploded around her. She
threw herself backward. Four more shots hammered into the
garage floor where she had been standing.

She ran sideways, away from the windows and the direct line
of fire.

The shooting was replaced by shouting.

Her heart pounded. She put her hand to the side of her head.
Her fingers came away dry. She hadn't been hit.

She raced through the garage, checking the motorcycles until
she found one with the keys in the ignition. The man with the
ponytail wasn't an ordinary householder looking to protect his
property with a warning shot. He meant to kill her.

She pushed the electric garage door opener, and as it began
to rise, punched the bike's starter button. The huge bike buzzed
into life like an entire hive of angry wasps.

The garage door was agonizingly slow to open.

The side door burst open. She fired two shots into the rafters over the top of the door.

She didn't look to see if she had hit him or anyone else. She leaned low, twisted the throttle, and raced under the half-open garage door.

Shots rang out.

Jess wrestled the big bike around the house. She glanced back. At any moment, they would reach the garage exit, and have a clear target. She needed another route.

The mountain road ran along the front of the house. It was too open, too exposed.

She turned another corner, around the far side of the house. There was no driveway or path, just a steep grass slope down the hill beside the house.

Two bike engines screamed to life.

She jerked her head in all directions, looking for another option. She needed cover and a fast route. She saw no viable alternatives. She had no choice but down.

She held her breath as she brought up the revs and eased in the clutch. The bike rolled over the edge of the hill, and her stomach lurched into her mouth.

CHAPTER FORTY-ONE

Tuesday, May 23
Santa Irene, Arizona

THE BIKE WANTED TO jackknife. It wanted to roll and tumble. It wanted to tip over and crush her into the slope.

She hunkered down, lying low on the gas tank, holding the back in check with ten percent rear brake and ninety percent force of will.

She hit the path that ringed the lake at an angle hard enough to snap her teeth together.

The big bike rocked. Its weight and momentum threatened to overwhelm her muscles. She put out one leg to stop the bike from falling and twisted the throttle.

The bike surged forward, blessedly taking the heavy weight off her leg and leveling out.

She heard roaring noises behind her.

She didn't look. She didn't need to. She knew everything she had to know about who was behind her.

She twisted the throttle as far as she dared.

The bike lunged forward. Bouncing and rocking over the hard-packed mud on the trail around the lake.

The ground undulated. Tire tracks lay ahead, but no graded path. The bike lurched wildly and threatened to throw her off.

She guessed the two chasing her rode the bikes around the lake regularly, and likely weren't slowed by the challenge.

She relaxed her muscles a fraction, and found the right rhythm, leaning forward and back as the bike rocked from one undulation to the next.

The suspension crashed, and the bike shook as she drove it faster and faster.

She heard gunfire, and a tree limb cracked and shook ahead of her. It angled down, and she lay low on the bike as she flew underneath it.

She needed more protection than the exposed lakeside path offered. There were openings between the trees, and she twisted her head to judge them as she passed, but each looked barely wide enough for the big bike.

A burst of gunfire rang out. Wood chips flew from the trees beside her.

Another gun boomed. Loud and heavy. A single shot.

She twitched her head right, looking in the direction of the sound.

Across the lake, she glimpsed black and silver. Wilson's boat. Racing in her direction.

Wilson stood in the middle, his Smith and Wesson pointed high in the air.

She heard a second booming shot.

Old school might be brave, but he was way too exposed.

An opening in the trees appeared. There was no way the big bike would fit through it. Her skin tingled. It was just what she needed.

She slammed on the brakes, and slew the bike sideways. The bike bounced and lurched. She threw herself off, and dove through the opening in the trees, pulling out her Glock.

She hit the ground with her gun trained on the space in front of her bike. Her pursuers had slowed. One of them loosed off shots across the lake.

Wilson's engine roared. He turned his boat away.

Jess lifted her head and fired. Her shots hit metal. The first bike. The sound was electric. Sharp and angry ricochets.

The man screamed. He fired wildly. Automatic fire.

The leaves over Jess's head shook.

The men shouted. She couldn't tell which one wore the ponytail from this distance.

The man in the rear swung his bike around and roared back along the path. The rider Jess had hit struggled with the weight of his bike.

Jess rose up, her gun out. "Freeze!"

He whipped his gun in her direction and fired.

Jess fired as she ducked. Her shots went high. She rolled right.

His bike engine screamed, and he roared off toward the house.

Jess ran to the path. He was beyond range, but she fired anyway.

Wilson brought his boat around in an arc, stopping close to the lake's edge. He emptied his gun after them, one pounding shot after another.

She watched the bikes disappear around the side of the house. The man she had shot struggled to turn up the slope.

She turned to Wilson. "I need a phone!"

He gave her a thumb's up and nudged the nose of the boat into the shore. "And I need more ammo. Let's go."

CHAPTER FORTY-TWO

Tuesday, May 23
Santa Irene, Arizona

JESS STOOD IN FRED Wilson's kitchen staring out at his private shooting range. His phone must have dated from the eighties. It was attached to the wall by an archway into the living room. A long spiral cord dangled to the floor. The numbers were arranged in a circle with a rotating finger plate.

She picked up the handset and twirled it to uncoil several knots from the length of cord.

Wilson stood in the living room. He gave a sheepish grin. "I don't use it much."

Jess dialed Mercer. The old phone made ticking sounds as she twirled the finger plate around to each number. It was oddly satisfying to let go of the dial and watch it spin back to zero.

She heard a slight buzz on the line, which Jess attributed to age and distance.

A click and Mercer answered. "Hello?"

"It's Jess."

"You sound like you're a long way away."

"Yuma National Forest."

"Not so far."

"Did you talk to the owner of the DIY store?"

"Bartlett. Yes. Not that he knew much. He remembered Melissa Green buying her place, but couldn't give a description of the man who bought plumbing supplies for her. Said he heard about it, but never saw him."

"Is he reliable?"

"Yeah. I've known him for years. He pulled a list of everything she bought. A lot of plumbing stuff, copper pipe and such. Electrical stuff, too. I expect it's all there in the remains of her house."

"You hear anything from the investigation at her house?"

"I'll give you two guesses."

"No."

"Nailed it in one. You found anything?"

"Every two weeks, Karen Warner had her hair done at a salon. The Crystal. On each visit, she used a phone while she was there."

"How'd you find that?"

"I have the best assistant."

"Seriously."

"Karen Warner was always well dressed. Her neighbor said she used a place on the west side of town, and my assistant called around."

Mercer made a clicking noise with his tongue. "There's no record of a salon in the Warner investigation."

"You have the records?"

"Just what's been entered into the databases, but yes, every pertinent fact. Certainly, everything used at trial."

"And there's no record of The Crystal?"

"None. But I think the fact she made a regular call from her salon is pretty significant."

"Yes. Except she didn't make a call, she received a call. In the employees' break room."

"What?"

"She had her hair done from ten to eleven a.m. But just before eleven she would go into the break room. The employees felt uncomfortable sitting around while a customer was there, so they left her on her own."

"And she received a call?"

"Apparently. Every two weeks."

"Damn. So she knew who she was communicating with."

"Right. And the calls stopped just before she was kidnapped."

"Give me the number. I'll get a trace."

"The calls came from a phone owned by a Fred Wilson. I've met him. I'm at his house now. He didn't know anything about the calls. But one of his neighbors used to come by. They were having trouble with their electrics, and borrowed his phone."

"Do the neighbors still have trouble with their phone?"

"No. They stopped coming after Karen was taken."

"Give me the address. I'll check on the homeowner. Get a name."

"I'll send you the details, but I checked on the home already. I met two men. They're the shoot first type."

"Meaning?"

"They shot at me and chased me on motorbikes. Fortunately, Mr. Wilson helped me fend them off."

"Where are they now?"

"Gone. They left in a hurry before we could give chase."

Mercer gave a sigh of relief. "Are you some kind of adrenaline junkie?"

"I didn't intend to be caught."

"No one ever intends to be caught."

"I hit one of them. He had a ponytail, and I'd swear he was the man at Melissa Green's house the other night."

"That's a pretty good link between the two."

"There's another link. I saw a lot of extra gasoline in the garage. I think they were planning to burn the place down."

Mercer whistled. "Gas?"

"The liquid sort in this case. But it was improvised. Not a planned affair like Melissa's."

"Send me what you have. Addresses, phone numbers, anything. Use this email address."

Jess scribbled down his email address as he spelled it out, letter by letter.

She frowned. "You use a free email service?"

Mercer gave a great sigh. "My daughter is making plans for her husband's funeral and my wife is trying to comfort our granddaughter." He was silent a beat. "I understand Santa Irene PD wanting to take over, but there is no way I'm going to sit back. I took a leave of absence."

"You're freelancing?"

He took a deep breath. "You mean, am I on a vendetta? Hell yes. But I took an oath to hold myself and others accountable for their actions. I didn't do that lightly."

"Believe me, I understand. But—"

"Two people were murdered at Melissa Green's house. There was a body buried in the backyard. We don't know much, but we're not dealing with a single crime here. And you know what that means."

Jess took a deep breath. She'd seen the evidence herself. Firsthand.

She looked in the direction of the neighbors' house and nodded. "They're going to kill again."

CHAPTER FORTY-THREE

Tuesday, May 23
Tucson, Arizona

CORA DROVE THE LAWSON'S Nissan. She stayed in the slow lane, keeping a safe distance between her and the car in front.

Hades sat in the passenger seat. Lawson was cuffed in the rear of the car. Hades had found a way to wrap the handcuffs around the seat belt, securing Lawson to the rear seat back.

Hades had called ahead to the brokers in Tucson to make sure they were available before they left the house.

He had his misgivings. While he and Cora were traveling to Tucson, Pony and Shorty were clearing out their second safe house. There wasn't much to do, but it had to be done. Lawson's hidden account had given them an opportunity, and he wasn't going to waste it.

It meant that Natalie Lawson and her daughter had been left in their house alone. They were bound to the tie-downs in the basement, but he wasn't going to trust that alone.

He had repositioned one of the security cameras in the basement. Its unblinking lens was pointed directly at the two women. Beside it, he had placed a box.

The box was filled with flour and sugar. It was heavy. It had thumped when he dropped it on the ground. He arranged two wires from the box to the camera.

The women had watched his every move. The looks on their faces were split among hatred, disgust, and fear. It was the latter that he hoped to use.

When his arrangement with the wires was complete, he patted the box. "Five pounds of military-grade plastic explosives. Enough to vaporize this basement and level the house."

The women glowered.

He patted the camera. "I see anything I don't like, and, *pfff*." He mimed an explosion with his fingers. "It's bye bye for you two."

As he left the basement, the look of fear that had settled permanently on the women's faces pleased him.

They passed a sign welcoming careful drivers to Tucson.

He checked his new watch. The online jewelers had been as good as their word, and the gold and diamond encrusted timepiece had arrived the morning after it was ordered. It was three in the afternoon. They would make their appointment on time.

When he had invaded the Lawson's house, he hadn't expected to be meeting with anyone, let alone a bunch of highly paid people from a finance office.

So, he had selected a suit from the eleven in Lawson's closet. They were different sizes, and the jacket had been tight until Cora had cut through the lining to allow the material more room to move. The result was a little odd, but he doubted anyone would notice for the few minutes they were going to be in the office.

The brokers were on the seventeenth floor of the Knox Building. Hades had checked out the building on the Internet. The leasing company had kindly provided a variety of videos to showcase their property.

The main entrance was a three-story atrium, but there were two other large exits as well as two exits through the underground parking garage. It was as much as he could hope for if anything went wrong.

There were five elevators, and three sets of stairs. A getaway down eighteen floors wasn't practical, but if they needed to evade anyone, they could use the stairs to move between floors.

Cora threaded her way through the grid of downtown streets. She stopped in a fast food restaurant's parking lot, two blocks short of the Knox Building.

Hades moved into the rear seat and pulled his jacket back to expose his gun. "One mistake and you're history."

Lawson studied the gun.

Hades covered his gun with his jacket and held out a small remote control.

"This triggers the bomb in the basement."

He turned over the remote to display a switch and a button. "When I turn this on, I have to keep this button pressed, or the bomb goes off."

Lawson stared at him.

"You understand what that means?"

Lawson nodded.

"You try anything, and my finger will come off that button, and *boom*, your wife and daughter are gone."

Lawson breathed in and out. "You lose as much as I do. You

blow them up, and there's no way you'll get the money."

Hades scoffed. The man had a good point, but he had no intention of giving him any hope. "I'll just move on. Find the next opportunity." He grinned. "How easy is it going to be for you to find yourself a new wife and daughter?"

Lawson pursed his lips.

"Exactly," Hades said. "So, do this right, and tomorrow we're gone. Then you get your life back. All three of you."

Several seconds had passed before Lawson nodded.

"Good," Hades said.

He stepped out of the car and used the gun under his jacket to gesture that Lawson should do the same. "Let's go sign this document."

CHAPTER FORTY-FOUR

Tuesday, May 23
Tucson, Arizona

THE ELEVATOR NUMBERS COUNTED up. Five, ten, twelve.

Hades held the remote in front of Lawson, pressed down the button, and flipped the switch from off to on. "It all gets serious now. One stupid thing, and…" He flexed his finger while holding the button down.

Lawson nodded.

"You understand?" Hades said.

"I do," murmured Lawson.

"Speak up. You're a man in control of his destiny. Talk to these people like you mean it."

Lawson swallowed. He took a deep breath. "I understand," he said, loud and clear.

Hades patted his shoulder. "Then we're all going to get along fine."

The elevator bumped to a stop. "My name will be Ken

Cooper, but you call me Ken every time," Hades said.

"I understand."

The doors opened onto a communal area.

Hades nudged Lawson out. "Look for this place. Find it. You do it. Because you ask me for anything, and I take my finger off the remote. Then I blow you away."

Lawson straightened his back. "I've got it." He ran his finger down a list of names on the wall beside the elevator. "Suite 1841." There was a map. The suites ringed the elevators with a corridor that ran in a rectangle.

Lawson walked to the left. They passed suite 1800. At the corner was Suite 1841.

The entrance door was solid wood. Lawson raised his hand to knock, then decided against it. He grasped the handle and opened the door.

Inside was a reception area with a bar-height counter. The walls were pale green with small bronze sculptures on tiny shelves at random, but pleasing positions.

A woman behind the counter stood as they entered. "Do you—"

"I have an appointment. Simon Lawson," Lawson said. He checked his watch. "I'm three minutes early, but I'm in something of a rush."

Her eyebrows raised a fraction. "Lawson. Yes, of course. Mr. Sedgwick is expecting you." She turned her back on Lawson and had a short, muted conversation on the phone before facing them again.

"This way please."

She led them down a corridor lined with gold-framed panoramic pictures of international cities before stopping at a glass door in a glass wall.

A conference room. A large table was ringed by a dozen high-backed leather chairs. The far wall was also glass. The view looked out across the city to the mountains in the distance. Hades figured they'd paid extra for the view.

A man was seated at the table, an inch-thick stack of papers in front of him. He rose as they entered, his gaze flitting from Lawson to Hades and back again. "I was expecting a Mr. Lawson..."

Lawson extended his hand. "Simon Lawson." He gestured to Hades. "This is Ken."

Sedgwick shook hands with Lawson first. Then Hades. "Ken?"

"Cooper," Hades said pleasantly.

Sedgwick cleared his throat. "I'm afraid company policy requires us to discuss our clients' affairs in private."

"I can waive that," Lawson said, flipping his right hand in the air. "No problem."

Sedgwick shook his head. "But I'm afraid I can't. Strict policy, unfortunately." He gestured to the glass entrance. The receptionist held the door open.

Hades cocked his head. Lawson hadn't had the chance to communicate with anyone. He'd been tied up in the basement since the invasion. His wife, too. If they had contacted anyone, the police would have been all over him already.

Finally, Hades shrugged. "Sure. No problem." He looked Lawson in the eye. "I'll be just outside."

A woman in a navy pantsuit passed by, a bundle of papers in her arms.

"This way," the receptionist said.

The company's policy was expected, but Hades had also expected them to accommodate Lawson's request. The question now was whether he could trust Lawson to do as he'd been told.

Hades exchanged glances with Lawson for a moment before he shrugged and followed the woman. As he walked away from the glass conference room, he kept his left hand in his pocket, his fingers wrapped around the remote to emphasize the danger to Lawson's wife and daughter.

The receptionist stepped quickly, expecting Hades to follow. When the glass door swung closed behind him, he didn't look back.

Hades rolled his shoulders. He checked the corridor, which was still empty. His VBR was under his jacket. He could reach it with his right hand, keeping his left on the remote. He flexed his fingers.

The corridor widened into the lobby.

Three men in dark jackets stood by the counter. They had the look of private security. One of them stepped back. He placed his hands on his waist, drawing his jacket open.

Hades curled his fingers around the grip of his gun. He inhaled slowly. He saw no holster on the man's shoulder, but no reason to be complacent either. Hades was out of his depth here. Anything could happen.

The receptionist pointed at a chair across the room. "If you'd like to take a seat." She turned to the man with his hands on his waist. "If you'd like to follow me."

She led the men down the corridor into the offices and toward the glass conference room.

Hades took up a position along the side wall where the corridor and the entrance door were in full view.

He kept one hand on his gun and the other on the remote. A clock behind the counter ticked. He took deep breaths, exhaling fully to quell his discomfort. The woman in the navy pantsuit left the offices. A bell chimed to announce the arrival of the elevator, and she stepped in.

A moment later, the receptionist returned with Lawson in tow. Lawson had a bundle of papers tucked under his arm.

"Everything okay?" Hades stood.

Lawson opened the glass entrance door. "Peachy. Let's go home."

Hades followed. The corridor was silent. No doors opened or closed. There were no muffled conversations spilling from the suites, nor the click of busy keyboards.

The elevator was slow to arrive. Lawson remained silent. He glanced, occasionally, at Hades. Hades kept his eyes moving. They could be approached from two sides and any of the five elevator cars. It was impossible to stand in one spot to monitor all angles.

He stood two paces behind Lawson. Close enough to grab Lawson around the neck, and far enough to show an attacker the gun he would jam into Lawson's spine.

An elevator bell rang. The doors slid open. The car was empty. Hades motioned to Lawson and followed him inside where they stood opposite each other.

Hades released his gun grip and used his right forefinger to press *door close*. He kept his finger on the button.

"You signed?" he said.

"Everything. All done."

"Twenty million?"

"Twenty-three million, and some. My whole life's savings."

Hades breathed heavily to control his boiling rage. He wanted to grab Lawson by the neck and strangle him. He wanted to beat and kick Lawson until he cried out. Then he wanted to kick him some more.

There was no way that a doctor like Lawson could amass such a fortune legitimately. He'd used some kind of scam. He must have. Only a questionable scheme that cheated a lot of others could have allowed Lawson to win so big.

Hades exhaled, relaxing his muscles. He selected the ground floor.

More than twenty-three million. Lawson had spent a long time in the winner's circle. It was long past time for him to taste defeat.

The elevator descended.

Lawson held out the papers. "Records. For what they're worth."

Hades took the papers with his left hand. The remote was in his pocket.

Lawson stared at him. Shock and horror crept across his face. Wrinkles lined his brow. He leaped forward, his fist clenched, his whole body driving his punch upward at Hades' chin.

Hades twisted, deflecting the blow. He curled a right hook at Lawson's ribs, but the man was moving. He rushed into Hades, banging him into the wall. The hand rail smashed against Hades' spine.

Hades brought his knee up into Lawson's groin. Hard. Lawson doubled over.

Hades raised his fist and smashed a hammer blow down on the back of Lawson's neck.

Lawson dropped to his knees.

Hades adjusted his fist, holding it ready.

Lawson rolled onto his side on the floor of the elevator.

Hades stepped back.

The display above the doors showed the elevator

approaching the sixth floor. If Hades knocked Lawson unconscious, he'd need to carry him past the guards in the building foyer.

Too suspicious. Too much risk.

Hades relaxed his fist. He stabbed the button for the fourth floor.

The elevator slowed.

Hades wrenched Lawson to his feet and rammed the VBR in his ribs. "I don't need you anymore, Simon." He jabbed Lawson with the gun again. "One stupid move and you're done."

Lawson grunted.

Hades ground the muzzle into the soft flesh under Lawson's arm. "So the remote is a fake. Doesn't matter. If I don't show up, your wife and daughter are dead anyway."

The elevator stopped. The doors buzzed open. There was no one waiting.

Keeping his arm wrapped around Lawson's torso to hold him upright, Hades shoved him out of the elevator and hustled for the stairs. Lawson limped and stumbled like a drunken sailor, but he didn't fall.

The stairs were bare concrete. Every sound echoed to the top of the building. Hades shoved Lawson in front, gripped the back of his collar, and pressed the VBR into the back of his neck. "Walk."

Progress was slow. Hades' tension rose as they passed the fire escape door on each floor. An employee's unfortunate decision to use the stairs would force him to take action he'd prefer not to take. No one had to die here if Hades could make it outside without further incident.

They passed the ground floor to the first parking level. Hades put the gun under his jacket and pressed it into Lawson's side. "Use the pedestrian exit. Don't talk to anyone."

Lawson's fear made him obedient. He followed a line painted on the floor to an exit ramp.

Hades sent a one-handed text to Cora. A moment later she stopped the Nissan at the curb. Lawson climbed in the rear seat. Hades followed and jammed his gun in Lawson's gut.

Cora pulled smoothly away from the curb. "How'd it go?"

Hades smiled. "I've never made an easier twenty-three million."

CHAPTER FORTY-FIVE

Tuesday, May 23
Yuma National Forest, Arizona

JESS SPENT AN HOUR in Wilson's kitchen describing her ordeal to Detective Beasley. Wilson nodded and *uh-huh'd* all the way through. A technician took their prints and swabs for gunpowder residue. He bagged Jess's Glock and Wilson's Model 29. Wilson seemed unconcerned to be deprived of his gun.

Beasley made several calls on Wilson's phone to verify Jess's background before he sat across from her at the table with a thump.

"Your ID checks out. But…" he leaned forward. "Explain why you're here again."

"Karen Warner, the woman who was kidnapped two years ago, received calls from that phone." She pointed to Fred's antique on the wall. "The calls were made by a man living in the house across the lake, and when I went to ask him about those calls, two men tried to kill me."

"They chased you on motorbikes."

"Shooting at me."

"You had stolen one of their bikes."

"They shot first."

"And the man with the ponytail?"

Jess sighed. "Was the man I saw burning down Melissa Green's house in Bear Hill."

Beasley turned to Fred. "Had you seen either of these two men before?"

Fred shook his head. "We pretty much keep to ourselves."

"The man who used your phone?"

"I saw him plenty, but he wasn't on the bikes."

"Name?"

"John Smith."

"You trying to be funny."

"It's what he called himself."

Beasley cocked his head and frowned. "Could you describe this John Smith to a sketch artist?"

Fred grimaced. "Doubt it."

"Did he have a scar?"

Fred shook his head. "That much, I'm sure of."

"You think the guy calling himself John Smith was really Hades?" Jess said.

"Why would I think that?" Beasley said.

"Because Hades kidnapped Karen Warner and he has scars on his face."

"He's reputed to have a scar."

Jess shrugged. "Have you found anything helpful at that house?"

Beasley scowled. "The house is almost empty. Looks like they were moving out. But we're not done over there yet."

"Who owns the house?"

"It's a rental property." He tilted his head. "Owner lives a couple of miles further down the road. He can't give a good description of the renters either. Apparently, they paid in cash in an envelope in his letterbox. First of every month. Regular as clockwork."

"Okay, I guess." Jess nodded. "But there's a definite link between Karen Warner, that house, and Melissa Green. The man with the ponytail. The phone calls. The fact that both sisters disappeared."

Beasley sighed. "The Karen Warner case is closed. No prosecutor will open it up again, without far more substantial evidence."

"But the Melissa Green case isn't closed." Jess heard the stubbornness in her voice.

"The Melissa Green case isn't my jurisdiction." He rapped his knuckles on the table before he handed her a business card and stood. "Anything more comes to mind about what happened here, let me know."

Wilson showed Beasley out and returned to the kitchen.

Jess pushed back from the table. "I'd better be going. Sorry about your gun."

"Yours, too."

"You probably won't get it back for weeks."

Wilson shrugged. "More where that came from."

Jess looked at him. They stood in silence a few moments before he grinned. "Can I trust you?"

"Absolutely," she said.

"All right, new school. I think I have something that might suit you. You are a lone female, after all."

CHAPTER FORTY-SIX

Tuesday, May 23
Yuma National Forest, Arizona

JESS WAVED GOODBYE TO Fred and walked back to her Mustang. Tucked into her bag was a Ruger 9E. The clip was fully loaded. Seventeen 9mm rounds. Fred had turned out to have a broad selection of guns in a large safe. He wasn't a survivalist, preparing for the end of the world, he just had a mechanical interest in how different guns performed. She promised to return the weapon in a few days.

She did a three-point turn and headed back down the mountain. The Mustang loved the extra assistance of gravity, and she had to keep her foot light on the accelerator to keep its speed under control.

Her phone picked up a signal as she approached the town of Death and Taxes. As she headed north, back to Santa Irene, her phone rang, and Mercer's name appeared in the display on the dashboard. She answered the call with the car's hands-free system.

"Captain Mercer?" she said.

"Can you talk?"

"I have two hours to talk. I'm on my way back to Santa Irene."

"I have news. It was Melissa Green's body in the woods. X-rays showed a broken and pinned right leg. Matches her medical records. They estimate she was killed about two years ago."

Jess whistled. "But she used her credit card a month ago."

"And she was seen in Bear Hill."

"Then it must have been Karen Warner. They were identical."

"It's the obvious conclusion. We just lack actual proof."

"CCTV footage?"

"Santa Irene PD are looking for it, but it's a long shot. Most places overwrite their recordings after a week or two."

"So, Warner is…or may be innocent."

"There's still a lot of assumptions, and don't forget their driver was killed as well."

"He was killed by Hades in the abduction."

"And there is a good trail of evidence to show they were communicating."

"Or Karen was."

"Maybe."

"But we definitely know Hades and The Devil Kings abducted Karen. If she is still alive, either they let her go, or she has become part of the gang."

"They wouldn't let her go. Hades is Norman Kemp. We have prints and DNA. We'd arrest him if we knew where he was."

"Stockholm syndrome?"

"It could be lots of things. There's just too many unknowns."

Jess pulled into a rest stop and parked away from the main cluster of cars and trucks.

"We keep dancing around the main problem. Karen Warner was physically kidnapped by Hades and The Devil Kings. Someone at the house by the lake made calls to Karen. Someone who doesn't like visitors. That same someone was at Melissa's house, and Melissa was killed about two years ago, too. They're all linked by one thing. Not Melissa, or Karen or Donald Warner, but Hades."

"And like I said, if we knew where he was, he would have been arrested by now."

Jess pulled Carter's notes from her bag and flipped them open. She sorted through the pages until she found a list he had made of people associated with the case. She ran her finger down one column and stopped at a name. "But he has a brother, Benny Kemp."

"Yeah. He's been questioned multiple times. Given statements. Short summary, he doesn't know anything about his brother."

"But he's his brother. He knows something about him. Maybe he sees him sometimes. Or gets calls? Or social media—"

"All of that has been monitored in the past. Big time. Trust me,. He doesn't just pop out for a drink with Hades in the neighborhood bar."

"It doesn't have to be blatant."

"Back when Karen was abducted, he was put under surveillance. Twenty-four hours a day. It was a pretty easy gig."

"Meaning?"

"He's in a wheelchair. Being a violent criminal is hard to imagine."

Jess sighed and finished the call.

Being in a wheelchair might slow Benny Kemp down, but it didn't rule out contact, or a knowledge of Hades' activities. She sent Mandy a message, requesting Benny Kemp's address.

A few moments later she got the reply, *Tomorrow*.

She put the Mustang in gear and headed back to The Bear Hill Hotel.

CHAPTER FORTY-SEVEN

Wednesday, May 24, 6:45 a.m.
Santa Irene, Arizona

JESS AWOKE LATER THAN she'd meant to. Her head felt stuffy from the hot, dry air.

She staggered into the shower, and a few minutes later steam increased the humidity in the room dramatically. She sat on the bed with a towel wrapped around her and checked her email.

No update from Mandy. She sent a single question mark. Moments later Mandy replied with, *working on it!*

A note from Morris, equally short. *Miss you.* He meant that he was worried. She hadn't called him yesterday because she preferred not to tell him what was going on here. He might have hopped on a plane. He'd done it before. Jess had spent a lot of years looking out for herself. She wasn't ready to surrender her independence. Not yet.

Henry Morris was a good man. No, he was a great man. He had risked his life for her. She needed him and wanted him in her life. But she had a job to do, too. And she wouldn't rely on him to take care of her.

She replied that she missed him, too, and she'd probably be home in a couple more days. Jess closed her laptop and vowed to figure out their relationship when she had more time to think about it.

She went downstairs to the breakfast buffet. She had barely eaten the day before, and she was famished. She consumed probably a thousand calories and downed three cups of coffee before returning to her room.

Her cell phone pinged when Mandy's email arrived. Jess read it twice.

Benny Kemp's address was on the south side of Santa Irene, twenty minutes from her hotel. Mandy had included a snippet from a newspaper funeral notice reporting Benny's death on May 9. His funeral was May 12, the same day as the traffic pile up. When Karen Warner's DNA was found inside the stolen van. His wife's name was Julia Kemp, and they'd had two children.

All of which meant Jess couldn't find out anything from Benny Kemp. She took a deep breath and squared her shoulders. Interviewing a widow was never Jess's favorite idea. She'd done it too many times. But it had to be done.

She checked that the Ruger was loaded and the safety engaged and headed out to her car.

Her phone rang. She recognized the number. "Captain Mercer."

"Where are you?"

"Just leaving my hotel."

"No easy way to say this." He cleared his throat. "Mitch Jackson died this morning."

Jess felt the air drain out of her. She leaned heavily against the side of her car. "Ah, damn," she whispered.

"I've known him since middle school," Mercer said, quietly. "Practically my whole life."

"I'm very sorry." She knew the words were of little comfort, but words were never adequate in such circumstances.

Mercer coughed. "That makes four."

"With Melissa Green, you mean."

"Yeah." He coughed again. "I'm going to get him. Somehow. I'm going to make that… I'm going to make him pay."

She heard his voice catch, and she paused a moment before she said, "Did you know his brother died? The funeral was the same day Karen Warner's DNA was found."

"How?" He cleared his throat.

"I don't know. But he had a wife and—"

"I'll be there in ten minutes."

"Let me try first. Sometimes a reporter can get people to open up when the police can't, Roy." She didn't want him tagging along, but she couldn't prevent him from going anyway.

"I've read the reports. Benny Kemp was a tough customer, and his wife wasn't much better. You'll need a badge just to get across the threshold." She heard his car start up. "I'll pick you up. If she knows anything that can help us find Hades, I want to hear it firsthand."

Jess bit her lip. "Okay."

Eleven minutes later, Mercer's black and white Ford cruiser raced into the hotel parking lot. He flipped open the passenger door. "Get in."

Jess wedged herself in between the equipment and the wires. A bundle of papers slithered across the transmission tunnel.

Some of the pictures she had taken in Melissa Green's kitchen were among them. "Light reading," he said, as he hefted them onto the rear seat.

Jess gave him Benny Kemp's address, and Mercer tore out of the lot.

Mercer didn't speak the whole trip, and they arrived fast.

Jess had not seen this section of Santa Irene before. The area might have been prosperous once, but now it was old and run down. Benny Kemp's street was a line of duplexes with barely a gap between them wide enough for the driveway.

Benny's house was in the middle of the block. It had bars on the windows, and the drapes were closed.

Mercer parked on the opposite side of the road. "Looks like she might still be in bed."

"Better let her wake up then," Jess replied. "No woman wants to meet strangers while she's dressed in her pajamas."

Mercer grunted, and they sat in silence.

Cars drove past. A few pedestrians walked by and stared at them. A silver Nissan was parked on the same side as Julia Kemp's place, but a few doors down.

Jess avoided looking at the windows to keep her patience in check. After forty-two minutes, a light went on in the hallway.

Mercer opened his door.

Jess put her hand on his arm. "Let's give her a few more minutes. We want her awake and cooperative."

Mercer closed his door. "From the reports I've read, you're hoping for a lot." He breathed heavily and fidgeted with the car's dials and knobs.

Jess watched the digital clock on the dashboard. She knew she was right to wait.

The clock ticked over. Ten minutes had passed since the

hallway light came on. Julia Kemp could have made coffee and shaken off her sleep.

"Okay. Let's go," Jess said.

Mercer was out of the car and across the road before she had closed her door. She ran to catch up and stepped in front of him.

He reached over her shoulder and pressed the doorbell. A buzzer echoed inside. He kept his finger on the button. The buzzing continued.

Jess pulled his hand away. "I think she knows we're here."

"We wouldn't be here at all if he'd done something about his brother a long time ago."

Jess took a deep breath. "I know you're angry. You have every right to be. But we need answers, not more enemies."

The door cracked open, held by a security chain. Through the gap, Jess saw a woman with thick golden brown hair and big dark eyes. Her friendly round jawline contrasted with her deep scowl.

"You're Julia Kemp, right?" Jess put a friendly tone into the words. "I'm Jess Kimball. This is my friend Roy Mercer."

"What do you want?" Her voice was thick with sleep.

"That coffee smells great." Jess smiled as she sniffed the aroma appreciatively. "Can we come in?"

Julia looked at them for a couple of seconds before she put her hand on the door to push it closed.

Mercer shoved past Jess and wedged his foot in the diminishing gap. He held his badge out at Julia's eye level.

Julia groaned.

"Either talk to us now or talk to us after I've arrested you."

"For what?"

"Littering. Spitting on the sidewalk. Broken headlight. You name it. I'll make it stick."

"Get the hell off my porch." She pushed the door hard against his boot.

"I mean it, Julia." He pushed back against the door, and the old chain snapped.

The door flew open. Julia staggered backward into the room. Only a firm grip on the doorknob kept her from falling flat on her ass.

Julia righted herself and glared at Mercer before she walked away.

"Thanks for inviting us in," Mercer said as he entered the house.

Jess followed him inside and closed the door behind her.

The duplex's kitchen was at the rear, and a sitting room was at the front. The two were separated by a half-wall. They followed Julia into the kitchen. What looked like two five-year-old boys sat at the kitchen table eating toast. Julia sent them to their room. They left silently.

They followed her into the sitting room. A desk was pressed against one wall. An old computer and printer sat on top. The keyboard was lost under a mass of junk mail. Julia bundled it up and stuffed it into a plastic bag from the local supermarket.

"I wasn't expecting visitors." She pointed to a two-person sofa. "Sit."

Jess pulled a fifty dollar bill out of her pocket and gave it to Julia. "For the broken chain."

Julia's eyes widened, and she stuffed the bill into her bra.

"We were sorry to hear about your husband." Jess sat and Mercer stood behind the sofa.

"Right," Julia said with contempt. "Like you cared one whit about Benny."

Jess looked at a photo of a man in a wheelchair on a table beside the sofa. "Is this Benny?"

"Guess."

Jess gave a sympathetic smile. "Was he in a wheelchair all his life?"

Julia shook her head. "Accident. That's what killed him."

"The accident?"

"He got a staph infection from the surgery. Got worse and worse. Antibiotics couldn't treat it." She paused and, after a moment, shrugged.

Jess nodded. "I'm really sorry."

Julia sneered. "What do you want?"

"Have you seen your husband's brother?" Mercer said.

Julia sighed. "Norman? Not since he was let out last time."

"Which was?"

She shrugged again. "Couple of years ago, more or less. He worked for Benny a little. Then I never saw him again."

"Cut the crap," Mercer said. "He's been seen in Santa Irene. You telling me he didn't come to his own brother's funeral?"

"How would I know?" She stuck out her chin.

Jess said, "Have you had any contact with him at all, Mrs. Kemp?"

Julia gestured toward the computer. "I expect you've been monitoring our phone and email. Just like you did when that Warner woman was taken."

"How did you feel about Norman's involvement in that?" Jess said.

Julia glared. "Seemed like that doctor got what was coming to him."

"Norman kidnapped Karen Warner," Jess said.

"We weren't his guardians." She flicked her fingers at Mercer. "We're not responsible for Norman."

Jess cleared her throat and waited until Julia turned her gaze away from Mercer. "Karen Warner's sister disappeared, too."

"Very sorry, but still not my problem."

"Melissa lived in Bear Hill."

Julia frowned. "How nice for her."

"You know the place?"

Julia shook her head. "Everyone's got to live somewhere."

"But here's the thing, Julia." Jess paused until Julia looked up. "She was found dead. Murdered. And someone burned her house to the ground."

Julia pressed her lips into a tight line.

"Bit of a coincidence. Two sisters." Mercer said. "And your Norman definitely kidnapped at least one of them."

"I told you. I haven't seen him, and my husband's dead, too. I've got enough problems of my own."

Mercer leaned over the sofa. He pointed a finger at Benny's photograph. "I find one shred of evidence that you've talked to Norman, or you're lying to us, and I'll make it my life's work to put you somewhere a million times worse than here."

"I've got nothing more to say to you." Julia walked to the front and opened the door. "Get out."

Jess followed Mercer back to his car. He wasted no time in swinging the cruiser around and peeling away from Benny's widow.

CHAPTER FORTY-EIGHT

Wednesday, May 24
Santa Irene, Arizona

HADES STOOD AT THE corner of Lawson's garage, deep in shadow despite the daylight outside.

He watched Cora ease the Lawsons' Nissan back into its space. She switched off the engine, and he pressed the button to close the door. He waited until the door was fully closed before moving out of the shadows.

He rapped on the windows. Julia looked at him from the rear seat.

Hades spread his arms. "Home sweet home."

Julia stepped out of the car, frowning. Her children wriggled out of the car behind her. Hades held out his fist and knuckle-bumped each boy in turn.

"We're done," Hades said.

Julia raised her eyebrows, questioningly. "What? What's done?"

"Inside first. We can talk inside." He walked out of the side of the garage, across the wide patio, and in through the large patio doors. Julia and the boys followed.

Shorty appeared at the bottom of the stairs. He raised a hand. "Yo, guys."

The boys ran over and hugged him. Julia waved.

Shorty gestured up the stairs. "Talk later. I gotta go back. Keep up the watch."

Cora sat on the sofa. Pony prowled the kitchen, picking at snacks in the cupboards.

"I don't understand," Julia said.

Hades shook his head. "I know, I know. We couldn't contact you. Couldn't risk it."

Julia looked at him.

Hades grinned. A big wide stupid grin. "We are inches from being millionaires."

Julia's mouth hung open.

Hades gestured to the house. "Look at this place. This whole house is what? Three mil? Four?" He shrugged. "Who knows, right?"

"Whose house is this?"

"Lawson's."

"Simon Lawson?"

"Yeah. This is his place. And look at it. It's worth millions."

"What are you going to do? Sell it?"

"Hell, no." Hades stood in front of Julia. "Are you ready for this?"

"What?"

"He wasn't just some doctor with maybe a million stashed away. People like that can't afford places like this." Hades grinned. "He had twenty-three million in a hidden account."

Julia's eyes widened, and her mouth dropped open.

Hades shook his head. "Twenty-three million. He scammed it out of people. Good people who deserved better. He took their money. Just like he screwed Benny. And now? He's going to pay for it. Because it's ours. All ours."

Julia looked at Cora and Pony.

Cora nodded. "It's not a joke. It's all ours. Or it will be."

Julia frowned. "Will be?"

Hades grabbed the papers from the brokerage account and held them up. "It gets transferred into our account at 2:00 p.m., our time." He checked his watch. "Four hours, Julia. Four hours and everything those scum did to you and Benny and the boys…" he lowered the papers. "It gets paid back." He laughed. "Paid back with interest."

Julia shook her head slowly. "It's just a lot to take in."

Hades threw his hands up. "It's twenty-three million to take in. I just wish Benny was here with us."

Julia swallowed. Everyone was silent. She sniffed. "The police were at my house today."

Hades frowned. "Today?"

"This morning. A lousy cop and he had a woman with him. Asking questions about you."

Hades scowled and leaned down toward Julia. "What did you say?"

"Said I hadn't seen you since you got out last time."

"What else?"

"Nothing. I told them to get lost."

Hades peered into the distance. "What police department?"

"I don't know. Some guy called Mercer. And I didn't get the woman's name."

"FBI?"

"Definitely not."

Hades looked at Cora and Pony and back at Julia. He sighed. "Four more hours. We just have to keep on our guard, and be ready to leave."

CHAPTER FORTY-NINE

Wednesday, May 24
Santa Irene, Arizona

JESS STRUGGLED TO FASTEN her seatbelt as Mercer slung the Ford through a ninety-degree turn to join the main road.

"I told you," he said, "The Kemps were no use at all."

Jess ignored the dig. "Did you have his computer monitored, back then?"

"According to the report, they searched it, but they didn't find anything useful."

"Any connection to Melissa Green?"

Mercer shrugged. "Don't know."

"Or The Art Market, or Bear Hill?"

"I can look."

"She seemed curious about the fact Karen Warner had a sister," Jess said.

"She missed a beat, but maybe she just didn't know?"

"Surely it was brought up at the trial?"

Mercer glanced at her. "Why would it be? She probably watched every moment of the trial, but I don't think Melissa was mentioned at all."

"It was a big trial. Got lots of attention. Whether it was relevant or not, the press would have done articles on every family member at some point."

Mercer grunted. "I guess."

"And she said Hades worked for Benny? Doing what?"

"Kemp did some construction work. I don't think it was very successful. I guess Hades could have worked for him."

"Construction? Like the kind of plumbing somebody did to Melissa's house?"

Mercer jerked his thumb toward the papers on the back seat. "It's in there somewhere."

Jess twisted around, shuffled the mess of paper into a single stack, and placed it on her lap.

She sorted through the pages until she found Benny's background. "General construction. I guess that includes plumbing. Or..."

"Or, what?"

"Benny couldn't have done that sort of plumbing from a wheelchair. But maybe Hades learned a trade while he was in prison?"

Mercer punched a button on his radio. It crackled and hissed. He punched the button again, and the radio turned off. "Out of range."

Jess fumbled her phone from her bag, the papers sliding around on her lap. "Who do you want?"

Mercer recited a number. She put the call on speaker. A young man's voice answered formally.

Mercer leaned toward Jess's phone. "This is Roy. Find out if

Hades, real name Norman Kemp, learned a trade during his last prison stint."

"Captain. I thought you were taking time off."

"Find out and text the answer back to this number, okay?"

"Sure. Few minutes."

Jess ended the call. "You're out on a limb here, aren't you?"

"And you're not? You've been shot at. Twice." Mercer grunted as he took the road for Bear Hill.

"You heard from Santa Irene PD?" Jess said.

He shook his head. "They're only going to talk to me if they want something."

"We could call on them."

"I'm on leave, remember?"

"I could do it."

He glanced sideways at her. "Maybe. Worth a shot for anything new." He took the next exit and doubled back down the service road to rejoin the road into town.

Jess straightened the papers on her lap again. Her photographs were at the top of the pile.

She pulled them out and waved a picture of the bike magazines. "Definitely not Melissa Green's reading material."

Mercer glanced at the pictures. "It did seem weird that there was a lot of food in the house, but given that it wasn't just Melissa Green, I guess that's not so strange."

Jess leafed through the pages. "The place was lived in. There was milk and perishables in the fridge. So they must have been getting the food from somewhere."

"Santa Irene PD were going to do a sweep of supermarkets and corner shops. They've been using Melissa Green's picture, but given they're identical, I guess it would do for Warner as well."

Jess studied a photograph of Melissa Green's kitchen. It was a sweeping view of a rear window, a gas stove, and the sink. She flattened it against the side window.

"What?" Mercer said.

Jess grabbed her phone. She found the same picture and zoomed in on the area by the rear window.

The counter top was some sort of stone-look plastic affair. Pressed into the corner was a pile of letters. She zoomed in as far as her phone would allow.

Her skin tingled. "Junk mail."

Mercer slowed the car. "So?"

"Wait," she said.

The envelope at the top of the junk mail was an advertisement that promised to increase the value of her home with a new wood floor. The company was called Wood Floor Whiz. Its logo was a simple black triangle on the corner of the envelope.

She searched the Internet for the company's name. There were several similar sounding matches, but nothing exact. She dialed the number on the envelope. An automated announcement for an insurance company asked her to wait for the next available operator. She hung up.

Mercer had slowed to thirty miles an hour, barely looking at the road ahead. Cars were zooming past. "Will you tell me what you've found?"

He stopped on the side of the road.

She tapped the picture. "I remember seeing this pile of junk mail in Melissa Green's house." She tapped her phone. "I've never heard of this company, and they don't exist. The phone number brings up an insurance company."

Mercer frowned.

"See this?" She pointed to the black triangle. "I saw the same logo on an envelope at Benny Kemp's house."

She slapped the picture down on the pile of papers. "Julia Kemp knew all about Melissa Green and Bear Hill. Benny was sending letters there. That's how he was communicating with his brother. He couldn't do it by phone or email because he knew those were easily monitored. So he used the postal service."

Mercer punched a button on the dash, and the lights and siren started. He stomped on the accelerator, and the Ford fishtailed onto the main road, headed back to Benny Kemp's house.

CHAPTER FIFTY

Wednesday, May 24
Santa Irene, Arizona

JESS PHONED MANDY AS Mercer threaded the cruiser through traffic. Mandy answered on the first ring.

"Jess?"

"I need details about a construction company owned by Benny Kemp. It might have gone out of business. See if you can get employee records. I'm interested in Hades, aka Norman Kemp."

"Based in Santa Irene?"

Jess looked at Mercer. He nodded.

"Yes," she said.

"Okay, I'm on it."

Jess hung up.

Mercer used the emergency lane to pass a slow car.

"You said Benny was investigated when Karen Warner disappeared?"

"He was. They monitored his phone and Internet. It's in the

reports. But it came to nothing." He shrugged. "I guess being in a wheelchair ruled him out of the actual kidnapping, and when they found no communication from Hades, they must have moved on."

Mercer swung the cruiser into Benny Kemp's street and parked opposite his house in the same spot he'd parked before. The drapes were closed and there was no sign of light in the hallway.

Jess extricated herself from the wires and checked the Ruger in her bag. Mercer was across the road already, knocking on the front door when Jess caught up with him. He had his badge out and his hand on his weapon.

Jess stood two paces to one side. She didn't really expect trouble from Julia, but no reason to make the two of them a single target.

Mercer rapped on the door again and held his finger on the buzzer.

The house remained dark.

He released the buzzer, placed his ear to the door, and shook his head.

Jess looked in the windows on either side of the door, but the drapes sealed all view of the interior.

She headed around the side of the duplex and a couple of minutes later, Mercer jogged to catch up.

The backyard was as unkempt as the rest of the place. The flowerbeds were nothing but weeds and the grass were knee high. She worked her way through the cloying grass to the kitchen window.

She could see through the kitchen and over the low wall into the living room beyond. The sofa where she had sat was empty. She saw no signs of life inside.

She shoved her face against the kitchen window. "We need evidence."

"If you're thinking of breaking in, forget it. If we need evidence, we need to stick to procedure to collect it," Mercer said.

She didn't mention the broken door chain on their first visit, and she didn't argue. "Okay, but take a look." She pointed to the desk in the living room.

The keyboard and mouse were shoved in one corner. She leaned over to get a different viewing angle on the desk and the floor around it.

"The computer and printer are gone," she said.

Mercer followed her gaze. "They weren't exactly portable."

"Right. And the bag Julia put the junk mail in is gone as well."

Mercer moved from side to side to get a good view around the desk and the room. "Damn."

"Julia's probably worried we're coming back with a warrant. She's trying to dispose of it."

Mercer said, "I'm going to check with the neighbors. See if anyone knows where she is."

Jess walked a path to the rear gate and checked along the alley at the back of the house. If Julia had dumped the computer close by, Jess couldn't find it.

Her phone rang. She answered it without looking. "Kimball."

"Mandy. Just sent you what I found on Benny Kemp's construction company, Goldleaf Builders. Sole proprietorship. Went bust two years ago. He filed for personal bankruptcy."

"Find any employee records? Names or addresses or anything?"

"Nothing so far, but I'll keep looking."

"What sort of construction did they do?"

"Retail stuff, mainly. He must have had a few people working for him. I sent you a list of his projects."

"Thanks, Mandy."

"Another thing. He had an accident. I found it in the papers. Scaffolding collapsed. After that, his company collapsed as well."

Jess frowned. "He was on the scaffolding?"

"Apparently."

"When did this happen?"

"A little over two years ago."

Jess whistled.

Mandy hummed. "It's all in the email. Hey look, I've got to go."

Jess thanked her and hung up.

Mandy's email was as organized as ever. Jess filtered through the details on her phone's small screen.

At the time Goldleaf went bust, Benny was working on two projects, refitting a bar and building an independent emergency room.

The bar was a fairly basic redecoration of an existing building. The emergency room was being built on a greenfield site. Mandy had included a snippet of the local Santa Irene newspaper article lamenting the loss of jobs at the emergency room.

Jess scanned down the page. The building was being constructed for a company called Argnot Medical Solutions, LLC.

She ran a search for the company in the *Taboo* databases and found a match. The company had only existed for seven months before closing down.

Jess compared the dates. Argnot had declared bankruptcy the

month before Goldleaf. Given the size of the emergency room project, one had likely led to the other. Goldleaf had declared bankruptcy a month before Karen Warner's kidnapping.

She scrolled through the information on Argnot. Only one company was listed as an investor. It had a Brazilian main address and several offices in the US.

Seemed like a typical US front to a foreign investor. The offices would probably be staffed with US nationals revealing little to indicate that the true ownership was offshore. The ordinary person's confidence in a domestic company would bring in further US investment.

She reached a page on Argnot's declared financial performance. The company was estimated at a little over twenty million. She frowned. There was no way a company valued at twenty million had offices across the width of the US. On top of which, why would they invest in one specific new emergency room?

She reached the end of the information on Argnot. The company had only one director, listed as S. Lawson. The address given was in Brazil.

The name Lawson was familiar. She ran back through her notes and found Warner's assistant had mentioned it.

She dialed Santa Irene General Hospital, and eventually was put through to Nurse Melanie Franklin.

"Melanie. This is Jess Kimball. We spoke yesterday. I have a question for you."

"Er… Okay."

"You said Dr. Warner had two doctor friends he worked with at the hospital."

"Yes. Simon Lawson. And Arthur Palmer. Good doctors."

"Is Simon Lawson a Brazilian national?"

"No. At least, I don't think so."

"Did the three of them try to build an emergency room?"

"Not that I know of. They weren't E.R. docs. But they were always talking business, you know? How to make more money. Saving for retirement. Investments. Stuff like that."

"Did they work together in the same practice?"

"They weren't partners or anything, but they referred patients to one another."

"Don't all doctors do that?"

"It takes time to build a reputation, and for doctors to trust one another. They form little cliques. Warner's go-to docs were Palmer and Lawson when the patient needed those specialties."

Jess thought about the prior conversation for a moment. "You also said something about their friendship cooling off at some point, didn't you?"

"Well, I don't know. I mean, to be fair, Dr. Warner had a lot of patients. Something's got to give when you're working all those hours. Social activities are usually the first to go, aren't they?"

"What about Palmer and Lawson? Were they still friends back when Karen Warner was kidnapped?"

"I wouldn't say they weren't friends, just, you know, I noticed they stopped doing things like going out to eat together."

"Did you ever mention this to the police?"

"Well, they interviewed everyone. Me and the doctors and everything. I guess if it was important, they would have said." She paused a moment and answered someone else speaking to her in the background. "I'm sorry. I've got to go. I wish I could be of more help."

"Not at all. You've been more help than you realize." Jess might have asked a few more questions, but Nurse Franklin had already hung up.

CHAPTER FIFTY-ONE

Wednesday, May 24
Santa Irene, Arizona

JESS RAN BACK TO the cruiser. Mercer was talking to one of the neighbors. She called out to him. "I've got something!"

He finished with the neighbor and jogged over.

"Donald Warner worked with two other doctors at Santa Irene General. Arthur Palmer and Simon Lawson. Apparently, they were a pretty tight clique. Referred patients to each other. Spent most of their free time talking medicine and business. And here's the important part." She paused to catch her breath. "Lawson was using Benny Kemp's construction company to build an emergency room."

Mercer frowned. "How did no one realize this?"

"Because Lawson hid the activities behind a shell company headquartered in Brazil."

Mercer shook his head. "I may not be qualified to investigate a complex financial setup, but there were plenty of resources put on the Warner case that could have spotted this right away."

"Looks like it was all done under the table. There's no legal link between Warner and Lawson."

Mercer sighed. "If there's no evidence to connect Warner to Lawson then we can't connect him to Benny and Hades, either."

"Did the neighbors offer anything helpful?"

He shook his head. "One of the kids said Julia Kemp left with her family in a silver car. Doesn't know what type. No one saw what happened to the computer or the junk mail."

Jess cocked her head. "Talk to Warner. Maybe he'll give us something."

"Maybe, but even if your guess is true, how does it help us find Hades after all this time?" He took his phone from his pocket. "I'll get someone to question Warner."

Mercer walked off down the street, searching for a stronger signal.

Jess leaned against the cruiser and looked up addresses for Palmer and Lawson. They both lived in upscale neighborhoods on the wealthier fringes of Santa Irene.

Mercer returned. "I've got someone who will talk to Warner, but don't get your hopes up. Santa Irene PD is not exactly thrilled at the idea of opening up the Warner case."

Jess's phone beeped. She read the message on the screen. "Hades did get some training while he was in prison. But the classes were all information technology, not plumbing."

She held her phone out for Mercer to read the message.

"Information technology," Mercer said, slowly. "The explosion at Melissa Green's was triggered over the Internet."

She kneaded her forehead to release the tension she was holding there. They had a lot of probable connections between Hades and that explosion, but nothing that indisputably laid a murder charge on his head. She needed solid evidence.

Jess called Santa Irene General. She asked first for Dr. Palmer and then Dr. Lawson. A few minutes later, she hung up. "Palmer has retired from the hospital. Lawson is on a week's vacation. His assistant doesn't know where."

"Sounds like a stock answer to give to a reporter."

"Maybe."

Mercer tapped his badge. "Maybe we should talk to Dr. Palmer in person."

Jess shrugged. "I have both home addresses now, anyway. Palmer is closer."

Mercer slid into the cruiser. "Then let's go check on Palmer."

CHAPTER FIFTY-TWO

Wednesday, May 24
Santa Irene, Arizona

JESS FED DIRECTIONS TO Mercer as he worked his way across town. Fifteen minutes later, he slowed to a stop on the road outside Arthur Palmer's house.

Trees poked over a high wall with heavy oak gates that blocked the view of the property from the road. A small pillar beside the gates contained a camera and a speaker. Mercer pressed the button and held his badge in clear view of the camera.

A woman's voice answered. "Can I help you?"

"We're here to talk to Arthur Palmer."

The speaker clicked as if the other end had terminated the conversation. Mercer took a deep breath, his impatience building.

The silence continued. He pressed the button and held it down. A few moments later, a man's voice came on.

"I don't care what you're selling. I am not—"

"Police. Use your camera, look at my badge, and open the gate. Or I'll come back with a squad and an arrest warrant."

The speaker clicked off. There was a full minute of silence before the gates swung open. Mercer drove up to the house.

The gravel driveway crunched under the cruiser's tires. The lawns weren't enormous, but they were a smooth lush green that was all but impossible to maintain in Arizona without incurring a serious water bill.

The house was a three-story colonial style reminiscent of a tobacco plantation. A large porch with Greek columns protected a tall front door. Four large windows were set on either side of the door. The arrangement of windows was repeated on the second and third floors.

The gravel driveway circled the house. Jess guessed it led to the garage. Mercer stopped directly alongside the entrance and jumped out. Jess unwound the cables from her feet and followed. Mercer was already knocking on the front door, which opened as she reached his side.

A man with neatly trimmed salt and pepper hair stood beyond the doorway. Plain Bermuda shorts, a trim pink polo shirt, and deck shoes without socks looked like he was modeling the clothes, not wearing them.

"Jessica Kimball, *Taboo Magazine*." Jess held out her card before Mercer could speak and screw things up.

He plucked the card from her fingers and looked at Mercer.

Mercer held up his badge. "Arthur Palmer?"

Palmer glowered. "Yes. What do you want?"

"Argnot and Goldleaf," Mercer said.

"What?" Palmer screwed his scowl a fraction tighter. "I don't—"

"How about we discuss this inside," Mercer said.

Palmer sighed and stepped to one side. "Come in."

Jess walked into a spacious hallway with a curved staircase that wound down from the second-floor balcony. A giant crystal chandelier hung on a long, gold chain from a towering decorated ceiling.

A blonde glowered down from the balcony. She had long legs and short shorts. She turned away and disappeared into one of the upstairs rooms.

Palmer led them through a set of double doors into a library. A large mahogany desk with a gold lamp and a phone on the top filled the corner at the far end of the room. Three walls of mahogany shelves were covered in leather bound books, which Jess suspected were rarely, if ever, read.

Two armchairs and a sofa were arranged around a fireplace. Palmer flipped a switch, and a fire burst to life. "Take a seat."

Jess perched on an armchair, directly opposite Palmer. "We understand you were once involved in business dealings with a company called Argnot."

He shrugged. "I've invested in a variety of businesses over the years."

"We're interested in Argnot. What can you tell us about it?"

He shook his head. "What is there to tell?"

"What was its purpose?"

"It's been awhile, but my memory is that Argnot was building a freestanding emergency room facility in an underserved neighborhood."

"A lofty goal." Jess took a breath and let it out slowly, relaxing her muscles. "What was your involvement with Argnot?"

"It wasn't my company."

"Were Dr. Lawson and Dr. Warner involved?" Mercer demanded.

"You'll have to ask them."

He glowered at Palmer, his lips pressed tight and his breath hissing through his nose. Jess thought he might attack Palmer, but he went to the window and took out his phone, dialing as he walked.

Palmer frowned. "What's going on?"

A muffled voice emerged from Mercer's phone. He listened and then said, "We're going to need the warrant. While you're getting that—"

Palmer rose halfway out of his chair. "What warrant?"

Mercer glanced at Palmer and went back to the phone. "We'll need the dogs. And send two cars. Lights and sirens. We want to make sure everybody in the neighborhood knows we're coming."

"What the hell is this?" Palmer said, rising from his chair.

Jess nodded as Mercer hung up after completing the ruse, and put his phone in his pocket. He pulled back his jacket to expose his gun. "Please sit down, Dr. Palmer. We won't have long to wait."

Palmer went for his phone on the big desktop. Mercer got there first and covered the receiver with his hand.

Palmer huffed. "I'm calling my lawyer. I have the right—"

"That clock starts ticking after you've been arrested," Mercer said. "At the moment, you're free to leave. We can wait outside if you prefer."

"What the hell is this about?" Palmer shouted and his spittle landed on Mercer's face.

"We can find room for you in the same prison as your pal, Warner. Assuming you want things to go that far." Mercer gave a hard glare as he wiped the spittle away with the back of his hand.

Palmer lowered his gaze.

"Please sit down, Dr. Palmer," Jess said.

He rotated his head slowly to look at her.

"Please," she repeated, waving to the chair he'd vacated previously.

He sank into the armchair. "So, tell me what you think I've done."

"First tell us about Argnot," she said.

He sighed. "Not much to tell. Argnot was organized for one thing, to build a specific emergency room. One of those pop-up ones. Just on a street corner in a neighborhood where we had no competition. Affiliate with a hospital and then sell it off after we got it running."

"Who are we?"

"Lawson and Warner, for sure. There might have been others."

"You don't know?"

"I wasn't in control of the company. I put some money into it. That was all." He looked across the coffee table. "Like I said, I invested in a lot of things. Still do."

"How much did you invest in Argnot?"

He shook his head. "I don't remember. Why do you care?"

Mercer glanced at his watch. "Forty-five minutes until we have that warrant and we can look it up for ourselves. Along with everything about you, right down to your underwear preference. We'll uncover things you didn't report on your tax forms, most likely. We usually do. And Uncle Sam is always interested in that stuff."

"You're a bastard, Mercer." Palmer shook his head, but all

the anger had gone out of him. He slumped deeper into the chair. "I put in a hundred thousand."

"That's all?" Jess frowned. "To build an emergency room?"

Palmer shook his head. "It… The idea was to get the building started, then get advances from investors as the work was done."

"And Warner and Lawson," Mercer interrupted. "Did they put in the same?"

"It was all we needed. In theory." Palmer nodded. "I mean… I didn't really know, but Lawson said he had done it before up in Chicago and it worked well. We could get in for relatively little upfront capital investment and reap big rewards when we sold the business."

"Only this time, it didn't work out that way, did it?" Mercer said.

Palmer straightened his back and shook his head again. "We closed down the company, and that was it." He paused. "So, now that I've answered your questions, you answer mine. What's all this about?"

"Goldleaf Construction," Jess said. "What can you tell me about them?"

"I never met them, but they were the builders." Palmer frowned. "Like I told you. Lawson had done this before. He was the one organizing everything. He was in charge. You should really be talking to Simon."

"How about David Warner? Did he have anything to do with the builders?" Jess asked.

"You'd have to ask him." Palmer shrugged. "Like I said, Lawson mostly kept us out of it. I looked at all the figures and the projections. It seemed like it would be a sound investment."

"So what happened? How did it go wrong?"

"Simple accounting. We needed to keep raising financing, but the banks in Santa Irene wouldn't loan forward like in Chicago."

"What do you mean?"

"Once you get one bank to loan on it, the others just follow. That's what Lawson said. We tried, but we couldn't get the first loan. So that was it. We chased the money for a while. Pushed on longer than we wanted to, trying to hold on. We got Goldleaf to do as much as they could. Lawson worked them pretty hard. Got them to invest a ton, and drove them to economize on everything." He paused, shrugged. "But it wasn't enough, and we all knew it. Some investments go bad. Win some, lose some. That's just how it goes."

Jess looked around the expensively furnished room. "You're not poor. You could have put more money into it."

Palmer shook his head. "We could have. All of us. But getting it up and running would have required a couple of million or more. That's a lot of money and a bigger risk. We might not have been able to sell it for a profit if we invested that much. So we cut our losses after the banks rejected us."

"And wrote the loss off on your tax returns, huh?"

He shrugged. "Our liability was limited. Argnot declared bankruptcy. Pretty easy really. We had a lawyer handle it."

Jess glared at Palmer. She breathed to calm her anger before she spoke. "It was easy for you because Goldleaf Construction was left holding the bag. Goldleaf lost everything."

He shrugged again. "Goldleaf was a construction company. They would have set up a separate company for that job, too. No great loss."

"Except Goldleaf wasn't a separate company with limited liability. Goldleaf was owned by one man. With a family. Benny Kemp."

"Well, obviously I didn't know." Palmer shook his head, sorrowfully.

"He went bankrupt," Jess said.

Palmer went a little green around the edges. "Well, I'm sorry… I really am, but that's business."

"Benny was hurt building your emergency room. Probably because he was cutting corners to help your *plan*," Mercer said. "In fact, it was Benny's injury on the construction site that halted construction and caused local banks to deny your loan applications, wasn't it?"

"I didn't know." Palmer frowned. His hands gripped the arms of his chair, white-knuckled. His voice a whisper.

"Benny Kemp lived the last couple of years in a wheelchair, with excruciating pain. He died two weeks ago, Dr. Palmer." Mercer's tone was cold, hard, unyielding. "His widow said Benny's cause of death was a staph infection he contracted during that first surgery. Didn't respond to antibiotics."

Palmer opened his mouth, but no words came out.

"You probably know Benny's brother, Norman Kemp?" Mercer smirked. "Professionally, he uses the name Hades."

Palmer's eyes widened, and he shook his head. "The criminal? The leader of The Devil Kings gang?"

"The one and only." Jess nodded. "You remember Hades, don't you? He killed Dr. Warner's driver and kidnapped Dr. Warner's wife."

Jess interpreted Palmer's expression as sheer horror.

"Hades is a ruthless killer, Dr. Palmer." Mercer's tone was laced with glee. "And you're the reason his brother is dead. We don't have to wonder how Hades plans to deal with you, do we?"

CHAPTER FIFTY-THREE

Wednesday, May 24
Santa Irene, Arizona

JESS WATCHED PALMER'S COMPOSURE crack into splintered shards. "How did you fund this scheme? You didn't have a spare hundred grand lying around, did you?"

Palmer licked his lips. His mouth must have been dry as dust. "Warner and I referred patients to Lawson. It was completely legitimate. Doctors do that. Send patients to specialists when they need a specialist's help."

There was a long silence.

"Sending Lawson work wasn't enough to make him rich, was it? Only so many patients he could see in a day," Jess said. "So, he scammed money off the insurance. That's how you and Warner and Lawson found the three hundred thousand startup capital."

Palmer pressed his lips tight together and looked at the ground.

Jess shook her head. "Weren't you scared when Karen Warner was kidnapped?"

He screwed up his face and shook his head. "Do you really think Hades took Karen because we couldn't get financing for that emergency room?"

Palmer was in deep, and he knew it. His expression was pained. Jess hoped he felt that pain for a long time.

But he had a point. She stood and gestured to Mercer.

"We need to talk." Without waiting for a reply, she left the room and walked outside to the cruiser.

Mercer followed. "What the hell are you doing?" He gestured back to the house. "We need to keep the pressure on him."

"If Karen hasn't been kidnapped and killed as everyone assumes then she has left Warner and joined Hades. But she wouldn't have just decided to do that. Not simply because some building deal went wrong. She had been getting to know him for some time before."

Mercer nodded. "We know that. The calls to the salon."

"Right. But suppose the relationship starts before the emergency room deal goes south."

Mercer cocked his head and narrowed his eyes.

"Lawson was pushing Goldleaf to get more done with less money, to cut corners." She waved her hand toward the house. "But Hades probably wouldn't even know about that, let alone be motivated to get involved with kidnapping and murder."

Mercer's eyes widened. "He did it for Benny."

Jess nodded. "I think so. It makes sense. Benny gets hurt, and his company goes bankrupt while he's lying in a hospital bed. It's the last straw. And Hades has a direct line right into the people that made it all happen."

"So he frames Warner. But Warner wasn't the main man on this deal or he wouldn't be in prison. Palmer and Lawson are still living large. If Hades is settling scores, surely he would have dealt with them already. Guys like Hades have notoriously short attention spans."

"Maybe he has." Jess nodded. "These people have plenty of secrets. Blackmail could be one more thing on the list."

Mercer unlocked the cruiser. "Like you said, it makes sense."

"How about we take Palmer's story to Lawson, get his story, and then take everything we know to the FBI. They want Hades. Maybe we can give them something that will help." Jess held up her phone. "I have Lawson's address."

Mercer got in the car. "Let's go."

CHAPTER FIFTY-FOUR

Wednesday, May 24
Santa Irene, Arizona

HADES SAT AT LAWSON'S computer. He refreshed the display for the thousandth time. The number hadn't changed. The money hadn't been transferred.

He walked the length of the living room and back. He hovered his hand over the refresh key, backed away, and walked the length of the living room again.

Julia said, "I'm getting itchy staying here."

"It will happen, right?" Pony said.

Hades nodded. "The brokers fell for it. If there was any trick or trap, they would have sprung it by now. We just have to be patient."

Hades pressed the refresh button.

Pony grunted. "Very patient."

"It's going to happen." Hades sat on the sofa with a heavy thump.

The house phone rang. Hades jumped up. The phone was on

a tall table in the hallway. He reached it not having made his mind up whether to answer.

It was a modern phone. The ring wasn't a real bell. A speaker played a canned tune. He picked up the handset. He put his thumb on the *on* button, but he didn't press it. The phone had an answering machine. If it was the broker, if there was any problem to deal with, he would be better off knowing what the broker had to say and having a plan before he spoke in person.

He let the handset dangle at his side. The ringing was replaced by Lawson's recorded voice apologizing that he couldn't come to the phone. There was a *bleep*, and the caller spoke.

It was a man. He sounded agitated. Out of breath.

"Simon. Arthur. I just had a police officer and some woman journalist at my place. Digging into Argnot. Playing good cop, bad cop. Threatened to get a warrant and things. Then they just drove off." Simon cleared his throat. "I didn't tell them anything. So…well, if they turn up at your place? Call me."

Arthur hung up.

Hades dropped the handset back onto its cradle. He could feel the adrenaline coursing through his blood.

Police? Journalist? He laughed. An interesting addition to his "farewell to Arizona" plans.

"Could be the woman from Bear Hill," Pony said.

"Could be." Hades grinned and pulled his VBR from its holster. "Get ready for company." He looked it over before tucking it away.

"Get the gas. It's time to break the news to our hosts."

CHAPTER FIFTY-FIVE

Wednesday, May 24
Santa Irene, Arizona

PONY AND SHORTY HUSTLED. They carried two five-gallon gas cans each. It was a short trip, from the garage through the back door and into each room in the house. They laid the cans on beds and chairs before running back to the garage and repeating the cycle. It took six trips to bring all the cans into the house.

Hades brought in a backpack. Inside were two-dozen small cans. He unscrewed the metal caps and pulled out a thick wick. Inside was a viscous liquid similar to Sterno. It was a slow burning compound that thinned with heat and soaked into the wick. Once lit, they were almost impossible to put out. He placed two of the cans in each room.

He met Cora, Julia, and Pony at the entrance to the basement.

Cora had a bundle of blankets. Pony had two cans of gasoline.

"Shorty is keeping watch," Cora said.

Hades nodded. "Ready?"

"Are we sure the money is going to transfer?" Cora asked.

"As sure as we can be. Whether it's transferred or not, the police are getting close. We need to move."

No one argued.

Hades flipped on the lights to the basement, and they descended the steps, leaving Julia upstairs in the hallway.

Pony set the gas cans down in a corner. Cora piled the blankets beside the cans.

All three Lawsons were where they had been left. Simon and Natalie on the floor stretched between the tie-downs. Amanda taped to a chair secured to a pillar.

Pony removed their blindfolds.

"The transfer hasn't gone through yet, but we're preparing to leave," Hades said.

Lawson made no reply.

"Sorry we had to put you through all this, but you must have been expecting something. Eh, Simon?"

Lawson frowned.

Natalie twisted to look at her husband.

Hades smiled. "Didn't he tell you?" He mocked astonishment. "Oh, perhaps he doesn't know? Or perhaps he's just being the same old Simon he's always been, and he doesn't care."

Natalie's head twisted to look at Hades and her husband.

Lawson shook his head and frowned.

Hades walked a circle around Lawson, mocking. "A couple of years ago, Natalie, your husband here planned to build an emergency room. Good location. An area that needed medical facilities. A noble plan. Simon and his doctor friends helping the community. Giving back."

Simon raised himself a few inches on his elbows. "I don't understand."

Hades turned to Natalie. "Did he tell you why he didn't build the emergency room?"

She didn't reply.

"We ran out of money," Simon said.

Hades tipped his head back and laughed. "Ran out of money!"

He stretched his arms out to either side. "Ran out of money? You live in a house worth millions. You have spent your life making money. One scheme after the next. You had twenty-three million hidden in an offshore account."

Natalie looked bewildered. "Is that true, Simon? *Twenty-three million?*"

"Oh, it's true, Natalie." Hades leaned toward Simon.

Lawson shook his head, not yet panicked. "We ran out of money, and couldn't finish it. We just couldn't get the bank to loan more money."

Hades kicked Simon in the side. Viciously. Above the hips, below the ribs. A soft, fleshy, unprotected area.

Lawson screamed and tried to curl up from the pain. He struggled against his bonds and the tie-downs that held him straight, cuffs cutting into his skin.

"How much, Lawson? How much were you planning to make on the deal?"

"It wasn't like that," Simon gasped. "It was…"

"Oh, for the love of God, Simon. Man up." Hades spat and kicked Simon again. Amanda screamed behind the duct tape covering her mouth. "You were in it for yourself. And when you thought the deal wasn't working out for you, you decided it shouldn't work out for anyone else, either."

Simon was crying now. "I-I-I don't understand."

"You and your pals were okay. That's all you cared about. What about the people working for you, huh? What about them, Simon?"

Lawson whimpered. His wife stared at him, her eyes wide. He breathed hard. "I didn't have a choice."

Hades' fury unleashed itself. He kicked Simon again. "What choice did you give them, Simon?"

Kick. "No choice at all."

And again. He'd have killed Simon right at that moment. Cheerfully. But there was more to do first. For Benny.

Hades took a deep breath and managed to tamp down his fury. "Julia! Julia, come down here!"

The basement door opened, and Julia descended. She glowered at Simon, whimpering on the floor, snot running from his nose. "You probably don't remember me."

He shook his head slowly.

"We met once. At the building site. Before the scaffolding fell."

Simon's silent whimpers were his only reply.

"You knew all about it!" Julia screamed, fists balled at her sides. "You sent Benny a hundred dollars in a cheap get well card. After you watched us lose everything."

There was a long silence.

"You killed him, Simon. His children have no father now. You're scum, Simon Lawson. You deserve whatever happens to you." Julia took deep breaths. "One thing you didn't know about Benny. Something important."

Hades peeled off his mask. "Take a good look, Simon."

"Meet Benny's brother," Julia said.

"Hades?" Lawson whispered.

Hades' lopsided grin was grotesque. "In the flesh."

Natalie spun her head around and buried her face in her hands. "No, no, no, no."

Pony and Cora peeled off their masks.

Simon gasped. His breath caught in his throat. He inhaled in short bursts. "*Karen Warner*? You set this up? You put David in prison?" He shook his head violently, side to side, as he cried. "But why? Why?"

"Think about it, Simon. You knew David well enough to know how he treated me. Controlling bastard. I'm sure you'll figure it out." Karen smiled. She dropped the mask onto Simon's crotch, turned, and walked upstairs.

Julia reached up and kissed Hades on his scarred cheek. "Thank you for this, Norman. Benny would be so proud of you."

Julia followed Karen out of the basement while Simon and Natalie and Amanda pleaded. Their voices tumbled over each other. One after another. Begging, begging, begging.

Hades shook his head in mock exasperation. "Goodbye, Simon."

He followed Karen and Julia up the steps and left Pony to pour ten gallons of gasoline over the blankets, the floor, and all three Lawsons.

All three of them were miserable excuses for human beings. They would burn here and burn in hell.

He would never waste an ounce of energy on them again.

CHAPTER FIFTY-SIX

Wednesday, May 24
Santa Irene, Arizona

MERCER HUSTLED THE CRUISER through the traffic. He reached for the siren on a couple of occasions, only to curse and take his hand from the switch.

"I know this feels like an emergency, but remember that what Lawson, Palmer, and Warner did happened more than two years ago." Jess ran her fingers through her hair and tried to get comfortable amid the cables and equipment crowding her seat. "Getting to Lawson quickly now won't fix what they did back then. We have to be clever about this."

Mercer glanced across the console. "Lawson set Hades on the path that killed my son-in-law, and Ernie and Jackson *this week*, Jess."

"Did he? Palmer might have been lying. Covering his own ass." Jess paused to gentle her tone. "And anyway, that situation is not your case. As much as you'd like it to be."

"All the more reason to get to Lawson. Find out." Mercer floored the accelerator.

Jess sighed. There was no point in arguing. She could hear Morris in her head, cautioning her not to let him make matters worse. She'd make sure he didn't go off the deep end. At least, she'd try.

Mercer slowed as they closed in on Lawson's house. The neighborhood was similar to Palmer's and Warner's, but even more expensive. These high-end properties were a mixture of well-spaced, one- and two-story residences in modern styles, set well back from the road. They had elaborate driveways and gardens and lawns that required a crew to maintain. Each property had fences and tall pines protecting the homeowners from prying by their neighbors.

Mercer came to a stop by a short brick wall and a wrought iron gate. A broad drive led around the house to a garage in the rear. The two-story house would have commanding views from its place on the hill.

Jess checked the number stenciled on the curb. "This is Lawson's."

No light shone through the windows. Plantation shutters were closed, and the drapes were drawn behind them.

"Big place," Mercer said. "But nobody home."

Jess squinted toward the house. "Doesn't it look like the front door is open?"

A bald man walked around the side of the house. He had broad shoulders and carried a cardboard box. His demeanor didn't suggest he had just finished a frantic phone call establishing an alibi with Palmer. He stopped on the driveway, frowning at the cruiser.

Mercer grunted as he rolled out of the car. He threw open the rough iron gate and strode toward the house.

Jess rushed after Mercer. The gate was swinging back closed when she slid through.

"Can I help you?" said the man with the box in his hands.

Mercer waved his badge as he approached. "Police. We're looking for Dr. Simon Lawson."

The man shot a glance at Jess as she reached Mercer's side. "I'm Simon Lawson."

"We need a few minutes of your time, Dr. Lawson," Mercer said, as if this was an official visit.

The man spoke to Jess. "Who are you?"

"Jessica Kimball. *Taboo Magazine*." She reached for a card but realized she had left her bag in the cruiser.

He looked back at Mercer. "What's this about?" He hoisted the box. "I'm kind of busy."

"Argnot Corporation and Goldleaf Construction," Mercer replied, matter-of-factly.

He frowned. "I've never heard of them."

"You were Argnot's president and managing member until you folded the company into bankruptcy a couple of years ago," Jess said.

"I'm not sure where you got that story from, but I'm afraid this isn't a good time."

"Perhaps it would be better if you came down the station," Mercer said. He turned and gestured to the cruiser. "Like, now."

The man shuffled his weight from one side to the other. He pressed his lips together and glanced back at the house and the open front door. "Okay. We can talk for a few minutes inside. I've got something cooking."

He led the way in through the front door. Jess followed Mercer. The hallway opened onto a sunken living room area to the right and a formal dining room on the left. A corridor with doors off it led straight ahead to a large kitchen and breakfast area. A faint, aromatic scent that Jess couldn't quite place hung in the air.

The man kicked the front door closed and whipped a gun from the box.

Jess stepped back. Mercer didn't move.

A man with a ponytail limped into the kitchen from the dining room. Jess had seen him twice before. Once at Melissa Green's house. The second time, at the lake house. He held a large semiautomatic weapon in front of him, pointed her way.

Another man walked up the two steps from the living room. "Well, well, well."

There was no mistaking that face. The scars were every bit as frightening in person as they'd been in the photographs.

"Norman Kemp," Jess said. "Or do you prefer Hades?"

He looked at Jess and licked his lips. "I do like a reporter who does her research." He laughed. "If only you had done a little bit more."

"I did enough to find you."

The man with the ponytail grunted. "You should learn to quit while you're ahead."

Jess eyed him warily. "I thought you should do the same."

He hoisted the gun. "Looks like I'm the one who's still ahead. Meet my friends," Hades said. "Pony and Shorty."

Shorty, the man who had claimed to be Lawson, rammed Mercer face-first against the wall. He ripped Mercer's gun from his holster and tossed it down the corridor.

Pony stood two paces from Jess with his gun lazily pointed at her stomach.

Shorty kicked the back of Mercer's legs. Mercer slid down the wall onto his knees. Shorty pressed the muzzle of his gun into the back of Mercer's neck.

Hades took two quick steps toward Shorty. "Take him downstairs."

Shorty pulled his gun back and dragged Mercer away from the wall.

Pony swung his gun in the direction of the door off the kitchen. "Out to the garage. Then down through the door on the left."

Jess sensed more than saw the barrel of Pony's gun move away from her. Without conscious thought, she threw her arm over Pony's gun hand and wrenched the gun toward the front door.

Pony grunted.

Jess closed her hand around Pony's trigger finger. The semiautomatic barked, loud and harsh in the confined environment. The recoil twisted the gun horizontally.

Hades yelped, dropped to the ground, and rolled backward into the living room.

Shorty grabbed his leg and screamed.

Mercer turned and drove a fist into Shorty's chin. Shorty rolled to the side and went down hard. His head hit the floor with a solid thump.

Pony heaved a punch into Jess's side, driving the air from her lungs. Her knees went weak. He ripped his gun arm free of her grasp.

Mercer pounded his fist into Shorty's face, wrenched the gun from his hand, and fired at Pony.

Plaster dust erupted from the sheetrock beside Pony. He dove around the corner, firing a wild burst into the ceiling.

Mercer fired two shots into the living room and ran after Hades.

Jess threw herself toward the kitchen. Mercer's gun was on the floor as the corridor opened into the kitchen. She crouched and ran for the weapon, her arms outstretched.

Somewhere in the house, multiple gunshots rang out.

The door from the kitchen to the garage sprung open.

Jess slowed.

A woman stepped into the doorway. She had a black gun in her hands. She held it like a movie star, elbows bent, pointing it upward. The woman was tall, her hair was dark, and her skin was devoid of makeup, but there was no mistaking Karen Warner's face.

Jess angled left, her hands reaching for Mercer's gun. She drove her shoulder into Warner's ribs. Below her arm, where the bones are barely covered with cushioning flesh.

The gun went off. Jess felt the hot exhaust gasses wash over her hand. The muzzle flash illuminated the garage and the steps leading down through an open doorway.

Jess stamped her heel on Warner's foot.

Warner snarled and ripped the gun upward and out of Jess's grasp.

Jess threw a punch. Warner jerked her head back. Jess barely made contact.

Warner grunted as she brought the gun back down to aim.

Jess grabbed Warner's elbow and forced her arm out straight to keep the gun pointed over her shoulder.

Jess leaned into Warner, her legs pushing hard.

Warner fell backward into the garage and stumbled through

the doorway into the dark basement. Jess kept hold of her arm. Warner took the brunt of the fall onto the steps as they tumbled down.

The aromatic smell Jess had noticed upstairs was much stronger here. The air was saturated with gasoline.

Warner hit the hard cement floor first. Jess wedged a knee into Warner's stomach. Warner bit down on Jess's arm. Jess head-butted her on the ear.

Warner screamed and twisted. Jess rolled to her feet, kicking the gun from her hand.

Jess leaped after the gun, following the sound of clattering metal in the dark. She tumbled forward then her feet pulled away from under her when she stumbled upon something soft.

Pain burned her elbows as she hit a wet concrete floor. She reached out, kicking herself forward, fingers searching for the gun. The gasoline fumes assailed her eyes.

Warner grabbed Jess's ankle.

Jess kicked as she wrapped her fingers around the gun and swept it forward as Warner dove at Jess.

The air was thick with highly flammable gasoline fumes, and the floor was soaked. The slightest spark would set it off.

Jess turned the gun in her hand. She raised the butt and brought it down with every ounce of strength she could muster on Karen Warner's temple.

Warner screamed. Short, sharp, and livid.

Jess deflected Warner's momentum and leaped to her feet.

Warner's screaming turned to moans. Jess heard shuffling and grunting in the darkness.

She stepped backward, putting distance and reaction time between her and Warner. Her shoes splattered the gasoline as she moved.

The grunting became more urgent.

The gunfire upstairs had stopped.

At the top of the stairs, light spilled in when the door was opened wider.

The light revealed Warner curled against one wall. She wasn't moving. In the middle of the floor were two bound figures. Against a pillar, a gagged woman was secured to a chair with duct tape.

The silhouette of a man appeared in the doorway at the top of the stairs, his breathing ragged and a gun in his hand.

Even with Shorty down, it had been two on one. Mercer against Hades and Pony. Not good odds.

The man stumbled down the first step.

This time, she had no choice. Jess raised her gun.

CHAPTER FIFTY-SEVEN

Wednesday, May 24
Santa Irene, Arizona

JESS GULPED. SHE WAS standing in gasoline. People were lying in it. A spark or enough heat, and it would probably go off.

The man leaned against the wall as he staggered down another step into the basement.

Maybe she should shoot low. Something to inflict enough pain for her to get control of the situation. She adjusted her grip on the gun.

The man slid down the wall and sat on the stairs. The outline became familiar.

"Mercer?"

He nodded. "Jess," he grunted.

Jess raced for the steps.

"Good," said a voice.

Jess looked up. The silhouette of another man was in the doorway. He was on his knees with a gun in an outstretched hand. His broad shoulders and size made him unmistakable.

Hades.

He fired. A fat, popping sound. The bullet went wide. Plaster exploded around her as it tore a giant hole in the wall by her head.

Mercer twisted around as Jess whipped her gun up. With the door open, maybe she'd get away without igniting the fumes. If not, she was going to die anyway. Hades would kill them all.

She squeezed the trigger one-handed, the gun still moving. The weapon boomed in her hand.

Hades' shoulder jerked backward.

She gripped tighter and squeezed the trigger. Again and again. Five booming shots as fast as her finger could move. The sound deafening in the basement room.

The swirling gasoline below her not gone, but forgotten.

Hades was tossed backward. He disappeared from view.

Mercer was on his feet, crouching and moving slowly up the stairs, gun first. He reached the doorway and knelt to examine Hades. "He's definitely dead this time."

"The others?" Jess said.

"Wait," Mercer said as he walked out of the basement.

Jess found the light switch at the bottom of the stairs and flipped on the sickly green fluorescent lights.

The figures on the floor were writhing. They were all gagged. The girl in the chair was rocking it back and forth.

Jess rushed to the chair, and eased the duct tape from her mouth.

"Thank God," she said. She nodded to the figures on the ground. "My parents."

Jess pulled the gags from their mouths. They panted and gasped.

Mercer limped down the steps. "Police and ambulance on

the way." His voice was curt and hoarse. "Get them out of here."

He cut the girl free from the chair. She slid to the floor and lay down.

Jess freed the couple's hands and feet. They cried as they curled into fetal balls. They could barely move. The girl dragged herself to their side.

"Simon Lawson," Jess said.

The man nodded.

Mercer helped the girl up the steps. Jess did the same with Simon and the woman.

In the corridor, Hades was on his back in a pool of blood. One leg was twisted under him, and his chest was a mess of wet flesh.

Jess ushered the Lawsons around him.

Mrs. Lawson stumbled to the kitchen and vomited. The girl rushed to comfort her. Mr. Lawson slumped onto the sofa.

Shorty was on the stairs, his head hung down, and his arms taped to the banister.

"I'm never going to look at duct tape the same again," Jess said.

Mercer grunted, and pointed across the kitchen.

Pony lay on his back. His blood-covered shirt was riddled with bullet holes, and his eyes were closed.

Julia was on the ground, her arms wrapped around an archway column and her wrists bound with handcuffs. Her eyes radiated hate.

Mercer patted the gun in Jess's hand. "Watch them."

She nodded.

He went upstairs. A minute later he returned with two little boys. They were pale. He walked them down the driveway and put them in the back of the cruiser. He started the engine, probably to turn on the air conditioning for them.

Julia shifted her weight. Jess adjusted her grip on the gun, keeping it pointed at her center mass.

Mercer limped in and out of the house. He carried large plastic cans of gasoline, and piled them at the far end of the lawn.

Jess kept her attention on the people in the house. Even so, she couldn't help but notice Mercer's limp and near constant grimace.

"I've carried out as much of the fuel as I could find," he said, drawing up a chair beside Jess. He looked exhausted. "I called for backup when I put the boys in the squad car. They should be here soon."

Mrs. Lawson talked quietly to her daughter. Simon Lawson sat motionless nearby.

Mercer and Jess sat in silence until a SWAT team appeared on the rear patio. They were covered in bulletproof gear and led with automatic weapons.

Jess made an exaggerated show of placing her gun on the ground and holding her hands up.

Mercer held out his badge.

The SWAT team spread out, evaluating the people in the house, assessing the dangers, securing the weapons.

They handcuffed the living and moved them into the backyard, away from the risk of fire. They separated everyone into two groups—the Lawsons, and those who had invaded the house.

Ambulances arrived. The medics stretchered away the injured. Simon Lawson was wheeled to the curb and into an ambulance.

CHAPTER FIFTY-EIGHT

One week later
Denver, Colorado

JESS HAD SPENT THE past week working on her article and listening to all the negative reports from her team of private investigators. Not even Mandy's new boyfriend, Trent Brennan, had found a new lead. With effort, Jess pushed her disappointment aside while she sat in Carter Pierce's office. He had his head down, reading her article.

Thelma brought coffee in a French press and a plate of cookies. She smiled, placed them on a table by Jess, and left.

Jess pushed the plunger down on the coffee and poured herself a cup. Carter didn't go in for mugs. He was a cup and saucer man, the aristocratic end of old school. She grinned. Perhaps she should introduce him to Fred Wilson one day. If nothing else, to see the look of horror on his face as Fred taught him to shoot.

Carter flipped over the last page and looked up. "I asked too much of you."

She blew on her hot coffee. "Not that you've ever done that before."

"I think on those occasions you were mostly responsible for your own dilemmas."

She laughed. "*Dilemmas*?"

He smiled. "It pains me to think of those situations as they really were." He waved her article. "This, too."

She sipped a fraction of her too hot coffee. "I lived to tell the tale."

"How's Mercer?"

"His leg is healing. He's on administrative leave. He should recover, physically. Santa Irene PD has recommended him for a medal."

"Good." Carter's smile faded. "Your biographies on Melissa Green and the police officers killed at her house were beautiful."

"Nothing is going to bring those men back, but I felt it was the least I could do for their families." She paused. "It's sad that I could find no one to mourn Melissa."

"We'll lead with this on the front page." Carter grimaced. "These men died in the line of duty. And someone should mourn Melissa, even if we're the only ones. It's not enough, but at least *Taboo* is doing something."

Jess nodded, but the lump in her throat prevented speech. Carter was one of the most supportive, kind men she'd ever met. His patience with her focus on finding her son bordered on saintly. His loyalty was absolute. And so was hers.

He took a deep breath. "Are you going back to Arizona to cover the court case?"

"I found a good lawyer for Benny's sons. She says she'll do the best she can to try to get money for them from Palmer, but the case is not solid." Jess shook her head. "Dr. Warner's murder conviction will be set aside, but it'll be done by consent without any kind of hearing. Nothing much to cover there. He'll be charged with fraud and tax evasion for his part in the emergency room scam. But if he's smart, he'll work out a deal and stay out of any public hearing on that one, too."

Carter said, "I meant the others."

"I'm not planning to. Shorty deserves what he gets. Julia," she shrugged. "And Lawson and Palmer will probably be sentenced to a fraction of what they deserve, but they'll be in jail right alongside Warner, if there's any justice in Arizona at all."

Carter nodded. "White collar crime. Lots of victims and not much recourse."

"True." Jess sipped her coffee. "Norman Kemp was a killer. But none of this would have happened if Lawson had dealt honestly with Benny."

"Pigs get fat, hogs get slaughtered," Carter said, clicking his tongue and shaking his head. "You didn't explore any of that in your article."

Jess frowned and her tone was as hard as diamonds. "Hades killed a string of people. I don't want to generate any sympathy for him."

Carter nodded. "And Karen Warner?"

"Like I said in the article, Karen Warner masterminded the whole thing. She grew up with the Kemp brothers and lost touch with them on her way to using her looks to capture a rich husband."

"But the pampered life bored her."

"She was always a wild child. When she visited the construction site for the emergency room, she recognized Norman and Benny. After that happened, she knew her husband and his two pals were responsible for Benny's ruin."

"So she set up the whole kidnap and ransom and everything else," Carter said.

"Right. She was the one who knew they could take over Melissa's life and not be found out." Jess took a deep breath. "Hard to say what the eventual charges against her will be. She's still living in some sort of dream world, but she caused a lot of heartache."

"I hope you're not blaming yourself for that. The woman would have killed you, and she did kill three people when she crashed the first stolen van. Not to mention, she killed her own sister."

Jess nodded slowly. "If she ever comes back, mentally, Arizona has the death penalty, and she'll probably get it. At the very least, she'll never get out of prison."

"Which is no less than she deserves. Still," Carter cocked his head, "It's a long way from bad girl to killer. Any idea what pushed her over that edge?"

Jess shrugged. "We'll probably never know for sure. But when Hades went to prison the first time, he was still a minor. He was charged with vehicular manslaughter following a joy ride in another kid's car. That's the accident when his face was cut up, and he got those scars."

"Let me guess. He was released on his twenty-first birthday, and the juvenile records were sealed."

"Yep. I don't know what happened there, exactly. But if we were betting, I'd say Karen Warner was the one behind the wheel all those years ago, too," Jess said.

"Norman took the heat back then for something he didn't really do."

They sat in silence for a few minutes before Carter put his hands together. "Okay, so you've been working hard. Now, you're entitled to some time off."

Jess finished her coffee. "I wouldn't know what to do with it at the moment. I don't have any promising new leads on Peter. I'd rather just work for a while and take the free time when I've got something to follow."

Carter laughed. "I thought you'd say that."

He stretched across his desk and handed her a plane ticket.

She glanced at the destination. "Barbados?"

"Consider it your next assignment. 3A. It's a window seat. I believe the man on the aisle is already packed."

She frowned. "I don't understand? What's the assignment?"

Carter pointed to the doorway.

Henry Morris held up a ticket. "Look at that. Mine's 3B. And you said you don't believe in coincidences."

She looked down. She felt a flash of heat across her skin. She wasn't good with emotions. She wished the ground would open up and swallow her.

It didn't.

She lifted her head. "Hello, Henry."

After a moment, she realized she was smiling.

And she couldn't stop.

THE END

ABOUT THE AUTHOR

DIANE CAPRI is the *New York Times*, *USA Today*, and worldwide bestselling author. She's a recovering lawyer and snowbird who divides her time between Florida and Michigan. An active member of Mystery Writers of America, Authors Guild, International Thriller Writers, Alliance of Independent Authors, and Sisters in Crime, she loves to hear from readers and is hard at work on her next novel.

Please connect with Diane online:
http://www.DianeCapri.com
Twitter: http://twitter.com/@DianeCapri
Facebook: http://www.facebook.com/Diane.Capri1
http://www.facebook.com/DianeCapriBooks